THYRA'S PROMISE

NATALIE DEBRABANDERE

ISBN: 1981969853
ISBN-13: 978-1981969852

DEDICATION

For Crystal, the real *Shining One*.

ACKNOWLEDGMENTS

Thank you to my readers! Thanks for sticking with me through all the books, loving the characters as much as I do, and giving energy to my dream with all the great Amazon reviews.

And Peter…
At the risk of repeating myself once again…
Yep…

THANK YOU!

PART ONE:
LEARNING TO DIE

CHAPTER ONE

897 A.D - in the Highlands of Scotland.

A thick layer of ice was on the ground that morning, not long after sunrise, when Thyra headed into the forest in the company of her brothers, Tait and Bjarke. They were dressed practically in woollen trousers and matching tunics worn over a thick, warmer undershirt. All three of them carried light bows and arrows on their back, and their short, sharp and deadly swords strapped to a leather belt around their waist. They had chosen to leave their heavier cloaks behind despite the intense cold, to be able to move faster through the trees. Today, they would be spending most of it out into the forest, hunting for game. It was one of Thyra's favourite winter activities, and something that she had always excelled at. She was excited and happy that morning. She had just turned twenty-one. She was a Viking warrior. The rather aptly-named Tait, which meant *cheerful* in the old Norse language, was her twin brother. He was Thyra's best friend, a talented, passionate poet, and a gifted young bard as well. Bjarke, who was ten years older, took entirely after their father.

He was a mountain of a man, taciturn and moody at the best of times. A warrior to the core, he really only lived to fight and conquer.

Every spring, without fail, he would leave their smaller settlement to go and connect with a larger group of Viking men who came from all over Norway, Denmark, and Sweden. Under the steely command of Gulbrand the Red, they then pushed further south, raiding and colonising territory as they went, as far as the Loire river into modern-day France, or even further than that. With those men, Bjarke had been involved in hard battles in Lisbon, Cadiz, and Seville. He had seen parts of North Africa, and the Sahara Desert. He enjoyed the warrior lifestyle. Still, every year when the weather started to change, he came back to spend the winter with his people. Covered in new scars that he wore as a badge of honour, and basking in triumphant glory, he was always welcomed back as a true hero. Then, he invariably enjoyed the darker season in the same manner; resting and recovering from his travels, feasting, and recounting tales of the fighting. He also often talked about the fascinating new people and cultures that he had encountered along the way. Tait was puzzled and rather disturbed by all this. *'How can you say that those people are interesting, when you always end up killing them all, brother…'* he remarked once. It had been a completely genuine and innocent comment on his part, although it earned him a hard fist in the face and a stern rebuke from Bjarke. *'Don't be so fucking soft',* the man barked.

Their clan was typically made up of several large families and their related members, over a hundred people in all. Asger the Great, Bjarke's and the twins' father, had been a celebrated warrior in his time, and he ruled undisputed over the growing community. A number of long-houses with attending barns and a courtyard in the middle constituted the bulk of the settlement.

And it was right next to a roaring fire in the centre of the communal main square that Bjarke usually held court. The young men from the village would gather around him, and listen avidly to his tales of adventure. Thyra could always be found sitting at the front of the group, eyes riveted onto her brother's face, trembling with excitement at the thought of one day being able to follow him over the water. It was simple curiosity and a strong desire to travel to distant shores, to meet and interact with the people he mentioned in his stories, which prevailed in her. She dreamed of tasting exotic foods, learning new languages, and experiencing different ways of living... Taking lives and violence in general did not feature very highly on her personal agenda, although something primal in her also responded to the lure of battle. She was a fighter, after all. She had been raised as one, trained to become a warrior, and she was strongly loyal to her people. The previous summer, she had begged and pleaded with Bjarke to be allowed to go with him. But the older man had simply laughed in her face at the suggestion.

"You're just a girl," he sneered. "Your place is not with the fighting men."

"No, you're wrong. I am a Viking, first and foremost, and a warrior just like you," Thyra replied.

He could feel her anger and hear the frustration in her voice. He relished provoking her a little more, lighting that spark in her, playing with fire.

"Just a girl," he muttered with a dismissive shrug.

"Come on, Bjarke, you know what I can do," she insisted. "You trained me yourself. Why bother with all that teaching, if all you want me to do is stay at home and wait? Please, let me come with you!"

"You're not ready."

"Yes, I am!"

"Shut up."

He slapped her across the face, hard enough to send her crashing to the floor. But then she rose, quick as lightning, eyes blazing with outrage and fury. He stood his ground in front of her. He smiled, amused and rather excited by her reaction. Like him, she had a short fuse. He pushed her a little more, just to see what would happen next.

"What are you going to do about it? Uh?"

He would have been glad if she had launched herself at him right there and then, the way she seemed ready to do as soon as she got to her feet. In the family hierarchy, she was well below him, and the slap had been there to remind her of that very fact. Bjarke knew that she hated it. The older she became, the more she struggled with her lower position. One day, it was all going to blow up sky-high, and something dark in him could not wait for it to happen. He would love an opportunity to really cut her down to size and put her in her place.

"What are you going to do, Thyra?" he repeated, taunting her. "I'm right here, sister. Want to fight? Show me what you can do? Go right ahead!"

But Thyra had taken the intelligent way out, and Bjarke was bitterly disappointed. Without a single other word, she had simply walked past him and straight out of the house. She was determined not to fight him. Bjarke stole a glance at her now, as she steadied her bow over her shoulder. In a strange way, he was proud of what she had become also. Although it was more because he believed that the gifted young warrior she had turned into was all down to him, and nothing to do with her own abilities, of course... Of his two siblings, weirdly enough, it was Thyra who had shown the most promise with weapons and fighting. Tait was always much happier when he was left to his own devices, to compose his poems and stories. He always was a dreamer and a gentle soul. But Thyra was made of different stuff. She could be extremely kind and gentle when she wanted to be, for sure, but she also had fire burning in her heart. She was driven and competitive, tough and relentless. And it showed. As she grew up, it quickly became obvious to Asger that his only daughter was different from the rest. Not for her to follow the path of other young women in the village, the girls who were taught to look after the household, cook for the men, and tend to the animals and the fields when their husbands were away fighting. No, Thyra was wild. She was stronger than most. She loved the forest and the mountains. She wanted to become a hunter, and a good fighter too. Asger could see no way of ever changing this, nor did he really want to. He was quite happy to raise her like one of the boys. And when his failing health no longer permitted him to see directly to his younger children's education, he instructed Bjarke to take them both under his wing.

With him, said education soon turned into warrior training of the hardest kind. Thyra took to it like a duck to water. Tait was reluctant. By then, he had taught himself how to read and interpret the ancient runes, and he could make astonishingly accurate predictions. He was extremely popular, well-liked in the village, and many thought that he would one day replace his father as clan chief. Bjarke did not appreciate this in the least. He was outraged at the mere suggestion of it. *'So, they want a woman as chief, uh?'* he once complained to Asger, frustrated beyond belief. *'My own brother, more interested in poetry than sword! And they want him to lead them?'* His father had simply laughed. *'Leave the poor boy to his studies',* he advised, wisely, *'and concentrate your efforts on your sister.'* Bjarke did just that, but he started to worry that she too would one day grow up to threaten his position.

And he was right. She was doing that now, quite unconsciously of course, definitely not on purpose; but all the same, he believed that he had to do something about it soon, before the situation got out of control.

He kept a close eye on her as Thyra led the way deeper into the forest, unaware of her brother's real, dangerous reason for taking her hunting in the first place. Tait was trailing at the back as always, lost in a world of his own, which was just as well. For once, Bjarke would have been happier if the boy had decided to stay in the village. But Thyra had insisted. *'Come on, you know it'll be fun!'* And as always, Tait had smiled at her, and agreed. It was hard to say no to Thyra. Bjarke met her gaze now, as she looked at him over her shoulder and flashed him a brilliant, excited smile. He tightened his fists in response.

"What?" he grunted.

"Oleg was out yesterday," she told him, referring to one of her young village friends. "He said he saw some deer just on the edge of the mountain."

"Why the hell didn't he kill a bunch of 'em then?" Bjarke muttered. "That bloody useless idiot is even more stupid than I thought."

She laughed, as if he were joking, which he definitely was not. He felt red-hot anger stir inside of him at the way that she appeared so free, so effortlessly happy. Thyra oozed confidence and charm. He suspected that she was destined for many great things, feats and achievements that he once might have hoped for himself but could never achieve. He was painfully jealous of her. She seemed to have it all! Life sparkled for her in a way it had never done for him, and everything about her simply served to highlight his own shortcomings. The people in the village loved her. So did Tait. And lately, Bjarke had begun to realise that they were all wary of him. *'A bully and a thug'*, that was what they thought of him. The people talked about him behind his back. He knew it, and the knowledge fuelled his anger even more. Recently, even Thyra seemed to be losing her respect for him. Well, he would show them. And he would start with her, right now, to reassert his authority on the family unit, and wipe that blazing smile off her face.

"You want to head for the hills on the east side today, yes?" she asked.

He did not respond and stepped in front of her to increase the pace. He was sweating now, a mixture of nervousness and anticipation. He knew she would not go down easily, because he had taught her so well. She was almost as tall as he was, slender-looking, yet all muscle. Dangerous. He shot a quick assessing glance toward her again. She missed it. *Good,* he thought. The twins had both inherited their mother's beautiful blond hair, and her piercing blue eyes. Tait and Thyra had been much too young when she died of a bout of the flu to remember her, but Bjarke did. He could not look at Thyra without being reminded of the mother he had loved so deeply, who had been taken away from him too soon; and that was another perfect reason for him to be angry at his sister. As far as he was concerned, Thyra was lethal in every way. And she was far above him in terms of intelligence too, which he could not tolerate either. *But not nearly smart or careful enough,* he reflected darkly, *not this time.* He was going to punish her for what she had done and bring her back in line.

"Hey, wait; we lost Tait," she said.

"He'll catch up," Bjarke snapped. "Keep moving."

CHAPTER TWO

The deer was hers for the taking, but he elbowed her out of the way to take the shot. Thyra swallowed back her irritation. Bjarke often did this. In past years, more often than not, he would do it with a smile and a teasing wink at her, and Thyra would laugh and push him back. It was always fun between them back then. Once upon a time, her big brother Bjarke had been Thyra's hero. He was the man she looked up to, the one she invariably went to for advice and guidance whenever she needed it. She trusted him unconditionally, and he loved her just the same. But a couple of winters ago, things had started to change. Out of the blue, Bjarke suddenly turned mean and bitter toward her. The once friendly and innocent banter between them only ever degenerated into full-blown arguments now. That none of those had turned into a physical fight yet was an absolute miracle, and solely due to Thyra's refusal to play his game. Bjarke was painfully cruel to Tait, too, whom she adored. He had stolen his writings once and burned them on the communal fire. When her twin brother burst into tears at the discovery of what he had done, Bjarke simply laughed and told him to toughen up. Tait hated him with a vengeance now, and Thyra felt deeply sad that Bjarke had managed to make somebody as pure and kind as Tait was discover the true meaning of hatred…

One day, she began to distance herself from Bjarke too. She simply had to. Something in him had gone dark and nasty, and even though she could not put her finger on exactly what it was, it still felt dangerous to her. Bjarke had started drinking heavily. He put on a lot of weight. Sometimes, she would catch him looking at her with a menacing glint in his eyes. It was profoundly disturbing, and she often felt unsettled in his presence. Still, he was her brother. He was family, and that meant a lot to Thyra. No matter what his problem was, she did not want to make things worse by calling him out on his failings. And so, on that day, when his arrow was not straight enough, not fast enough, and nowhere near powerful enough to kill the deer immediately, she jumped up and ran to it. She drew her sword and finished the job for him, quickly and efficiently. Thyra was an accomplished hunter, one of the best they had, which meant that she respected the animals that she killed. She would never allow one to suffer unnecessarily on the brink of death. Obviously, she had no idea that this time, Bjarke had intentionally misfired… And as she turned to look up toward him, with a smile because she did not want him to feel bad, he kicked her in the face. Thyra was completely unprepared for this, and she hit the ground hard. For a couple of seconds, she lost track of time and her surroundings, and just lay there in a heavy daze, completely stunned by the blow. It was only the sound of his whip slashing through the air that started to bring her back to a semblance of awareness. And only a second later, she felt the sting of the braided leather on her back, easily cutting through her tunic and her undershirt, slicing her skin open, and drawing blood. It took her breath away. Bjarke managed to do it twice more in rapid succession before she finally regained her senses enough to turn around. She grabbed hold of the whip with her left hand, just as he was about to hit her again.

"Stop!" she cried.

She felt the thick length of corded cable wrap around her forearm like a live burning snake. She was not wearing her protective arm bracers that morning, and it hurt. When Bjarke pulled, it took a big chunk of skin off her arm too. But despite the pain, Thyra kept a strong grip on the whip, and she used it to get herself back on her feet. Bjarke snorted, and he smirked at her. Then, rather unthinkably, he drew his sword. Hers was still lying on the ground, right where she had dropped it when his booted foot connected with the side of her face. It was way out of reach and completely useless to her at this particular moment, even if she had been crazy enough to want to use it against her own brother.

"What are you doing?" she yelled. "Are you mad?"

"Oh, I think you know full well what I'm doing, don't you?" he replied.

He pulled on the whip and laughed when she stumbled.

"Call yourself a warrior, do you, girl?"

He moved forward with his sword raised over his head, and her response was simple. She grabbed onto his wrist, took two steps back, and, aided by his momentum, fell backward. She brought him down with her, raised her feet, and planted them against his chest. She pushed. Bjarke went flying through the air, and he lost his precious sword in the process. Thyra stood up, brushing blood from her lip. She was bleeding heavily from her nose and a cut on her forehead that looked deep and extremely painful. She glanced at him and shrugged.

"Yeah, I do," she said. "How about you?"

"You little shit," he growled.

She had thought this would be the end of that, but before she even fully realised what he was doing, he regained control of the whip and cracked it against her right leg. Her knee buckled.

In a flash, he was on her and punching hard. She was able to block his first blows, and even return a few; but the last one, a heavy fist to the centre of her chest, managed to slip right past her defences. Winded, she went down heavily. He jumped onto her again, wrapped the length of well-oiled leather around her neck, and used it to snap her head back.

"So, you thought you could fool me, uh?"

His breath was hot and unpleasant against her face. Just a little more pressure from the restraint, and she would pass out. They both knew it.

"What?" she managed to gasp.

"You've been lying to me, Thyra."

"No. I… What do you mean?"

She really had no idea what he was talking about. She struggled to free herself, but he was too heavy. The whip was cutting into her neck, and the roaring in her brain turned from simple noise to acute pain. Her whole head suddenly felt like it was going to burst from the pressure. He was slowly strangling her and laughing about it. *Keep fighting,* she thought, as she desperately tried to stay conscious. *Keep fighting, Thyr…* But despite her best intentions, the lack of oxygen started to take its toll. She shuddered. Her body started to go limp underneath his. Her vision blurred even more. Bjarke recognised that she was right on the brink. He relaxed his grip on the whip, put a little less pressure against her neck. She lowered her head and coughed out blood onto the snow.

"You have been trying to join the Volsung clan, haven't you?"

Damn it, Thyra thought with a sudden surge of panic that woke her up nicely. *How does he know about this? I only ever told Tait, and he would never speak…*

"Bjarke, listen to me. I…"

11

"Why?" he interrupted loudly. "So that you can go to war under their banner, uh? Because I told you that you couldn't come with me, you think that you can bypass my authority and betray your people?"

If she had been able to breathe better, she would have burst out laughing at that. *So that's what you think, you idiot? That I want to join their ranks and fight for them?* It was ludicrous, and she had to make him see sense.

"Bjarke, you don't understand. I never even..."

"Shut up! I know what you did."

"You don't know anything!"

Over the mountain, about twenty miles away from Asger's own settlement, the Volsung clan lived and thrived. They were a long-established line of Vikings with ancient roots in the deep forests of Sweden and Norway. Their warriors had fought in all the great battles, and they had also laid claim to a large area of territory across the highlands, in a beautiful valley nestled by the side of a sheltered lake. The soil over there was much better for growing crops. In the past, before Thyra had even been born, there had been severe tensions between the two groups. Asger had tried once to push the Volsung people lower down into the valley. He wanted their piece of fertile ground for himself. But the Volsung warriors had other ideas about this, of course, and a fierce battle had ensued. Asger and his men were soundly defeated. Since that day, the two communities had stayed well away from each other, but it would not take much to ignite tempers again on both sides of the fence. War between the rival clans was still a real possibility, even now, twenty-five years later...

Despite knowing this, Thyra had wandered a little closer to the Volsung area during one of her solitary hunting expeditions. Truth be told, it had not been by mistake. She really wanted to go there. She had heard many fascinating stories about the Volsung, and she was insanely curious about them. Those Vikings seemed to be better, smarter, fiercer than her own tribe. It was said that they were feared and respected throughout the land. Paradoxically, they were peaceful, too... How could that possibly work? Last but not least, their leader was a woman. As soon as Thyra heard this, it became an obsession with her, and she could no longer let it go. She had heard of female warriors and chiefs, of course. Female commanders were not unheard of in Viking culture. But none so close to her own village. She badgered her father for more information about the woman.

"What does she look like? How old is she? Can she fight? Is she a healer too?"

But Asger flat-out refused to answer any of her questions about the Volsung commander. Bjarke did the same when she went to him.

"A filthy lot is what they are," he simply barked at her when she asked him. "Stay the hell away from those people."

So, on that fateful hunting day, Thyra got lost on purpose. And on the shores of the lake that afternoon, she discovered more joy, happiness, and hope than she had ever thought might be possible in her life. Now, fury flooded through her at the thought of Bjarke even thinking about causing harm to the Volsung clan... And especially to their legendary female chief, the great commander Kari Sturlusson. In spite of all the dire warnings Thyra had ever heard about her, Kari had quickly become a cherished friend to her. The woman who was renowned all over the Scottish Highlands and far beyond as *The Shining One* became the main reason for the young warrior's secret and frequent trips over the mountain that summer; and well into the autumn and winter months too. But Thyra had been extremely careful. *So, how the hell does he know?*

"Bjarke, let me go," she murmured.

It was hard to breathe, let alone speak with that whip still wrapped so tightly around her neck. It was extremely painful. It made her voice sound raw and raspy when she spoke, and she struggled to make herself heard.

"It's not what you think…"

"Like hell it isn't," he replied. "You got it in your head that you can do this without any consequences, uh? Well, listen good, girl. I'll see to it that no sister of mine is going to get away with being a traitor."

He pulled her to her feet and dragged her roughly to a nearby tree. As he had predicted, she did not make it easy for him. She managed to turn around, and she kicked him hard in the stomach. He grunted and lost his handle on her for a second. She punched him in the face then, and even thought that she might be able to get away. She absolutely did not want to fight against him any more than this. But she was feeling weak from her recent injuries, and he still carried his sword. Without hesitation, he slammed it down against the side of her right leg. This was no training hit with a flat edge. This time, he really meant it, and the sharp blade went in deep and hard, slicing through her thigh muscle and almost all the way through to the bone. She screamed in excruciating pain. It was bad enough to almost make her pass out again. She slumped onto the ground, and he grabbed a handful of her hair.

"Now, stay still," he yelled.

He pushed her down once more and tied her wrists around the tree with a length of rope. Obviously, he had been planning all this. He was well-prepared. When he raised his whip again, Thyra glanced up toward him. She was utterly shocked by the look on his face. This was no longer the man she used to know and respect, not the brother she had loved so much, far from it.

He was breathing hard now, and his eyes glinted with the intoxication of his own power. He was having fun, and Thyra felt angry with herself all of a sudden. *I should have fought him harder. I shouldn't have let him gain the upper hand…*

In a real fight, if she really had given it everything she had, it was more than likely that she would have come out on top. But again, he was family, and because of that, she had not for one second believed that he would take it this far. This was no regular argument between them now, no ordinary punishment either. It was madness, pure and simple. Her injuries were serious, and if left untreated, the one to her leg could be life-threatening. Her thigh was gushing blood onto the bright white snow, and already, she had lost all feeling in her lower leg. Her back stung with every breath that she took. Her left arm was throbbing, and so was the side of her face. It should have been enough already, but it looked as if he had only just started with her. The thought crossed Thyra's mind that he actually meant to kill her. She averted her face as she saw the tiny flick of his wrist on the whip's handle. He was really going to do this, no doubt about it. Bjarke sniggered at her reaction.

"Thirty lashes, that should do it," he muttered.

He's enjoying doing this, Thyra realised, and she steeled herself for the first strike. She knew he would not hold back. *I will not scream…* But she almost did, surprised even though she was prepared at the violence of the blow, and the way that it literally made it impossible to catch her breath for an instant. It burned through her skin, and deep into the very fabric of her soul. She started to get scared. *My brother has lost his mind…*

"One," Bjarke called out. "Two… Three…"

At first, there was just enough pause in between each hit to allow her to recover and absorb some of the pain. But pretty soon, the pace started to increase.

"Seven, eight, nine…"

Then, there was no longer any respite, and agony was all she knew.

"Eighteen!" Bjarke shouted.

He sounded drunk. The urge to shout back and to beg him to stop was pretty overwhelming by that point. But Thyra suspected that it would be useless, and probably just encourage him to hit her harder. He would see her pleas as a sign of weakness and attempt to beat it out of her even more savagely. She bit on her lower lip so hard that she started it bleeding again. *Don't say anything. Don't let him win this. Don't show him how much you're hurting.* At the count of twenty, everything started to go blessedly dark and soundless for her anyway. And as she slowly sank into a sea of warm and soothing darkness, where none of the pain could penetrate, instead of her brother's harsh counting as he was killing her, the brilliant smile of the woman they called *The Shining One* flooded through her consciousness. Thyra melted into the memory. In a flash, she was gone.

CHAPTER THREE

She was feeling hot as hell, a little bit tired from her long and arduous hike over the mountain, and the lake looked like the best thing in the world to her at that particular moment. Thyra only hesitated for a second. She shot a careful glance around her, to make sure that she was alone. Once satisfied that no one else was around, she stripped off all her clothes, and stepped out into the water. The lake was ice-cold, as she had expected, and felt absolutely wonderful. It was late spring, sunny and warm out, and it had taken her just over half a day to make it this far into Volsung territory. She had run some of the way. Part of her was feeling slightly apprehensive at the idea of encountering people now, and yet, it was precisely the reason why she had lied to everyone at home that morning, including her beloved brother Tait, about where she was going and the reason why. The Volsung had been on her mind for a few weeks. Thyra had waited eagerly for Bjarke to disappear off on one of his early campaigns to take the first step. If she met anyone, she was just planning on saying hello to them. Surely, this would not be reason enough to start the next war, right? Her plan was to hang around the lake for a bit and see what happened. It would be very unusual if no one from the clan came to fish, wash clothes, collect water, or simply enjoy a swim, just as she was doing now.

17

What she had not anticipated was that she would come out of the lake to find that her clothes, and crucially her weapons too, had disappeared. As she ran out and started to frantically search for them, a voice suddenly echoed behind her back.

"Well, you've got some nerve, warrior."

Thyra whirled around at the sound of the female voice, and her face instantly dropped at the sight of her own sword resting in the woman's hand. From the way the newcomer was holding it, it did not seem as if she were a stranger to fighting at all. That was bad news. In the other hand, the woman carried her clothes. Trousers, shirt, both arm bracers, boots, the whole lot. Thyra swallowed hard.

"Give me that," she ordered.

The woman smiled easily.

"What?" she asked. "Clothes or sword? You can only have one, so take your pick."

Thyra frowned. *What the hell?* And how could she have been so stupid in the first place? Even Tait, who did not care about such things, would have laughed at her for making such a stupid, rookie mistake. Now, Thyra was naked on all counts, and vulnerable. No laughing matter, for sure. She hesitated. She considered rushing forward, tackling the woman down, and grabbing what was rightfully hers. But something about her appearance made her hesitate and think twice about it. The stranger was just as tall as she was, older, but obviously in peak physical shape. Very able-looking, and with a confidence that bordered on smug. *But then again, why the hell not?* Thyra reflected a little ruefully. She was not the one who had let herself get caught like this, all naked and defenceless. Thyra carried on observing her, frantically thinking through her limited options. The woman watched her back with an amused smile dancing over her lips. *Now, what will you do?* she seemed to be thinking.

She was dressed in light linen trousers, laced-up leather boots similar to Thyra's, and a sleeveless grey tunic belted at the waist. She also carried a large knife on that belt, and her own sword tucked against her side in a weathered black leather sheath. These weapons were obviously not for show and had been used before.

"So, what will it be?" she asked.

Long, silky auburn hair threaded with a little white here and there cascaded over her tanned shoulders, and as Thyra stood staring at her in stunned silence, the woman's eyes slowly travelled over every inch of her naked body. They lingered over her small yet perfectly formed breasts, perhaps a little too long... Yeah, definitely too long. And damned if the woman did not smile again then, and even lick her lips. Anger flashed through Thyra at the exact same time that her cheeks flushed a darker shade of pink.

"Sword," she snapped. "Then, I'll just take the rest from you."

The woman laughed, green eyes shining with approval.

"Yes, you look very capable of doing so," she reflected.

"Then give it back."

"In just a moment, perhaps. For now, I don't think you are in a position to argue with me much. Like I said, you do have some nerve, coming to swim here without permission. Tell me, what is your name, warrior?"

The weapons she had found waiting on the lake shore were a clear indication that this was indeed what this naked stranger was, a warrior; her flawlessly chiselled body also hinted at that fact. There were a few scars on her, which may or may not have been acquired in combat. Her clear blue eyes burned with outrage, indignation, and a hell of a lot of aplomb too. It was a pleasure to watch her and guess at what she would do next.

19

"Give me my stuff back, and then I'll tell you my name if you want," Thyra replied.

She was quite furious, along with a mixture of embarrassed and keen, as she suddenly realised from what the woman had said that this was a member of the famous Volsung clan. As bold and beautiful as Thyra had suspected they might be, and already in full possession of everything she owned. Weapons, clothes... And from the superior look on the woman's face, probably also staking claim to the rest of it that very second. *How could I be so dumb?!* But with no other solution at this point, other than to go along with her, Thyra decided to pretend as if none of it really mattered. If it came down to it, she had complete confidence in her own fighting abilities. In a confrontation, naked or not, she would win, for sure. So, she made a conscious effort to relax. Two could play this silly game, all right.

"I didn't know the Volsung owned the water," she said, matching the woman's smile with one of her own. "What about the air I'm breathing now, you own that too? My name is Thyra, daughter of Asger."

She noticed the almost imperceptible tightening of the woman's hand on the handle of her sword when she said this. And the way that she stood a little still too. Obviously, stories went both sides, and they travelled far. What sort of things had this woman heard about her own clan, Thyra wondered. That they were as fierce as the Volsung? That they should be feared just as much? Well, if that was the case, she had probably just single-handedly destroyed years of glowing reputation with one thoughtless, awkward move. *Thyra the Naked,* she reflected glumly. Definitely not so fierce now. Not so proud. Maybe her own brother Tait would write an epic poem about her failings one day. She pursed her lips in silent exasperation and struggled to keep her temper in check.

"What's your name?" she asked.

But the woman simply carried on ignoring her.

"It seems you may have ventured a little too far from home today. Have you not, Thyra, daughter of Asger the Great?" she remarked.

She was pointedly using the famed designation to show Thyra that she knew exactly who she was and belonged to. A rival clan, a dangerous tribe. The enemy, pure and simple.

"If you say so," Thyra replied with a light shrug.

The woman threw her a piercing look.

"Are you alone?"

"What do you think?"

"Do you come as a friend?"

"Yes," Thyra replied sharply. "As you can see, I've got nothing to hide. Now, are you done playing with me? What is your name?"

The woman laughed easily, and in the next instant, she did the very one thing that Thyra would have least expected of her. She stripped off her own clothes. When she was done, she walked up to Thyra, who remained standing there looking a little shell-shocked, simply watching her approach. With her clothes on, the woman had looked quite beautiful. Naked, she was simply magnificent. She put her beloved sword back into Thyra's hands. She locked eyes with her and smiled again.

"My name is Kari Sturlusson," she informed her at last. "Clan chief, and rightful owner of this land. The Volsung are my people, but I assume you already knew this, right? They call me *The Shining One*."

And on that bombshell, she walked straight past Thyra and out into the lake. She only paused for a second then, to glance back over her shoulder at the startled young woman.

"Are you coming, warrior?"

There was only one answer to that question, and it would seal their fate.

"Yes," Thyra replied.

And without even thinking about it for another second, she dropped her weapon once more.

∞

That first swim together led to a lot more over the course of the long, hot summer. It sparked some random walks all over the green valley, and entertaining, animated conversations between the two of them. Much laughter as well, and a growing sense of togetherness and appreciation. Over the following days and weeks, Thyra made a lot of new friends. She was regularly invited back to the Volsung settlement after a swim or a walk. Just for food, or some more spirited talking. She relished it all. Over there, the commander-in-chief enjoyed the privilege of having her own private quarters, situated on the side of the main long-house where the warriors lived. The first time that Thyra went, Kari's bodyguard and second-in-command, Hrorek, flat-out refused to leave them alone when she asked him to. The big bearded warrior spent the entire evening sitting at the back of the room, staring suspiciously at Thyra the whole time, and with his hand clasped tightly over the handle of his sword. Thyra herself kept him in her field of vision all the while. They did not say a single word to each other that day, and Thyra was relieved when an exasperated commander eventually managed to get rid of the man.

One morning shortly after, Thyra spotted Hrorek practicing with his men as she arrived in camp. He was everything that Bjarke had once been. Strong, fast, extremely skilled. She could not keep her eyes off him. Likewise, he spotted her immediately.

"Show me what you can do, warrior," he yelled.

Thyra shot a quick glance toward her companion.

"Go," the commander said simply.

With an eager smile on her lips, feeling excited at the unexpected challenge, Thyra immediately drew her sword, and she ran into the middle of the training ground. It was the first time that Kari had seen her in action, and she was impressed to see how good a fighter her new friend really was. In just a short amount of time, Thyra demonstrated that she was more than Hrorek's equal, and quite fearless with it too. For a little while, the clan chief simply stood aside, and she took pleasure in watching her move. Yes, this one really was excellent, she reflected. *Well, when she does not allow herself to get caught with her pants down, literally…* Kari smiled at the memory of their first encounter, and how very beautiful Thyra had looked on that day. She had only known her for a few short weeks, yet it felt like a lot longer, and in the very best possible way. Eventually, she called the young warrior back to her side. It was pretty clear from this demonstration that the two fighters could go all day without breaking a sweat, and without a single one gaining any real advantage over the other. Also, Kari wanted her near.

"Thyra, come on back," she invited. "Enough of this now."

Thyra glanced at her, and she nodded her agreement. She turned to go, but Hrorek held her back. She found that he was looking at her a little differently now. Any suspicion he might have felt toward her was gone, clearly, and a healthy amount of respect seemed to have replaced it.

"Hey, you're good, Viking," he said. "I'm impressed."

A brilliant smile illuminated Thyra's features, and deep pleasure at the honest, heartfelt compliment shone in her eyes. She could not recall her own brother ever telling her something like this; that she was good or doing well. Not even when Bjarke used to be okay with her. She felt her throat tighten at the realisation and sought to dispel the instant feeling of sadness that it sparked in her.

"Well, don't look so surprised," she joked.

Hrorek chuckled at that and clapped a friendly hand over her shoulder.

"I'm not. You really are."

"Thanks. You too."

He nodded, apparently satisfied with their little session, and went back to his training. A few days later, when Thyra was back in the village, he asked her a pointed, loaded question.

"So, tell me now, warrior. If I were to go and visit your clan tomorrow, would they welcome me in the same friendly way that we have welcomed you here?"

Thyra hesitated for a split second too long.

"I knew it," Hrorek laughed. "The Asger people still hold a grudge, even after all these years. Ha! A sign of weakness if ever there was one."

Thyra was slightly irritated at his instant condemnation and dismissal of her kin. It felt too quick, and certainly too easy to her; but all the same, she was not in a position to argue with him over the matter. Hrorek was entirely right. She could not in all honesty tell him that members of the Volsung group would be welcomed with open arms by her own people. Bjarke, for one, certainly would want to fight and draw first blood before he even heard what a delegation had to say. Indeed, it was a sign of weakness and inadequacy. It occurred to Thyra as well that in any fight that might ever take place against a man of Hrorek's calibre, Bjarke would probably not come out a winner either. Her expression darkened suddenly, and she shivered at the thought of a violent confrontation between the two men. She hoped she never had to witness something like that.

"I'm sorry," she murmured. "But yes. I don't think you should go there tomorrow. And actually, maybe not for a long while either."

Kari was quick to notice the hint of tension in her voice. In response, she rested a warm and reassuring hand over her shoulder, and caught Thyra's immediate, grateful smile toward her. She held her gaze for a few seconds and marvelled at the openness reflected in those clear blue eyes. She could feel Thyra's frustration, and she also understood perfectly her disappointment at having to answer in this way on behalf of her people. But it only made Kari appreciate her straightforwardness even more.

"It's all right," the commander reflected in a satisfied voice. "It is a start in the right direction, and we will build on it. Isn't that right, Hrorek?"

The man nodded to his chief. Then, he held out his right arm to Thyra. Surprised, but pleased with the gesture, she gripped onto his forearm. He smiled at her and gave her a frank, open look of his own.

"Yes, it is a start. And an excellent one at that," he agreed. "I'm glad you've come here, warrior. And now, you and I are friends. Yes?"

"Yes," Thyra said, relieved. "Thank you, Hrorek."

He squeezed her arm and pulled her into a brief hug. Kari nodded in full support of this little exchange, and when they found themselves alone again at last, she shared her approval with Thyra.

"You are a sparkling representative of your people, and I thank you for sharing of yourself with us, Thyra. Whether it is you or your brother Tait who succeed your father as chief, we will have a wonderful opportunity to put old misunderstandings to rest. And maybe even sooner than that."

Thyra agreed, although she was taken aback slightly by the rather stiff, official-sounding comment.

"Well, I hadn't really thought about that," she replied with a light shrug. "But I guess you're right. The thing is though, the one in line to succeed my father is Bjarke. And he will take some heavy convincing."

That evening in the valley, thunder was rolling around the peaks. From time to time, a flash of lightning would illuminate the room where the two women sat in front of the fire, sharing a simple meal of smoked salmon, apples, rye bread, and a drink of mead.

"Never thought about it?" Kari repeated, looking genuinely surprised. "But I thought that was the reason you wanted to get to know us in the first place…"

Thyra shook her head, puzzled. *What?*

"No," she replied. "Like I said, I just wanted to come and meet you, that's all. I had no ulterior motives, and certainly not any political ones of any kind."

Kari squeezed her shoulder again.

"Well. Here is a rare and amazing display of pure Viking spirit," she exclaimed, delighted. "Curiosity, fearlessness, and a willingness to explore. You are one of a kind, Thyra."

It was supposed to be a compliment, and meant as such, but Thyra simply stared at her in complete silence this time. She looked crushed. Kari's smile faded.

"Are you all right?" she asked.

"I'm fine. I just…"

Thyra bit on her lower lip, shaking her head in sudden reluctance.

"Just what?" Kari prompted. "Thyra?"

"Nothing. I should go."

CHAPTER FOUR

Thyra looked upset as she stood up and reached for her cloak. It was raining hard outside, and she had already stayed far longer than she had anticipated. Tait was covering for her back at home, but all the same, it would not be wise to push it too far. Eventually, she had felt it necessary and wise to tell him all about the Volsung and her new friendship with their chief. It was the most exciting thing that had ever happened to her, and she wanted to share her joy with him. He was thrilled as well, and pleased for her, as she had known he would be; but also, quite worried about the whole thing. *'If Bjarke ever finds out...'*, he warned her. But Thyra was adamant. *'I'm being careful. He will never know.'* As it was, Bjarke was the last person in the world that she was thinking of now, as she prepared to go. She really was not looking forward to walking twenty miles in the pitch black and the pouring rain, to climb up and over the mountain range back to her own settlement. But what Kari had said to her stung quite badly. So, that was what the commander thought this was to her. An attempt to patch things up with their people. A political and diplomatic move. Nothing else. Nothing more. Yes, it was definitely time to leave now.

"Thyra?"

"I'll see you soon, okay?" Thyra replied evasively.

She avoided eye contact with the chief. All of a sudden, she could not get out of there fast enough. The need to walk away and be alone totally overwhelmed her. She felt ashamed and deeply hurt. *A sparkling representative...* Was this really all she meant to this strong and beautiful woman? *How stupid of me to hope for more...*

It had not taken long at all for Thyra to develop the most profound respect and admiration for Kari. The commander was both gentle and kind, yet equally unyielding and tough with her men whenever she needed to be. Never unfair in any way though, and Thyra had witnessed this on several occasions. Kari was never harsh without cause, the way that Bjarke so often was. Unlike him, she was a true leader, and one that Thyra would have gladly followed into the hell of any battle Kari decided to fight. But obviously, after this last remark, she realised that it was all one-sided. Indeed, it was time for her to get out. And go lick her wounds on the way home.

"Thyra, wait..."

Kari touched her arm, but Thyra shook her off impatiently, even a little harder than she may have intended. The chief looked surprised at the gesture, but she appeared instantly sad instead of angry, which Thyra had not expected. It threw her off slightly, but only for a brief moment.

"All right, what did I say?" Kari enquired.

"You didn't say anything," Thyra repeated.

Oh, but she can be so stubborn, and proud, Kari reflected. She really loved that about Thyra. Her energy, her stark intensity. She felt herself grow strangely emotional now as she watched her standing rigidly there, with her eyes burning and her cheeks aflame. Obviously struggling with something deep inside her head that she did not want to or felt that she could share. Kari held her gaze, and she waited.

"It's fine," Thyra muttered.

Kari suppressed a small sigh. It was an extremely long time since any woman had challenged her in quite the same way that this young warrior did. Right from the word go, Kari had been attracted to her. It was her athletic looks, her vivid intelligence, and the way that Thyra smiled so brightly every single time that she looked at her, as if she really loved what she saw. Her skills with the sword were pretty exceptional, too... When Thyra stood next to her, Kari felt both safe and empowered, supported and understood, all at the same time. This had been a huge surprise for her. She was used to power and always being in command. This was not an act with her, no accident, but deeply embedded into the very core of her spirit. She did not need anyone. And she did not know how to be anything else, either. Did she even want to? She was not sure, and yet, with Thyra, she got the sense that it would be all right to allow herself to depend on someone else. There was huge vulnerability in that, which was frightening to Kari. But she had to admit that it was also weirdly seductive and attractive at the same time. She sighed again, quite audibly this time. Being with Thyra made her feel like a living, breathing contradiction. It was both frustrating and exciting, irritating and thrilling. And lately, not being with her had started to feel completely wrong too...

As if to reflect Kari's inner raging thoughts, all of a sudden, there was a brilliant flash of lightning on the outside, and a violent boom of thunder made the walls of the small dwelling shake.

"You are not going out in that," Kari declared.

Thyra just shrugged, unconcerned it seemed. She reached for the door without uttering another single word. Kari stopped her.

"What's wrong, Thyra?" she insisted. "Talk to me."

With an irritated shake of the head at being forced to explain herself, when all she really wanted to do was leave, disappear, and be alone with her disappointment, Thyra finally turned to face her.

"Don't worry, it's my fault," she snapped. "I just thought that the friendship between us was a little more personal than what you just said. But you're perfectly right. This will be good for our two clans. I guess I should focus on the bigger picture, just like you do."

Kari felt a sudden jolt of electricity tingle at the base of her spine. *So, she feels it too...* Once again, Thyra reached for the door, and once more, the commander held her back.

"Don't."

Thyra flashed her a dark, simmering look.

"In case you forgot, I don't take orders from you."

"I know full well that you do not, and I would never expect you to," Kari replied evenly. "And that's not what this is about, anyway."

With another gentle smile, she tightened her fingers over Thyra's wrist and slowly reached for her hand. She felt her grow tense, and she noticed her eyes widen ever so slightly. This was no casual touch between them, and they both knew it.

"It is personal," Kari confirmed in a murmur. "Please, will you stay and talk to me?"

Now, Thyra felt rooted to the spot. Her heart was pounding hard inside her chest. There was only one thing she wanted to do, and chatting was definitely not it. Impulsively, she raised her free hand and rested it on the side of Kari's face. She caressed her cheek with her thumb and stepped a little closer to her. Now, it was her turn to watch the other woman grow slightly uncertain.

"I think I'm done with the talking," she said.

"I am way older than you, Thyra…"

"So, what?"

"So, are you sure that you…"

"Yeah, I'm sure," Thyra interrupted.

She smiled at Kari, leaned forward, and kissed her. She had imagined this scene in her head about a thousand times. She thought about it whenever she went off to bed at night, or on one of the long walks that kept taking her back to the Volsung village. She had been unsure of how the gesture would be received, if she were ever to try such a bold move. She figured that if she was lucky, it would spark the same kind of response from Kari. If not, it would probably earn her a punch in the mouth. The commander was hard to read sometimes. But even though Kari held back a little now, the intense look in her eyes and the way that she gripped onto Thyra's hand spoke volumes.

"Okay…" she murmured. "Okay."

And then, it was just as if she had finally stopped arguing with herself inside her mind and decided to go for what she truly wanted. She wrapped her arms around Thyra's neck and lifted her legs up and around her waist. She enjoyed the small gasp of surprise the gesture elicited from her, and the instant delighted grin that followed.

"Bed," she whispered, before finding her mouth once again.

Thankfully by now, Thyra had a pretty good handle on the layout of the place. Immediately, she walked them straight to the bed, without once having to break the kiss. She sat down on it with Kari still in her arms and looked up into her eyes.

"There is something I would like you to do for me," Kari whispered.

Beautiful green eyes flashing with raw need and passion. Her cheeks were flushed as well, and she had a serious look on her face that immediately made Thyra want to take back what she had said earlier. There was nothing she was not prepared to give to this woman. No order she would not be willing to follow. It was a dangerous way to feel, but somehow, she suspected that it was safe to be that way with Kari.

"Anything you want," she replied.

Kari nodded just once and pulled her tunic over her head in one swift and easy move. She felt the slow tremble that immediately started in Thyra's legs. She pressed herself against her. No further words of encouragement were needed after this. Thyra softly wrapped her lips around Kari's left nipple, and she started sucking on it, slow and gentle. Kari was unprepared for how good that would actually feel, and she stiffened. She had to bite down hard on her lower lip not to whimper out loud at the sight and feel of her young lover doing this to her. She noticed Thyra close her eyes, and how she seemed to lose herself in the sensation. This pleasure was obviously shared both ways. Kari kept her arms draped loosely around her shoulders, caressing her cheek and running her fingers lightly through her hair, as Thyra maintained her slow rhythm, shifting from one breast to the other, sometimes only pausing briefly to glance up at Kari and make sure that she was all right.

"I want you to lie down now," Kari whispered to her after a few minutes. "My turn."

Any more of this, and she would surely start to moan in pleasure. The very last thing she needed was Hrorek crashing into the house, rushing to rescue her from a non-existent threat. She took the rest of her clothes off, and helped Thyra to do the same quickly, feverishly. Any doubts she may have harboured about making love to her had completely disappeared now. It was what they both obviously desperately wanted, and so, Kari would make it happen. To hell with the consequences, if any. She stretched herself out against her lover's strong, heated body.

She leaned over her and paused for just an instant.

"Are you all right?"

"Yes," Thyra murmured.

Kari kissed her again then. She made that next kiss deep and intimate, deliberately slow and teasing, and she reached for Thyra's breasts at the same time. Thyra made a strangled sound in her throat that sounded a little like a sob. The trembling in her legs intensified. Her skin was burning, and even though they were lying close to the fire, she knew it had nothing whatsoever to do with that, but with the incredibly erotic way that Kari was touching her. It felt insanely good to her. She allowed it to go on for a while, luxuriating in the wonderful sensations... And yet, she soon decided that her place was back on top. She started to roll over, but Kari pushed her down.

"Stop fidgeting, warrior. I am not done with you yet."

With a low chuckle, Thyra wrapped her arms around her shoulders and did what she had in mind in the first place. She went back to running her tongue over Kari's nipples, enjoying the gentle quiver in her body every single time that she took one deeper into her mouth.

"Hey," Kari protested.

Not one for being ignored, she grabbed a handful of Thyra's ash-blond hair and pulled her head back sharply. She thought that her lover might well appreciate a little rough gesture, and she was right. Thyra gave her one of those loaded, charged looks in response. Hungry, wild, and so unbelievably sexual.

"What is it, Chief?" she asked, breathing hard.

Kari grinned at her, amused at the cocky response. She was enjoying every sizzling second of this new game they were learning to play together.

"You may be stronger," she stated in a low, teasing voice, "but there are things I can do to keep you still, you know?"

Thyra laughed again, and her eyes sparkled in renewed delight.

"Oh yeah?" she challenged. "Well, I'm sure that you..."

But Kari did not allow her to finish her sentence this time. She reached in between her legs and pressed her fingers against her most sensitive point. She started a gentle circling movement, applying just enough pressure to get her notion across. Thyra shuddered all over, and immediately went a little limp on top of her.

"Thyra?"

"Uh... Um?"

Thyra heard her as if from a very long way away. She was completely and utterly lost. If Kari took her hand off her now, she would burst into tears. And beg her for more. She knew that for sure.

"Look at me," Kari whispered.

Thyra struggled to raise her head. She gave a little wasted smile.

"Yeah," she panted. "I... I guess you can do this..."

When Kari pushed her down again, all Thyra wanted to do this time was follow her lead. And the older, more experienced woman recognised this. She never once took her hands off her. She kept her lover feeling safe, grounded, and her fingers firmly in place, massaging gently. Her touch had grown as light as a feather, which was a good thing really, because Thyra did not think that she could take much more of this kind of treatment without hitting the ceiling at some point.

"Have you done this before?" Kari murmured.

Thyra looked at her, and she blinked to clear her head. She had never done this before, not really; except on her own a few times, on the rare occasion when she needed the kind of release that even running all day through the forest could not give her.

Some of the young village men had made it clear that they would help her with whatever she needed in that department, so long as she was open to the idea. One even tried a bit of a rougher and more direct approach one day, and ended up with a broken hand, a busted lip, and a fantastic black eye for his efforts. But this, right now, and with this particular woman... This was what Thyra wanted to discover more than anything in the entire world. She shivered all over again at the delicious sensation of Kari's fingers gently stroking her.

"Kari, I've not... Well... I don't know..." she mumbled.

"Sshhh, it's okay," the commander told her gently. "You are so beautiful, you know that? We'll take it slow, I promise. We've got all night."

And with that, she slowly drifted down lower, and her tongue went to replace her fingers. She felt Thyra's body grow instantly rigid and tense. She saw her throw her head back, and her hands tighten into fists over the covers. She rested a calming hand over her hard stomach and watched as a drop of sweat glistened over the tight muscles there.

"Are you all right?"

"Yes," Thyra whispered. "Please, don't stop..."

"Good," Kari smiled. "And don't worry. I won't."

She followed those words with another one of those heated kisses that seemed to be her specialty. Thyra melted into her. She felt herself sink into the bed. She could no longer move. Her eyes fluttered closed.

"Oh, Kari..." she sighed.

"Told you I could keep you still, didn't I?"

Kari's voice was at once playful and loving, teasing and reassuring. All that Thyra could do was simply nod and chuckle weakly in response.

"Yeah," she murmured. "Yeah..."

This was an entirely new and startling experience for her. She was not used to dropping her defences in front of people. She did not respond well to orders, or to letting anyone else lead. Bjarke was the exception, of course; and then, only because it was supposed to be that way in the hierarchy of the family and of the clan. When he was away, she was normally the one who took charge. But now, for the first time in her life, Thyra found herself willing to relinquish all control. What she had found with Kari was so incredible that she had never even expected it might exist. It was the gentleness of a woman's touch. The reassuring, protective shelter of pure female energy, coupled with the steely hard strength of a true leader of men. Thyra had no defence or shield against that explosive combination of powers. And even if she had possessed a thousand weapons, she would gladly have dropped every single one for Kari Sturlusson, *The Shining One*... She forgot about time, about getting caught, about Bjarke, and every single rule in the book. She followed Kari's hand when her lover led her over the edge, and when it was done, she claimed her turn and she took her there too. They carefully learned and caressed every single line of each other's bodies, over and over with undiminished passion, even after the fire went out and it became cold in the room. They made love like this all night long and well into the morning, until they were both too exhausted to carry on, and finally drifted off to sleep in each other's arms.

CHAPTER FIVE

Thankfully, Bjarke never got to yell twenty-five on that fateful day in the forest, because Tait finally caught up with his siblings, and put a stop to the madness. One look at the older man and another one at his twin sister, who was lying slumped against the tree, tied up, unconscious and bleeding, told him everything he needed to know about the situation. This was fucking bad. With no hesitation, he collected a rock from the forest floor, and crept up behind Bjarke. The man was so caught up in his action that he never even heard him coming. Tait was quick and accurate with his improvised weapon. He raised his arm and hit his brother hard against the side of the head. Bjarke collapsed. With his heart thundering in his chest, terrified that he was going to find her dead, Tait then rushed over to Thyra. He pressed his trembling fingers against her neck and checked her pulse. She was still breathing. Heaving a huge sigh of relief, he used his knife to cut through her restraints.

"Thyra!"

He grabbed her by the shoulders and shook her vigorously.

"Thyra, come on now! Wake up!"

Only half conscious, and with her eyes still closed, her first instinct was to swing a loaded fist toward his head, but he had been expecting it. He managed to dodge the punch and seized onto her wrists.

"Stop. Open your eyes, Thyra. It's me, Tait!"

Thyra quite obviously struggled to follow even that simple command. Blood from the cut on her forehead had dribbled all over her eyelids. It had started to thicken and form into a harder crust. Tait rubbed a handful of fresh snow all over her face in a clumsy attempt at helping her to regain her senses more fully. When Thyra finally managed to crack one eye open, she fixed him with a blank stare.

"Tait. Where… Where you been?" she muttered.

"I got lost, but don't worry about that," he replied. "What I want to know is what happened between you two here to lead to this kind of carnage!"

"Uh? What carnage?"

She looked confused, and he was immensely glad when she looked past him at the unconscious Bjarke, blinked hard a couple of times, and he noticed her gaze finally clear up. There, she was back for good. No long-term damage by the look of it. But then, her eyes suddenly grew wider, and she gripped onto his arm in genuine alarm.

"What did you do?" she exclaimed. "Tait, tell me you didn't…"

Tait gave a casual shrug in response, as if he really could not understand why she would worry about it. Especially after what Bjarke had just done to her.

"Don't fret about him, he's not dead. Just knocked out good and proper for a while," he explained. "I had to do something to get him off your back, you know? And somehow, I didn't think that simply asking him to stop would be enough. What the hell, sister?"

Thyra grunted, and she attempted to stand up. The pain in her leg when she moved was so intense that it almost stopped her breathing again. But never mind that.

"Help me, Tait," she requested through gritted teeth.

He grabbed onto her waist and pulled her to her feet. The sudden rush of blood to her injuries made her instantly dizzy. She fought not to give in to the urge to just bend over and vomit. Leaning on her twin, panting hard, she took several deep breaths to clear her head.

"Thyra, what is the matter with him?" Tait insisted. "Why was he beating you up so savagely? I mean, the guy was literally frothing at the mouth!"

She gave a heavy sigh.

"He knows," she murmured.

Tait immediately understood what she meant by that, and he looked frankly horrified at the news. It was the very thing he had dreaded would happen all along, and he fully understood the implications. Bjarke would never let this go. He would never forgive his sister either. If it stopped there, it would be bad enough. Unfortunately, the situation had the potential to unravel into everyone's worst nightmare.

"But how?" he exclaimed. "How did he find out?"

It was Thyra's turn to give a shrug, a silly gesture that she instantly regretted when it sent a ball of scorching fire between her shoulder blades and down along her wounded back.

"Wish I knew," she replied. "Beats me…"

It suddenly dawned on Tait that she might suspect he had something to do with it. After all, he was the only one she had confided in, and trusted enough to let into her secret. He paled quite visibly at the realisation.

"Hey, Thyra," he murmured. "I swear I didn't say anything to him. You know that, right? I would never do something like that."

She managed a much stronger, reassuring smile for him.

"Of course, brother. I know. Can you get me my sword?"

He ran to pick it up for her and paused on his way back to check on Bjarke.

"He's still out cold," he announced.

Thyra only glanced once at the older warrior, as she secured the weapon to her belt.

"Good," she approved.

"But you can't be here when he wakes up."

She was feeling slow and really sluggish again. Hazy and cold. Her head was pounding, and it was hard to think. All of a sudden, the impulse to lie down and close her eyes became pretty hard to ignore.

"Thyra, did you hear what I said?"

"Yeah," she murmured. "I heard you. But... Why?"

Tait looked at her as if she had gone completely mad. He was beginning to feel increasingly nervous himself about this situation.

"Because Bjarke didn't look like he was ever going to stop hitting you, Thyr," he pointed out to her. "You know what I'm saying? He looked like he was enjoying doing it. Killing you! You have to go away for a while and stay there until he calms down."

Thyra gave a weary nod of agreement. She suspected that Tait was right, and that it was probably the wisest thing to do at this point. She had to warn Kari and the rest of the Volsung people. She suspected that Bjarke would not calm down after this. And if his rage and fury got the better of him, things had the potential to grow a lot worse extremely quickly. If the man believed that he had been slighted by the Volsung in any way, and that his pride had been injured, he would want to go to war against them right away, no questions asked. Bjarke was mad all right, but he still yielded a lot of power and authority over the rest of the young Asger men. They would follow him, for sure.

Reluctantly, perhaps, at first; but they would eventually. And if Bjarke really wanted to launch an attack, there was no guessing the lies he would tell them to get them moving and do his bidding. Thyra's blood turned to ice at the thought of it.

"Thyra, are you with me?"

"Yes. Yes, I'm with you, Tait."

She rubbed a tired hand over her eyes and straightened up as best she could. *Come on now, this is no time to be weak!* She gathered all her strength. There was no two ways about it, she had to do this. She rested her hands over her brother's shoulders and stared intensely into his eyes.

"Will you be all right with him if I leave you now?"

"Yes, of course. I'll get Oleg to come and help me."

"And you can find your way back home in this fog? You're sure?"

He flashed her a warm, confident, and slightly teasing smile in response. This was pure Tait. Underneath his gentle and kind ways lurked a fierce intellect and an even sharper wit.

"Don't worry, sister. You know me, right? I can do anything when it really suits me, I just have to feel motivated. I can handle him. So, you can leave. Go back to your friend, have your leg looked at, and make sure that the Volsung know what's going on over here."

Thyra glanced toward Bjarke, and she hesitated again. The thought of leaving Tait alone with this brute was making her feel sick to her stomach.

"I'm wondering if maybe I shouldn't just…" she started.

"No, Thyra, you have to go," Tait interrupted.

His tone had turned urgent.

"I hit him hard, so he won't be so feisty when he wakes up. And I'll get help. I'll be all right, I promise, but you need to go now, before he comes to. It's not safe for you here anymore."

Her body felt utterly broken, and the twenty-mile hike in bad weather over the peaks would feel like double the distance, if not more, in the sorry state that she was in. Thyra felt a sudden rush of intense love for her brother. She did not want to leave him! At the same time, the thought of seeing Kari soon kept her energy up and her mind clear. She had something important to do, she just could not fail. She hugged him hard, one last time.

"I love you. Please be careful."

"I will," he grinned in reply. "And you too. I'll see you in a few days."

There was nothing left to say. Thyra stumbled away on unsteady legs and with a growing sense of unease. But she reminded herself that Tait was smart, way smarter than Bjarke was. At any rate, she had no other choice but to trust that he would manage the situation well.

For a while, she simply ran, ignoring her growing fatigue and the pain in her wounded thigh, eager to put some good distance in between her and Bjarke. But as soon as she left the relative shelter of the forest and started climbing higher, the weather turned nasty. Snow had come early this year. That very same morning, when she had gone to the river to collect water for the rest of the household, she had been forced to break through several inches of ice to get to it. And now, a violent blizzard was in full swing. She would not normally have attempted to cross over in those conditions, it was plain crazy. But once again, she had no choice. She just kept thinking of Kari, her beautiful lover, *The Shining One*… Thyra had asked her once the reason for that name. Kari replied that it was because she often travelled overseas in order to build alliances, new trade routes in the south and all along the Rhine river. She worked to create lasting friendships and a trusted bond with all the people she encountered along the way.

"I find that peace is the way forward, definitely not war."

People said that everything always seemed to shine a little bit brighter after one of her visits.

"Hence the nickname," Kari concluded.

"All right. I like it. I just thought maybe it was because of your smile," Thyra reflected casually.

She was effortlessly supportive and kind, and it was some of those qualities that Kari appreciated so much about her. That the woman would be an asset to any clan, on any battlefield, was also never in doubt with her. But hopefully, Thyra would choose a different path. And Bjarke really was right, in a way. Kari had not tried to recruit her as a warrior. But she had invited her to travel with her.

Next summer. Will you come with me?

Thyra reminded herself of that invitation, as she slipped on a patch of ice for the third time in about as many minutes and fell heavily to the ground. She tried to catch her breath, as the biting wind cut into her skin, and the lacerations on her back bled openly. She kept her mind on Kari. She imagined the warmer and gentler climes that her lover had described and pictured herself there with her. She fought to keep going in a whirlwind of snow and ice, knowing that if she allowed herself to stop and rest for even just a few seconds, there would be no getting up again. It was simply a case of 'walk or die', and despite her weakened condition, Thyra was acutely aware of that fact. She kept her head down, and she carried on putting one foot in front of the other, turning the snow bright red all the way to the Volsung settlement. And when she got there, she just dropped.

CHAPTER SIX

The commander-in-chief of the Volsung clan had learned over the years to remain impassive and to not let her emotions show, no matter what tricky circumstances she may have found herself in, or whatever might be going on with her personally under the surface. But she was clearly deeply affected when she opened the door to her most trusted lieutenant and found him standing there looking both solemn and grim, carrying her unconscious, precious lover in his arms. If Hrorek had not suspected before that the two women had become extremely close over the course of the summer months, the commander's startled and highly emotional reaction pretty much gave it all away now.

"What happened?" Kari snapped. "Get her inside, quick!"

Hrorek stepped in out of the raging blizzard and walked over to the bed. He laid Thyra on top of it and moved out of the way to allow his frantic chief access to her.

"She's covered in blood," the commander exclaimed. "What the hell happened? Who did this to her?"

She turned to him, in shock and barely contained fury, as if he should know.

"I'm sorry, Kari," he replied. "I found her lying in the snow by the side of the horses' barn. I tried to wake her up, but I could not..."

Kari turned back to Thyra, almost as if she had not heard him speak. *Oh, my darling.* She wrapped her fingers around her wrists and leaned over her.

"Thyra," she murmured intently. "Thyra, can you hear me? Come on, wake up!"

She felt growing panic at her lack of response. The young warrior who was normally so full of life, energy, and laughter now appeared deathly pale and seriously hurt; perhaps even fatally wounded. Kari narrowed her eyes at the lacerations on her back. She knew exactly what sort of violent treatment would have caused such severe injuries. Her pulse quickened at the thought. She winced at the sight of the deeper cut on Thyra's thigh, and the dark bruises on her face. She spotted the red marks and painfully raised lines around her neck and wrists and knew instantly that she had been restrained at some point too. *Who did this to you?* She felt wild, red-hot rage flood through her at the thought of anyone daring to hurt Thyra like this, intentionally. A terrible urge to punish them in kind suddenly seized her. Kari Sturlusson, *The Shining One*, never resorted to violence to solve her problems. She did not want or ever need to. But she was finding herself severely tested now. She turned back to look at Hrorek, who just stood there watching them both in worried silence. She knew that he too had grown very fond of Thyra.

"Are you all right?" she asked him.

He nodded, although without much conviction it seemed. She saw him clench his fists, and a muscle in his jaw tightened. *Yes*, Kari reflected. He was probably thinking just the exact same thing that she was. Right now though, they both needed to take action of a different kind.

"Get Sigyn over here," Kari instructed.

"Yes. Right away, Commander."

They were extremely good friends, and most of the times, she was simply Kari to him. But in a challenging situation like this one, he would refer to her as *commander*. She was the one in charge, and even though they were close, he never allowed himself to forget that fact. He had a job to do as well, and it made things easier when under pressure to remove any personal feelings between them. He ran off to find the clan healer. Kari returned her attention to her wounded lover.

"Thyra..." she whispered. "Open your eyes, my love..."

She brushed her lips lightly over hers and framed her face in both her hands. Thyra was so frighteningly cold. She had a lot of blood stuck in her hair. The back of her tunic and the thick shirt that she wore underneath had been all but shredded by the violence of the blows she had received. Kari swallowed hard. *Whoever did this to you...* The measured and wise woman who was renowned for her peaceful ways once more could not shake off the feeling of murderous rage that threatened to overcome her. She was trembling with it. And there was a lot of fear mixed in with that reaction too. Thyra was lying way too still. What if she never woke up?

"Commander."

Startled, Kari whirled around at the sound of the healer's voice behind her.

"Sigyn!"

She had not heard or even noticed her walking in, so intently focused was she on Thyra. Hrorek was standing by the side of the door, watching her with growing concern. Kari met his gaze, and she issued her orders.

"Muster all the men," she instructed. "Make sure everyone is aware and alert. I want armed guards posted at every corner of the settlement, from right this minute and until further notice, you understand?"

"Yes, Commander. Understood."

Kari gave him a sharp nod. Hrorek walked back out into the freezing night to get his warriors organised.

"Sigyn," Kari repeated intently. "Can you help her?"

She had no idea how old the medicine woman could well be. It felt to her as if Sigyn had always been around somehow, forever a reassuring staple of the Volsung world. And Kari felt her heart beat faster with sudden hope when the usually quiet, reserved, and mysterious woman looked her straight in the eye, gave her a slightly crooked smile, and rested a confident hand over Thyra's shoulder.

"We will get her warm now. We'll clean her wounds. She is young, this one, and there is a lot of life still in her. She will be fine. And so will you."

It was the most words Kari had ever heard the ancient woman speak, and she was beyond grateful for her kind message of optimism. She nodded, took a deep breath to calm her racing heart, and prepared to assist her in her work as best she could.

"Tell me what you need," she said.

They took her wet clothes off first, and covered her freezing body with dry, warm blankets. Kari used a soft cloth to clean the dried blood off of Thyra's face, out of her hair, and the sides of her neck. Sigyn wrapped a protective bandage over the cut on her forehead. Next, they moved on to her back. Thyra did not stir or flinch once, not even when the healer started to pick bits of bloody clothing off her skin, pieces that were embedded deep within the lacerations. Sigyn worked quickly. She was almost furiously focused, and not too gentle with her patient. Kari kept an anxious, close eye on her lover's face. *How can you not feel this, Thyr?* It was worrying to say the least, but to her immense relief, once Sigyn began to pour liberal amounts of alcohol straight into each cut, Thyra's eyes snapped wide open. She gave a yell that was quite loud enough to alert the entire camp. If Kari had not been there to stop her doing it, she would probably have seized the old woman around the neck and squeezed her until she dropped.

"Aha!" Sigyn shrieked in triumph.

She seemed both highly satisfied and greatly amused by Thyra's reaction, and it dawned on Kari that this had probably been the old woman's goal all along, to wake her up in this strange way eventually. Whatever the case may be or the reason why, her lover was back now, and it was all that mattered. Kari instantly prevented any more violence by gathering her up into her arms and holding her tightly against her chest.

"Calm down, my love, it's all right," she soothed. "I've got you, Thyr. You're safe now."

The first rush of adrenaline and disorientation over and done with, and with the added power of those wonderful words to reassure her, Thyra sank a little deeper into her embrace. Her eyes fluttered close again. *I made it…*

"Kari…" she murmured. And then, more urgently, "Kari?"

"Yes, I am right here," the commander replied. "It's okay."

Thyra struggled to glance up toward her, but then relief soon flashed through her usually sparkling blue eyes when she managed to do it.

"Hey…" she sighed.

Her eyes were a little red now, hazy and kind of confused. Kari wondered if perhaps tears were not far off either. She sure felt increasingly like it herself, especially when Thyra flinched sharply again at the feel of Sigyn plunging a bone needle deep into her thigh. The healing work had to be done though, and that wound definitely needed stitching up tight. Kari was grateful for Sigyn's expertise and the speed at which she worked.

"This will be over soon, darling," she promised. "Last little bit, all right? Just relax for me."

Thyra nodded, and she attempted to respond. She tried to stay awake and present, but the pain was much too great, and she blacked out once more for a while. She was not even aware that she had done so, or how long for. But when she opened her eyes again, Sigyn was gone. There was a fresh bandage wrapped around her leg, and the same to protect the cuts on her back from further contact with anything that might inflame the delicate skin. She tried to lift a hand to her forehead, to see what was there, but she was feeling too weak to even manage that. She dropped it, closed her eyes, and sighed. She started to drift off again. But in the next moment, she became aware of warm fingers caressing her cheek, and the amazing sensation of her lover's lips brushing carefully over her mouth.

"Thyra? Are you awake?"

Kari's voice. Such a warm, peaceful, gentle whisper. Thyra badly wanted to see her face now. She fought to stay conscious, she struggled to open her eyes. Her heart was beating wildly against her ribs when she finally succeeded in doing both. She was out of breath and sweating from the effort.

"Take it easy," Kari advised. "I'm not going anywhere, all right?"

She flashed her another bright, encouraging grin, and Thyra reflected that it had to be the most beautiful smile she had ever seen. She kept her eyes firmly fixed on Kari and vowed not to let anything take her down again.

"All right…"

She started to relax again. But only just one second later, a sudden picture of her brother's face surged through her mind, and a stab of fear rippled through her entire chest. *Tait. Please, please, let him be all right…* Instant panic flooded through her.

"Thyra, what's wrong?" Kari exclaimed in alarm.

She moved quickly behind her once more and attempted to comfort her. But Thyra was as tense and as rigid as a piece of steel in her arms, and she would not be soothed.

"Bjarke," she exclaimed. "Bjarke knows I've been spending time with you! He thinks I want to fight with your side, and against him somehow!"

"Thyra, please calm down…"

"But he knows, Kari!" Thyra interrupted, and she was quite frantic about it. "You have to tell Hrorek. You have to tell him to be ready."

"Okay, I will. Just…"

"And get the rest of the warriors ready too, in case Bjarke decides to come here. Do you understand?" Thyra insisted in an increasingly ragged voice. "My brother is a dangerous man. He is not thinking straight anymore!"

Kari recognised fear and raw emotion in her voice. She felt her heart tighten suddenly. The emotion, she had expected. But the fear surprised her, coming from someone like Thyra.

"Is he thinking of war, then?" she enquired.

"I… I think so…" Thyra replied. "Yes."

She was clearly exhausted after that outburst, and as she fell back onto the blankets, coughed a couple of times, and struggled to catch her breath, the Volsung commander simply nodded quietly.

"All right, then. Thank you for warning me."

While Thyra had been sleeping, she had already given further orders to that effect. She had not known about a specific threat at the time, but it did not take a genius to envisage the eventuality. Her warriors were ready to face anything that might come at them. And so, it simply meant that right now, Kari had an even more pressing question for her lover.

"How did Bjarke find out about us?" she enquired.

Thyra shook her head. Tired, reluctant tears shone in her eyes.

"I have no idea," she murmured. "But Tait is not to blame for this, I can promise you. He would never do anything to put me at risk, and he knows damn well how I feel about you too. I have complete faith in him."

Kari was not going to push for further reassurance on the matter. Thyra's absolute conviction about her brother's integrity was more than enough proof for her. There was really no need to debate this.

"Our warriors stand ready," she confirmed.

And then, she felt her heart swell at the way that Thyra pressed herself a little tighter into her embrace, and curled up against her chest, as if unconsciously looking for protection. Kari caressed her hair gently. She kissed the top of her head, and she was pleased to feel her breathing slow and relax once more after a short while. *Just one last thing to get straight before I can let you rest, my love…*

"Who did this to you, Thyr?" she whispered. "Please, tell me."

She had a pretty good idea of what must have happened by then, and that it certainly had something to do with Bjarke, but she still tensed with unspoken anger when Thyra said his name out loud.

"Yeah, it was him," she admitted.

"Oh, Thyra… I am so sorry."

"But it's probably my fault too," Thyra added in a small, broken voice.

"What?" Kari frowned in disbelief. "You're all black and blue. Your injuries are severe. How could any of this be your fault?"

"I just didn't read him right," Thyra replied with a heavy, tired sigh. "I didn't think he was serious, you know? And so, I didn't put him down when I had the chance. I didn't want to hurt him. And then, when I realised what he was going to do, it was too late."

Kari was both deeply impressed and shocked at the same time. She felt a strong rush of pride and affection toward her lover at this striking admission. Thyra had not wanted to hurt her brother, and she had almost paid for that with her own life. It was admirable in a way, if not absolutely crazy. And now, Kari worried about what would happen the next time he tried to hurt her. She suspected that unfortunately, it would only be a matter of time; probably sooner than anyone had ever dreamed it would be, and with devastating consequences for both clans involved. As far as Kari was concerned, the man presented a grave threat to them all now. They should stop him at the first opportunity. But how? Some of the rage that she had felt before at the thought of it still simmered undiluted inside of her. She took a few deep breaths to bring her emotions under control. But then, Thyra sent her right back up there with the next thing that she said.

"I have to go back," she murmured.

Kari could not quite believe her ears.

"Absolutely not," she snapped. "Why?"

"I have to make sure that Tait is all right."

"No. You are wounded. You are not going anywhere."

Thyra did not reply this time, but her silence was enough. It spoke volumes. Kari waited several long seconds to see what she would say next; still, her lover did not speak. The commander sighed in utter frustration. There was not a lot she could do to stop her if Thyra really wanted to go, but...

"Then, I will travel with you," she declared.

"No, you can't do that," Thyra argued.

"Well, try and stop me, warrior."

This was insane. Thyra opened her mouth to object again, but then she spotted the hesitant smile dancing on her lover's lips. There was a hint of uncertainty in Kari's clear green eyes, as if she knew that she was skating on thin ice, trying to impose her own ideas on her like this. But what prevailed was compassion, kindness, and deep understanding. No one had ever looked at Thyra with quite so much love and concern in their eyes before. She recognised what Kari was doing, and she knew the reason why. *I am worried about you too...*

"All right, I don't think I would want to do that, Chief," she murmured. "Try to stand in your way. But I need to look after my brother."

"And so, I will not attempt to stop you either, I promise," Kari answered, relieved. "But for now, please, will you try and get some sleep? The quicker you recover, the sooner you can go, all right?"

Thyra nodded. She started to say something else, twice, but stopped herself both times before she could say it. Kari thought that she felt her struggle not to cry.

"What is it?" she murmured.

There was another slight hesitation. And then, it only came as a whisper, as if Thyra was afraid to ask. In fact, she had never requested this sort of thing of anyone before.

"Can you stay with me?" she murmured.

"Yes. I will not leave your side, Thyra."

Somehow, the way that Kari said this sounded like a much bigger, more solemn promise. But Thyra was too tired to pursue it. Reassured, she just rested her head over her lover's chest, closed her eyes, and drifted off into a deep, dreamless sleep.

CHAPTER SEVEN

Over the next few days, the storm worsened quite significantly. It was as if the Universe was granting Kari's not-so-secret wish for her lover to stay in camp and allow herself to heal properly. Hurricane-force winds ravaged the mountain and the valley. It snowed incessantly, and the entire surface of the lake froze solid, several thick inches deep. A few of Kari's toughest and most experienced warriors, which included Hrorek amongst them, attempted to go up and over the mountain pass, but the conditions up there were so atrocious that even they could not get through. This was excellent because it afforded the Volsung settlement the best protection in the world, although it also meant that Thyra was now completely cut off from the rest of her clan. Under normal circumstances, the situation would not have been a problem for her, and probably just the opposite in fact. But now, she knew that Tait was stuck on the other side, having to deal with the whiplash effect of her actions on his own. She was worried sick about him. Still, even she had to admit that the storm gave her a much-needed opportunity to rest and recover. Yes, she was young and strong, and yet, her injuries were significant, and required several days of complete rest before she started to feel better. And of course, it was also pretty wonderful to be granted some all-alone time with Kari...

The commander kept her in bed for most of it, and they devised ingenious ways of making love that did not start Thyra's injuries bleeding all over again. Kari fed her delicious lentil and chicken broth, rich honey-cured salmon, and wonderful herb-flavoured wine. They snuggled together, warm and safe inside the chief's private quarters. And mainly, they talked.

"Such wanderlust," Kari observed one morning, laughing at some of Thyra's more pointed questions about her recent travels. "Yes, I have heard of the hot sandy deserts of which you speak. But I have not seen those lands myself. How did you hear of it?"

"My father used to tell me all kinds of good stories," Thyra replied. "And then later, Bjarke did too. I really want to go one day and see it all for myself."

She looked quietly thoughtful, as Kari knelt in front of her by the side of the fire, changing the bandage on her thigh. So far, they had managed to avoid discussing many of the delicate subjects that still weighed heavily on their minds. But it had stopped snowing during the night, and the winds had eased up. This was a clear sign that they would not be able to hide away from everyone else for very much longer. Thyra was keenly aware that soon, Kari's duties would claim her back to the real world, and she would have to face her own clan and family. Over the turbulent weeks and months that were to come, she would look back on these stolen moments together with a mixture of sadness and gratitude. But for now, her strength was quickly returning, and she was not thinking about such things.

"And so very restless too," Kari smiled. "Although I have to admit that has its uses sometimes, and I rather enjoy it."

She threw a teasing, knowing wink in her direction. Thyra turned instantly bright red at the memories of what they had got up to in bed, but she did not miss a beat.

"Oh. Enjoy pinning me down, do you?" she challenged.

Kari's smiled widened even more. She chuckled in reply.

"Only when you struggle. Now, how's your leg?"

"Great. Like I never even got hurt."

"Really?"

Kari raised an incredulous eyebrow. Thyra gave her a light, slightly impatient shrug in response. She hated not feeling a hundred percent fit for duty.

"Well, not really," she admitted. "But it won't be long."

She finished getting dressed in the brand-new clothes that Kari had procured for her. Warm trousers, a well-cut tunic, and a pair of sturdy boots that would last her a long time. Best of all was the thick layer of protective leather that went over the tunic like a sleeveless top, and which fitted over Thyra's chest and torso like a second skin. It was custom-made especially for her. Not only did it highlight her athletic figure and make her look amazing, but no whip would be able to cut through that thing. Kari had made damn sure of it.

"This is perfect," she approved, as she ran her hands over the material and kissed Thyra at the same time. "Now, let's just add a few more things."

There was a large belt with a special loop to fit her sword through. And a pair of arm bracers of the finest quality, made of pure leather and bronze.

"Kari, these are beautiful," Thyra reflected, in awe.

"Yes, they are. How do you feel?"

"Safe. Thank you."

Kari glanced at her, surprised at the softness in her tone. Thyra looked sharp, strong, and pretty invincible in her new fighting clothes. What a strange thing it was then that the sight of her like this only made Kari want to protect her even more, and do everything in her power to keep her out of harm's way...

"That's good," she agreed. "I'm glad, and you're welcome. But I meant your head, Thyr. How are you feeling?"

Thyra had woken up crying from a nightmare in the middle of the night, with a blinding headache and raging fever to add to the bad dream. It had only lasted for about an hour or so, but it was enough to put her down for the count. Now, she looked fine once more, but Kari was still worried about her and keen to check.

"Oh, that's all right now," Thyra confirmed easily. "I'm feeling good."

She closed her eyes and smiled when Kari rested her hands over her cheeks. Thyra wrapped her arms around her shoulders and pulled her against her chest for a gentle hug. She thought that Kari clang to her a little harder than maybe necessary.

"Are you all right?" she whispered.

She felt the commander nod against her shoulder.

"Yes, fine. I've just never been too good at waiting."

Thyra knew that she was referring to Bjarke because she was feeling the exact same way. What was her brother up to at this very moment? She would have given a lot to be able to find out what his plans were.

"Come on, why don't we go out and get some fresh air?" she suggested. "Then, we can figure out what to do next, and how to put an end to this stupid game."

"Good idea," Kari approved. "Just one more thing before we do."

She pulled back and reached for the heavy torc of braided gold that she wore around her neck. The necklace had been in her family for generations. It was a symbol of her clan, and also a mark of her authority and status as commander-in-chief of her community. The torc had been moulded to include the Volsung symbol of a wolf on one open end of it, and a raven on the other.

This was in reference to the Viking god Odin, of course. Kari smiled when she spotted the startled look in Thyra's eyes, as she took off the torc and raised it up to her neck.

"What are you doing?" Thyra protested. "Kari, I can't wear this."

"Can you not? Tell me why."

"It's too much. It's too beautiful for me, and I'm…"

"If that is what you think, then you can stop right there," Kari replied, interrupting her before she could say anymore, and rather sharply too. "You are beautiful to me, Thyra, and I want you to have it. Now, you don't just look like one of my warriors. This marks you as one of the Volsung, for sure, but even more importantly, it identifies you as a member of my own family. I want everyone to see this, and to know how much you mean to me."

She paused, as if she had suddenly realised something else important.

"Of course, I will understand if that is not what you want."

Thyra was a little puzzled at how quickly Kari had gone from confident and assertive to quiet and withdrawn, and so heartbreakingly sad with it too. She immediately reached for her hand.

"Hey…"

The chief raised her eyes to her, looking serious and slightly afraid. Now, for the first time, she really felt exposed and at her most vulnerable. But of course, Thyra would never ever think of hurting her. She could not for one second understand why Kari would feel so unsure of her still, so worried about how she truly felt about her.

"Kari, I love you," Thyra said to her simply. "You have no idea how proud I would be to wear your torc. And for everyone to see it and know that I belong to you."

They had shared a lot of things over the last few days, some deeply personal and private, some even painful, and yet, neither of them had ventured quite this far yet. Thyra was well aware of that, and she intentionally used powerful words. She said, '*I belong to you*'. Not 'to your family', not 'to your clan'. *I belong to you*. If she had not already managed to show Kari that she was hers through her actions and her behaviour, then she wanted to make certain that the woman heard it from her own voice now. She saw the sudden flash of emotion that flickered across her lover's features. She spotted tears welling up in her brilliant green eyes.

"Please, don't cry. I love you. I will never leave you."

Kari shook her head. She could not speak.

"Come here," Thyra whispered.

The usually controlled and emotionally-reserved Volsung commander allowed her younger lover to pull her into her arms. She enjoyed the strong wave of comfort and protection that instantly enveloped her when Thyra tightened her embrace on her body and stepped even closer to her. She felt the cool brush of new leather against her cheek, and the warmth of her fingers as Thyra gently massaged the back of her neck. She did not say anything else as Kari cried, reluctantly at first, and then harder, sobbing as if she would never be able to stop. Thyra stood waiting calmly and patiently, simply allowing her to do so. She had no necklace to give, no gold or new clothes to offer to the woman she loved, but one thing she could give her was warmth, support, and strength when it was needed most. No questions asked, and certainly no conditions imposed. Thyra was prepared to spend the rest of her life holding her like this if that was what Chief Kari Sturlusson required of her. She closed her eyes; she lowered her head slightly; and she kept her arms safely around her lover, as Kari let go.

After a while, the hard sobbing finally stopped. Kari gave a heavy, exhausted sigh. She shifted a little in Thyra's strong embrace.

"Sorry," she murmured.

"Doesn't matter," Thyra replied.

Kari made a single half-hearted attempt to pull away then, because she felt that it was what she should do now. But she was grateful when Thyra tightened her arms around her in response, and shook her head no.

"Wait..."

Neither of them was ready to let go just yet.

"So long as you were not crying because I just told you that I love you," Thyra whispered. "Um? You were not doing that, right?"

There was such genuine tenderness and compassion in her voice. Kari smiled at the gentle teasing that was also expertly weaved into the question, just to help her get over the tears and the emotion.

"Not in a million years," she promised. "And I love you too."

"Good, because you're not having your neck thing back."

Kari chuckled softly. More humour to fight the pain. This was a true warrior's way. She did pull back then and rested the palm of both hands over Thyra's chest. She looked at her. She spotted concern and just a trace of hesitation in her limpid blue eyes. But Thyra was much too respectful to ask any probing questions. And Kari was not certain that she would have been able to offer any answers anyway.

"I'm not really sure where that came from," she admitted.

"Well, I don't need to know. Are you feeling better?"

"Yes... Thank you."

"Good. Here, drink this."

Thyra passed her a fresh cup of water, and then she gently brushed her thumbs all over her lover's face. Over her eyes and cheeks, restoring colour to her skin, kissing and erasing traces of the painful tears that she knew Kari would not want anybody else to see. Kari let her do this. She allowed herself to be touched in this way, to be soothed and comforted in this way. Now that Thyra's injuries had almost healed, her strong protective side was re-surfacing once more, and Kari was a little stunned to discover how much she actually enjoyed being on the receiving end of it. She shook her head in amazement. Indeed, life with Thyra was full of surprises.

"Right, Chief. Now that we're done with this, do you think I can finally be allowed to go and eat something?" Thyra enquired suddenly.

She stood watching Kari with a pretend anxious look on her face, and that sexy little smile of hers dancing over her lips. Once again, she knew just what to say to rescue them from another emotionally charged moment. Kari burst out laughing.

"Absolutely," she declared. "Let's go, my warrior. I think you've more than earned it."

They stepped outside into a world of brilliant sunshine and rapidly melting snow. After so many days of enforced inactivity, the entire camp was now buzzing. People walked past, busy with their work, raising their hands for a quick greeting when they spotted their chief, but otherwise barely paying attention to them. Satisfied, Kari took Thyra by the hand. She laced her fingers through hers, as they started to make their way toward the main square and the dining room that was there. Before they could make it though, and tuck into the hearty breakfast that Thyra had in mind, Kari looked over her shoulder at the sound of heavy footsteps behind them.

"Commander!"

It was Hrorek, coming toward them at a dead run. Two of his warriors were with him. Thyra stopped at the sight of the men approaching so fast, and her entire body immediately grew rigid when she spotted the grim look on Hrorek's face. No way this was going to be good news. Kari threw her a sharp glance. She knew, too. Instead of letting go, she tightened her grip over her fingers.

"Commander," Hrorek exclaimed as soon as he caught up with them. "A group of ten men have just been spotted coming down from over the mountain pass. They are on horseback and headed straight toward us."

"Fighters?" Kari enquired.

"Yes, Commander, it looks like it. They are flying the Asger flag."

On hearing the news, Thyra's right hand instinctively flew to the handle of her sword. Hrorek glanced at her. Kari noticed how his eyes first stumbled and then lingered over the distinctive necklace that Thyra now wore around her neck. It sparkled in the sunshine with her every movement, and it would have been hard to miss. The man looked surprised at the sight of it, slightly taken aback, but only for a brief moment. He met his chief's gaze once more, flashed her a quick smile of approval, and lowered his head as a sign of respect. Kari nodded back to him in the same way.

"Close down the settlement, and put your men in place," she instructed. "You know what to do. Then, the three of us will go out there and meet the Asger party."

"Yes, Commander!"

Once Hrorek was gone, Kari turned to her lover. She met her gaze.

"Are you all right with doing this, Thyra?" she asked. "Do you want to ride with us?"

Thyra looked both surprised and pleased to be consulted on the matter. With her mouth feeling slightly dry, and her heart beating fast inside her chest at the prospect of an imminent encounter with her dangerous older brother, she just nodded once.

"Yes, Commander. I'm happy to go with you."

Kari flashed her a gentle smile. *I love you, Thyra.*

"Then, let's go," she said.

CHAPTER EIGHT

They rode three-a-side, with Kari in the middle and Thyra close to her on her right. They were just getting out of view of the Volsung settlement when the Asger party of ten came into their line of sight. The men had slowed down.

"Thyr, can you make out who this is?" Kari asked.

It was immediately obvious to Thyra who the men were.

"Yes," she said. "This is Bjarke, riding in the middle on the big black horse. And he's brought all of his best fighting men along with him."

"In this case, we should stop right here and let them come to us," Hrorek suggested.

"Agreed," Kari approved. "Thyra?"

"Yes," Thyra replied. "Let them bridge the gap."

This did not take very long. Soon, the Asger group stopped coming forward as a whole, and Bjarke cantered over toward them on his own. Kari took a couple of deep calming breaths to steady herself before the encounter. A disturbing picture flashed through her mind of Hrorek, carrying a wounded Thyra into her home on that cold and stormy night. She was glad when the debilitating anger that she had felt did not immediately come flooding back through her again. She needed a clear head to deal with this Bjarke, and blind rage would certainly not help her achieve the positive result that she was after. She watched him approach in total silence. She was not surprised to find that he was an imposing-looking man, even from a distance. He still carried a full head of hair, although it was turning slightly grey at the sides; and a thick curly beard too, which was a deep, dark-auburn in colour. His eyes were small, icy blue, and set a little too close together in his curiously puffed up face. This no doubt was the result of an unhealthy relationship with alcohol in general, and mead more specifically. There was nothing at all forthcoming or intelligent in his gaze, and actually, quite the contrary. Nevertheless, when Bjarke brought his powerful horse to a stop in front of them, in a flurry of freshly fallen snow, Kari nodded respectfully toward him.

"Welcome, Bjarke of Asger," she greeted him in a strong, clear voice.

She saw no harm in addressing him the same way that she would have any other traveller. All who came as friends were welcome on her land. That was her personal rule, and she had yet to find out Bjarke's reason for showing up. It might not be what she feared, after all. She had to work quite hard not to dwell on the fact that this was the brute who had almost beaten to death the woman she loved so dearly. But she knew she had to remain totally in charge of her own thoughts and emotions. Otherwise, she would only have revenge and murder on her mind, and she would be no better than him. This was the only reason why Kari was allowing him the benefit of the doubt; to preserve her own sanity and the integrity of her beliefs. To keep her lover safe, of course. And to protect her warriors, and the rest of the villagers as well. He seemed surprised by her attitude and unsure of how to respond. He barely glanced at her and did not return the greeting. Instead, he frowned at Hrorek, and positively glowered at Thyra.

"So, missed me?" he sneered.

Thyra had been looking intently toward the group of Asger warriors, searching for her twin brother. She recognised them all, but Tait was not amongst them. Now, she returned her gaze to Bjarke when he spoke to her, and simply shrugged.

"How's your back, sister?" he continued. "Itchy yet?"

This was typical Bjarke. He loved to push people, bring up unpleasant stuff, and provoke them into an argument or a fight. But Thyra knew his MO better than most. She remained calm, and again, she did not reply. She refused to play his game, and Kari watched attentively as the man's expression slowly started to darken. *Well, it did not take long…* She felt a definite shift in the air around him. This was not a man in control.

"So, what is the purpose of your visit?" she asked.

He shot her a furious look, as if she had no right to be there.

"I came to speak to my sister. Nothing to do with you."

Kari glanced briefly toward Thyra. She noticed the easy way she sat on her horse. Thyra was relaxed, with the fingers of one hand curled loosely over the reins and the other one resting comfortably on her thigh. She appeared confident, calm, and in total control. Looking like a seasoned warrior, which was the complete opposite of her brother.

"Well, she's right here."

"In private, Volsung," Bjarke spat.

Kari suppressed a smile at this weak show of temper, and she waited to hear what Thyra would say. She appreciated the straight-forward, heartfelt answer that came from her lover.

"Whatever you have to tell me, you can say in front of my friends, Bjarke."

"Friends?" he snarled.

"Friends. Family. Both are true and apply equally in their case."

This was a provocative statement, expertly delivered and without any emotion, which made it even more powerful. It hit home. Bjarke was clearly fuming. And it also became obvious to him from her demeanour that Thyra would not budge either. He decided to allow her this little advantage just now, to make her believe that she was ahead of him. And then, he would screw her into the ground.

"Very well," he declared. "First of all, know that you have been banished from our group. You are no longer a member of the Asger clan. The way you have conducted yourself is totally disgraceful. Leave, and don't come back."

"I already left, and I'm not..."

"Shut up!" Bjarke yelled, as was his habit.

"... I am not planning on coming back," Thyra finished in an even tone. "I just want to see my father one last time and say goodbye."

"That old senile fool!" Bjarke exclaimed, as if her love for her father was a personal insult to him. "Why would you bother with him?"

She sighed and shook her head in obvious wonder at his profound stupidity.

"If you don't know, then I don't think explaining it to you will help," she remarked. "And I want to speak to Tait as well. After this, I will disappear and you will not have to see me ever again, I promise."

Secretly, Thyra was hoping that her twin brother would decide to follow her. In fact, she was pretty sure that he would. As a keen writer and a talented poet, he had expressed a strong desire to travel, and done so more than once. It was clear though that his wish was not to be carrying a sword and fighting for his brother when he eventually got around to doing it. Tait would choose to come with her, Thyra was absolutely certain of it now.

She felt quietly excited at the thought of being reunited with him soon, as Bjarke carried on with his list of announcements, and both Kari and Hrorek waited patiently for him to finish.

"Second of all, understand that I am now in command of the Asger clan."

Thyra did not let it show, but she winced inside at the news. She was not overly surprised, of course. She knew that Bjarke had been struggling under their father's lead for a while now, and the old man was a little too old and weak to put up much resistance against him. But she wondered how the rest of the people felt about this sudden change of rule. She suspected that anyone who dared to challenge Bjarke about it would meet a swift and painful death. Maybe some already had… Thyra shot a quick glance toward her lover. Bjarke assuming command was bad news, and Kari knew it too. But the chief refused to give voice to her disappointment. Instead, she kept focusing on what she wanted.

"I hope that you will consider allowing our communities to grow closer, Commander," she suggested to him. "The Volsung people have enjoyed getting to know Thyra, very much so, and we are looking forward to much stronger links with your clan. For trade and travel, of course, and even more importantly, for friendship and exchange between us all. I believe that we can do this, if only we…"

But Bjarke threw his head back, and he laughed. For the first time that morning, Thyra felt herself about to lose patience with his antics. How dare he behave in such a way? Why did he not show Kari the respect that she deserved, and that she was granting to him right now, even as he took the liberty of stepping onto her land unannounced and without permission? Thyra fought the urge to jump off her horse and pull him off his mount. She was really itching to deliver a nice hot punch to his fat and ignorant face that would make him think twice about laughing. When she looked at Hrorek, Thyra received instant confirmation that the Volsung warrior was not impressed by her brother's behaviour either. There was a strong expression of distaste on his face, as Hrorek continued to watch and carefully assess the man.

"Friendship?" Bjarke exclaimed in disbelief. "You must be mad!"

"Bjarke, don't you understand that this is the only way forward?" Thyra snapped. "Aren't you fed up of holding on to stuff that happened before you could even walk? What the hell can it really mean to you now? Let it go!"

But Bjarke had delivered his message, and he was clearly done with the talking.

"You," he snarled, pointing his finger at her in a stabbing gesture, "are now the enemy, you understand? Just a wretched Volsung dog, like the rest of them! If you come anywhere near the village again, my archers will shoot you dead."

Thyra had expected this might happen, and she had steeled herself in anticipation. She did not flinch at his words, even if it broke her heart to hear him say that to her. She had loved him so much once... He was her brother, her own flesh and blood. No matter what, she still did love him, and she did not want to lose him. As their gazes met, he could not have failed to realise her true feelings. But he simply spat on the ground and turned his horse around.

"Bjarke," Thyra called sharply after him. "I will not stay away from Tait, and he won't either. You cannot do this to us, do you hear me? BJARKE!"

Only with this last call did she raise her voice in frustration and allow the full range of her emotions to truly show. Only then did Bjarke stop, and glance back at her over his shoulder.

He was smiling now, pleased to have sparked an emotional reaction from her at last. It felt like victory to him. After all, she was the woman he had always viewed as his biggest challenge, a threat that he had to contain, and eventually, hopefully, disable for good.

"What's the matter, sister?" he chuckled darkly. "Feeling a little rattled all of a sudden, are we? Never been too good under pressure, uh?"

Kari witnessed the exchange between them in dismayed silence and with a growing sense of alarm. In spite of herself, she shuddered at the thinness of the man's smile, and the emptiness that she could see reflected in his eyes. Everything about his demeanour and his attitude spelled out rage, jealousy, and pure hatred toward his younger sister. How was it even possible for a second that this violent, blood-hungry man and her beautiful, kind, compassionate lover could be related in any way? Kari wondered. It was simply astonishing. And of course, by assuming total command of his entire clan, this bully was now going to turn into a despot. All the signs were there. It was frightening, demoralising, and Kari suddenly realised with an icy shiver of impending doom that this day would probably not be the last that she would hear from him. A man like Bjarke would be looking for any excuse to launch a war. And if he could not find a good reason, he would just make one up. The love of her life was caught right in the middle of this nightmare, and Kari was totally committed to her. She was also in charge of the safety and well-being of her entire community. Men, women, and their children. People who trusted her with their lives.

"Almost forgot about that precious little brother of yours," Bjarke said with a belligerent shrug, interrupting her thoughts. "You really love that boy, don't you, Thyra?"

CHAPTER NINE

Bjarke snorted in disdain at the instant charge of emotion that flashed across Thyra's eyes when he mentioned her twin. He had always been jealous of their bond. *Oh, well.* He reached for the large satchel that he carried slung over his chest and threw it on the ground in front of her.

"Here's a little memento for you, sister."

And on those puzzling and rather ominous words, Bjarke threw his horse into a furious gallop, and headed straight back toward his waiting men. Thyra did not bother to watch him go, or even call after him this time. Instead, she immediately jumped off her pony. She looked impatient, frustrated, and slightly worried too, as she hurried to pick up the satchel. Kari would never forget what was about to happen next. She had her eyes firmly fixed onto her lover when Thyra reached into the bag and looked to see what was inside. At first, an expression of total incomprehension registered over her features. But then, she blinked hard a few times, and Kari watched her eyes grow wide. She saw her shake her head, just once, and frown in disbelief.

"Uh…" Thyra said.

Kari slid off her own horse and started walking toward her. Something was wrong, she could already tell by the look on her face. She just had no idea yet how horrendous it would turn out to be.

"What is it, Thyr?" she asked. "You okay?"

Thyra did not reply. She reached for what was inside the bag, and a split second later, finally managed to make true sense of what she was looking at. It was repulsive, revolting, totally unthinkable. And as the picture finally crystallised into reality, she let out a wounded scream and fell to her knees. The bag slipped from her fingers. The bleeding, severed head of her cherished twin brother hit the snow with a sickening thump. Even Hrorek recoiled in shock. Kari gasped in sudden horror.

"Is that what..." Hrorek started.

But Kari did not even hear the rest of his question. Only one thing was on her mind at that particular instant, and it was Thyra. She threw herself at her and grabbed onto her shoulders roughly. She attempted to turn her away from this appalling scene.

"Just look at me," she urged her intently. "Thyr, listen. I want you to keep your eyes on me, all right? Just keep looking at me!"

But Thyra's gaze was riveted onto her brother's head, and Kari may just as well have been talking to a wall. She shook her harder to catch her attention.

"Thyra!" she yelled.

She could not get her to glance away, or even move. When Thyra did take her eyes from Tait, briefly, it was to stare at the blood on her own hands. Her twin brother's blood. *He's dead. Dead. Tait is dead...* Kari noticed her grow even paler, and visibly sway.

"Take a deep breath," she instructed. "Stay with me, Thyra. Come on, I will get you through this."

But Thyra was not listening. Her breathing had deteriorated even further and was now dangerously out of control. In the next instant, she began to shake violently as well.

"Tait!" she cried out in a strangled voice.

Big painful tears that she was not even aware of poured down her entire face, as she struggled to reconcile the ludicrous discovery of her brother's head stuffed inside a bag like this with her sense of a good, solid, functioning reality. She simply could not wrap her mind around it. It was too hard, too ghastly; it made no sense at all. Thyra suddenly became aware of a startling new sensation at the back of her head. It was like being dragged down into a deep, pitch-black hole. There was no air. It was like drowning. And it only became worse with every breath that she failed to take in.

"No," she moaned. "It's not real. Can't be. This cannot be real!"

"All you have to do is stay with me," Kari repeated to her. "Keep breathing with me, nice and slow. Thyra, come on. You can do this. Just listen to my voice, my darling. Focus on me."

She tried to hold her gaze, to keep her from sinking deeper into an even more devastating panic. But she could not reach her this time. Thyra was already too far gone, lost in a world of grief and incomprehension, plummeting lower down and further out of touch with every passing second.

"Tait... I can't... No, no, NO!"

Her voice broke on that last yell, and she staggered to her feet.

"Where is he?" she panted. "Where is Bjarke?"

She looked toward the mountain, but the Asger party had already completely disappeared from view. Thyra swore in fury, drew her sword, and started running toward her horse. Kari had not seen this coming.

"Thyra, don't!" she shouted. "Wait!"

But her urgent plea fell on deaf ears.

"Hrorek, stop her! Don't let her go!"

Kari realised that Thyra's only desire right now would be to catch up to her older brother, and just sink her blade through his body. To bury her sword as deeply and as hard into Bjarke as it would go, to cause maximum damage and pain. Maybe she was thinking of slicing his head off in revenge too, who knew? But there was no way that Kari could let her do any of this. First of all, Thyra would not stand a chance against the ten Asger men put together. Secondly, if she started any kind of a fight with Bjarke, it would give the man his perfect, ready-made excuse for war. Maybe it was all a part of his sinister plan anyway. Perhaps he had already set up a deadly ambush for his sister and was only waiting for her to come running into it. Third but certainly not least, this was not the way that Kari Sturlusson operated. Definitely not a path *The Shining One* would ever follow.

"Thyra, wait! Don't do this!" she exclaimed with mounting urgency. "Listen to me at least, before you go and do something stupid!"

But her words did not register with Thyra. She was already on her horse, and about to launch into deadly pursuit of her brother. As she flew past him, already close to maximum speed, Hrorek jumped up and grabbed her around the waist. As the horse carried on, he wrapped a strong hand around Thyra's belt and pulled her off the racing pony. They both fell heavily to the ground. Oblivious to the intense rush of pain that shot through her already wounded leg, Thyra was the first to get back on her feet. Sword still firmly in hand, she started to move ahead of him. But Hrorek would not call it quits so easily. He grabbed onto her ankle with both hands and gave it a sharp pull to trip her up.

"Stop right there!" he shouted.

Thyra stumbled, almost fell, but she kicked back hard, and managed to shake him off. She did not hear him grunt in pain.

She did not notice the sudden stream of blood that came pouring out of his injured nose. Once again, she straightened up to her full height, and kept on going. Only this time, it was *The Shining One* herself that she found standing in front of her, blocking her way. The commander's request was subtle. It was not a shout, not an order. It came laced with immense love and compassion. And it was delivered calmly and evenly, yet with tremendous power infused into one single word.

"Stop."

In her blind rage, it looked for an instant as if Thyra would just blow right through her. Kari was standing in a risky place, right in between the young warrior and the fast horse that she desperately needed to catch up to Bjarke. Breathing hard, and looking dangerous, Thyra took a single additional step toward her. But Hrorek was ready to make another move. She felt him get into position. She heard the light crunching of the snow as he prepared to grab on to her. Thyra was faster. She immediately whirled around to face him down.

"Stay back, Hrorek," she muttered. "Don't touch me, all right?"

She did not raise her sword against him. Of course, she would never do such a thing. But she did put up her hand in obvious warning, a sure signal that he should not attempt to come any closer or suffer the painful consequences of it. She did notice him bleeding then, and felt a single stab of regret at the realisation that she had caused this to happen. But she could not stop going. Could she? No! She could not let this go. She stood her ground in front of him. Unbeknownst to her, behind her back, Kari also made a quick soothing gesture toward Hrorek for him to stand down. He nodded to both of them in response and relaxed his stance. One more time, Kari attempted to get through to Thyra.

"Thyr," she invited. "Listen to me, please."

Thyra turned around to face her. Truth be told, she could barely see her lover anymore through all the tears burning in her eyes. Her entire world was spinning out of control. It had turned cold suddenly, so bone-chilling cold. Nothing about the situation felt real to her anymore.

"Let me go after him, Kari," she said.

"I can't do that. They would kill you!"

"Then give me some of your men!"

Kari shook her head in a negative gesture.

"Why not?" Thyra pleaded intently. "If we take him out now, there will be no war! I promise, Kari. I will take control, and I will not let it happen. Please. Help me go after him and bring him down. HE KILLED MY BROTHER!"

That last sentence was delivered in a scream. Kari felt her own heart breaking at the despair that she could hear searing through her lover's voice. She took an impulsive step forward and rested a soothing hand over Thyra's right cheek. She could feel her trembling still. She could sense how much horrible pain she was in. It hurt her very deeply too.

"Oh, baby," she whispered.

In spite of herself, Thyra leaned into her touch, and she closed her eyes for a brief instant. Kari was deeply moved at this raw display or trust and affection, especially during such a heart-wrenching moment in time. She reached for Thyra and pulled her into her arms. She held her hard and tight against her own body.

"Thyra, I love you more than I ever thought possible," she murmured. "You know I do. And that is why I can't let you do this. I just cannot."

CHAPTER TEN

As Kari had anticipated, Thyra soon attempted to pull back and away from her. She was enraged, and on top of it, also feeling deeply lost. She was terribly let down by what she perceived as such an apathetic reaction from the mighty Volsung commander. Kari was her lover. She was a powerful woman. And she was on her side, Thyra knew that. So, why the hell would she not want to help her achieve revenge against Bjarke, especially when she had all the means to do so?

"Let go of me," she snapped.

Kari released her instantly, reluctantly. She did not attempt to force the embrace again, even though she would have loved to keep her arms around her lover and attempt to comfort her. But she could see that Thyra was in shock, and not thinking straight at all. It would not be wise to insist. Kari was desperate to carry on talking to her though. She wanted to keep doing it until she could get her to calm down. In her current state of mind, Thyra was not only a danger to the Volsung people as a whole, but to herself as well. Kari could not let this go, not when there was so much at stake.

"But why not?" Thyra kept repeating and asking her over and over in an increasingly ragged and worn-out voice. "Bjarke killed Tait. Do you understand? He mutilated... He..."

She stumbled over the rest of the words, simply unable to articulate the description out loud. Just imagining the dreadful scene in her mind's eye was enough to cause the blood to completely drain from her face once more. She looked like she was going to faint, or be sick, and maybe both.

"Do not think about it, Thyra," Kari urged her again. "Do not think about how it happened. It's over now. Tait is at peace. The only one you are really hurting by dwelling on the details is yourself."

"But I can't, don't you understand?" Thyra shouted.

She looked all around unsuccessfully for something to slam her fists against. She was feeling so betrayed. Of course, what Bjarke had done to Tait was all that she could focus on! What else? Her mind was full of screaming, horrible questions about it. *Was it quick? Did he suffer? Did he know it was coming? How many strikes did it take to do it?* She glanced toward the ground, shivering in fearful anticipation. But Hrorek had acted quickly and respectfully for her. He had already recovered her brother's remains. There was not even a drop of blood left in the snow now. As if it were all just a dream. Thyra shivered again.

"Why, Kari?" she insisted. "Do you really expect me to just let this go? To simply do nothing, and pretend as if it doesn't matter?"

"Of course not," Kari replied, in a firm yet gentle voice. "But you have to understand that sometimes, not responding with crushing violence to such a disastrous act is actually the best and most powerful thing you can do."

"I don't see how."

"Think about it, Thyr. If you go there now, and if by some miracle you manage to kill him without losing your own life in the process, we will have a war on our hands."

"I don't care if I die," Thyra murmured.

"Well, I do," Kari shot back sharply. "Listen to me, please! You were raised and trained the warrior way, I understand; and you are an excellent fighter, I know that too. But that does not automatically make you into a mindless killer! Don't let Bjarke win this fight by turning you into another just like him. Realise that you can become a *Shining One* instead, like me; and that you can be the one to end all war across this land. For good!"

Thyra was not having any of it.

"How?" she growled. "By being weak?"

Kari flashed her a gentle smile in response.

"Do you think I'm weak, Thyra?" she murmured.

Thyra stared at her lover, as silent tears continued to stream down the sides of her face. The magnitude of the love that she felt for her was stronger than any rage or fury she might have experienced. She slowly shook her head no. She slumped to her knees in front of her, and Kari followed her there.

"You're the strongest person I've ever met…"

Kari rested a soothing hand over her shoulder. She took a deep breath and lowered her voice.

"Maybe so. And the only reason for that is because I have strong principles, and I stick to my mission. I do it regardless of what happens to me, or in the world around me. No matter how cruel or soul-destroying it may be. I stand for peace, now and always, and I act accordingly. You told me once that you want to travel the world with me, and help me to grow friendship and cooperation between the people?"

"Yes… I do."

"But how will you be able to do this if your heart is full of death and violence? The change has got to take place within you first, Thyra. Trust me, because I speak from experience. Killing, war, and revenge will not bring you the peace of mind you seek. It is a losing battle, and in the end, it will only destroy you too."

Kari remained kneeling in the snow in front of her lover, and now, she also reached forward and raised her face in both her hands to take a better look at her. Thyra locked eyes with her. She appeared exhausted, tragically sad, and painfully defeated. But she was still there all right, no matter what. She was still listening and paying attention. Kari had never loved anyone more.

"I know this is hard, and that it goes against your every instinct," she said.

Thyra nodded just once. '*Hard*' sounded like such a flimsy, inadequate word to describe what she actually felt. Completely ripped apart and shredded to pieces was more like it.

"Yeah," she murmured with a bitter shrug. "It's hard."

"And that is precisely why you cannot afford to fail. You have to make the right choice, right now. Become the broken link, Thyra, and help me to stop this senseless violence once and for all."

Thyra glanced at the heavy sword that she was still holding in her right hand. She stared at the razor-sharp blade that was glinting in the sunshine, and a sudden image of it dripping with Bjarke's blood flashed through her mind. She squeezed her eyes shut and shook her head to get rid of the image. If what Kari said was true, then she could not allow herself to think of him right now.

"I guess you want me to get rid of this, too?" she asked.

"No." Kari smiled. "I want you to keep it and use it well, whenever you need to defend yourself and protect others. But never to attack, Thyra. And never to retaliate either. No matter what happens, no matter how harrowing it may be."

The undeniable wisdom and true power of Kari's argument were starting to sink in, but it was so hard. *Tait, my brother...* Whenever he popped into her head, Thyra could barely breathe.

"I understand," she forced herself to say.

"Good. Now, you must focus on what you want."

Thyra looked up and she met her lover's gaze. She even managed a weak, broken smile for her that never quite touched her eyes. But she was trying and doing the best she knew how to do. Once again, it certainly did not go unnoticed.

"Focus on what I want?" she murmured with a light shake of the head. "I don't know what I want, Kari. I don't know what you mean..."

"What I mean is this," Kari said gently. "You cannot change what happened. But how can you make sure that this tragedy does not break you? That it serves and elevates you instead, and everyone else in your world?"

Thyra stared at the ground once more. She fought the urge to rebel against Kari's words. *Tait was murdered! How can such a thing ever be forgiven? How can it be 'elevating'?* She shook her head in furious rage, and once again, she half-attempted to pull away from her. But Kari did not let her go.

"I just want to kill him..." Thyra muttered. "I want to kill Bjarke."

"I know you do," Kari replied. "But what I need you to do is answer my question, Thyr. I would not be pushing you so hard if there was another way forward."

Thyra struggled to think. This was the most devastating thing she had ever been faced with. And if anyone other than Kari had been holding on to her right now, she would have been tempted to sink her blade through their chest in punishment for the outrageous and shocking demands that they were making. She took a hard breath. And then, through the mist of rage and fury that she felt, and the overwhelming sadness that accompanied it, something came to her at last. It was a single easy thought that she heard delivered in her brother's voice.

"I think I could work to create a world that Tait would be proud of," Thyra murmured. "Is this the sort of thing you want me to say?"

"Yes," Kari approved intently. "How does it feel?"

Thyra looked at her, eyes still full of tears.

"He would have loved you, Kari," she replied. "Tait would be excited about this change you talk about. And I suspect that you're right, too. It all starts with me. If I can break the cycle of violence, and if I can do it in his name..."

She let her voice trail off, staring into the distance.

"You certainly can, and I know you will," Kari said. "And you know what else too?"

"What?"

"Sometimes, you really have to be completely destroyed in the process of finding yourself in life. To be able to discover your true reason, and your purpose for coming into this world in the first place. I think that yours are becoming quite clear now."

Thyra was still fighting against the anger that threatened to pull her apart if she even relaxed for a second.

"Yeah?" she muttered. "Well. I feel pretty destroyed."

"It won't last, I promise. Come on."

They both stood up, and Thyra was grateful for Kari's help doing it because her legs were wobbly and weak, and she still felt incredibly nauseous. Amazingly though, there was also a new, fragile sense of possibility emerging from inside of her now too. She could be in total control of her rage. No, she would not turn into another Bjarke. Never. She would take her cue from Kari and become just like her instead.

"I have your brother, Thyra," Hrorek confirmed when she met his gaze, eyes full of the burning, unspoken question. "Don't worry; we will go back now and take good care of him."

"Thanks," Thyra murmured.

She was grateful beyond words to him for doing that, and thoroughly ashamed of her own disgusting behaviour. She could not remember kicking him so hard, but the warrior looked awful now.

"I'm sorry about your face, Hrorek," she apologised.

"No problem, my friend. I have a tough nose."

Kari rested her arm around Thyra's shoulders.

"Hrorek, can you please take the horses, and go on ahead?" she instructed. "Gather the people in the main square. I want to speak about this situation."

"Yes, Commander. Kari. I will."

Kari flashed him a quick smile as he went, before returning her attention to Thyra. She pulled her closer against her side and brushed a gentle kiss over her cheek.

"You and I can take it a little slower, all right?"

"All right, yes," Thyra murmured. "Thanks."

She was pale. There was a hollow and far-away expression in her eyes that Kari knew would not last forever, but that she did not enjoy seeing on her all the same. She wanted to give Thyra some more time to regroup after such a shock. And what a horrible surprise it had been. She was suddenly reminded of the way her lover had woken up from her nightmare in the dead of night, complaining of a violent headache and raging fever. She wondered if perhaps Tait had been killed at that very moment. It would make a lot of sense. Given the exceedingly strong bond between the siblings, Kari was pretty sure that Thyra would have been able to feel the moment of his death. She did not mention it to her or ask any more questions. Right now, she just wanted to keep Thyra with her and close by her side. Protected, and safe.

"I love you," Thyra mumbled.

"I love you too, Thyr."

Kari was about to say something else as well, but there was a sudden unexpected shout from behind. She frowned in alarm at the sight of Hrorek and his entire contingent of men running back out toward them. *What is he doing?*

"Kari!" Hrorek shouted. "Chief! Asger is returning! They're coming back, watch out!"

Kari stared hard toward the mountain. Her eyes widened at the sight. *Oh, no...* Now it was not just ten men, as before, but it looked like a little over fifty. All mounted on horseback and coming at them with breakneck speed. Their swords were raised up in the air, and they were screaming their battle cry at the top of their lungs. Without saying a word about it, Thyra grabbed hold of Kari's arm, and she positioned herself as a shield in front of the Volsung chief. All of a sudden, the deadly sword was back in her hand, and ready to be used.

"What are you doing?" Kari screamed at her.

Thyra spared her a single glance over her shoulder.

"My job, protecting you. I won't let anyone hurt you."

Hrorek got there at the exact same time. He was back on his horse too, and with his arm held out toward his boss. At the same time, his eyes remained fixed onto the rapidly approaching swarm of enemy fighters.

"Get on the horse, Chief, I'll take you back."

Already, the Volsung warriors had run past them and were getting within fighting distance of the attacking force. Soon, the sound of clashing swords could be heard in the distance. Thyra knew exactly where her place was, and it did not look like the back line to her.

"Get out of here," she urged Kari. "You're the clan chief, you cannot afford to get caught in the middle of this fight. Go with Hrorek."

"Come with me, Thyra!"

"No, I'm staying right here."

Thyra turned just once to glance over in the direction of the fierce battle already raging between the two opposing clans. When she moved back to meet her gaze, Kari spotted immense focus and steely determination burning in her eyes.

"Go with Hrorek," Thyra repeated urgently. "I won't fight in anger, I promise."

She flashed her lover a brief, intense smile.

"I am fighting for you, and for peace. Now, get to safety."

"Commander, get on the horse!" Hrorek shouted in echo.

Knowing that it was madness to keep them all stuck in this awkward position, Kari threw one last look toward Thyra, and she jumped behind Hrorek.

"Don't you dare get yourself killed," she yelled after her.

"No way in hell, Commander," Thyra yelled back.

And after one last reassuring smile and a heavily loaded look exchanged between them, a promise of sorts, she started running toward the fight.

CHAPTER ELEVEN

She was true to her word. She did not fight in anger, but to protect the woman she loved and honour the memory of her brother. If anything, she found that it gave her added clarity of mind, focus, and extra strength she was even surprised to find that she possessed. She had never been in a real battle before, true. But on that day, Thyra proved herself to be one of the most valuable and committed warriors the Volsung men had fighting on their side. She recognised a few faces from her own clan. One man in particular stood out from all the others; and when he came at her with terrible bloodlust in his eyes and his sword raised high over his head, clearly intent on harming her, she felt a rush of disbelief mixed in with intense frustration. She had trained with this guy. She had shared food with him. She had always considered him a good friend, and she knew that he felt just the same about her. She dodged his first strike and hit back just enough to show him that she meant business. Before he could launch himself at her again, she yelled out his name.

"Audun! What are you doing? Why are you fighting me?"

He stood in front of her, panting, snarling, clearly lost in the mists of a deadly fighting trance. All around them, the snow had turned red with the blood of stricken men. Thyra's blade was dripping with it. She had blood on her hands and all over the leather that covered her chest. And throughout the chaos and mayhem of battle, the banging of swords, and the screams of wounded fighters that echoed throughout the valley, she could not find any meaning for any of it. The more she fought, the sadder it made her feel. *What a waste…*

"Hey, I am your friend, remember?" she shouted. "Wake up, Audun, and stop fighting. This is all wrong!"

But it was like talking to a wall. It was clear too that a lot of the men involved in the battle did not belong to the Asger clan. It was fast becoming obvious to Thyra that Bjarke must have been planning this attack for a while, and that he had managed to assemble a generous army from other separate Viking groups. How on earth he could convince those men to fight for him and against Kari, of all people, Thyra had no idea. But mercenaries abounded in those days, and she knew for certain that there were warriors out there who could be hired to fight for almost nothing, simply because they liked to kill so much.

"You betrayed your own blood, *bikkja*! Now, you will die!"

What crazy lies has Bjarke been feeding all those guys? she wondered. But Thyra did not have time to respond to Audun's outrageous statement, because the man immediately ran at her again, and attempted to bury his sword into the centre of her chest. She blocked the strike and punched him in the face extremely hard. She broke his nose. He screamed in pain and staggered back a few steps.

"Stop fighting me, you idiot," she shouted.

She did not want to have to kill him. For the first time, she realised how very right Kari was about all this, and about her. She may have known how to fight and handle a weapon better than most, but she took no pleasure in killing people, not even the ones who seemed to harbour such hate toward her. She would never be one of those warriors who kept count of their kills by carving deep lines into the handle of their sword, the way Bjarke did. The more she got drawn into this brutal battle, the more she realised the futility and stupidity of it. But not so with Audun it seemed, who tried once more to slash her throat. If he kept going like this, at one point he might eventually get lucky... Thyra decided that enough was enough. This man would never stop, and she did not have much of a choice anymore. She had to make him. She made sure that it was quick and painless for him. And then, she took one precious second to kneel by the side of his body afterward and touch his shoulder. *I'm sorry, friend...*

"Thyra!"

She whirled around at the sound of Hrorek's voice calling her name. In all the confusion, she had not seen him come back. But from the look of him now, all covered in sweat and blood, just like she was, it was obvious that he had been fighting quite hard for some time too. She ran over to him, only stopping once on the way to disable an enemy fighter with a single expert strike of her sword.

"Is Kari all right?" she yelled. "Is she safe?"

"Yes, she's back and organising our defence. But look over there," he replied.

More men were coming up now from the eastern side of the mountain, pouring in from out of the deep forest. Thyra felt her heart almost stop at the sight of them. They were headed straight for the settlement. And there were so many of them...

"We have to get back," she exclaimed. "Give the order, Hrorek, now!"

Without waiting, she started running as fast as she could toward the village. This was now a full-scale attack, and as she reached the main square, she realised that some of the fighters were already inside and setting fire to the nearest dwellings.

Women and children were streaming out of the burning houses, and Thyra suddenly spotted Kari in the distance, sword in hand, fighting two men at the same time. She gritted her teeth and rushed straight over to them, ignoring everything and everyone else around her. She threw herself in front of her lover. Before the first man could react to her, she plunged her blade into his throat, and when she turned around to deal with the other one, she found that Kari had already dispatched him in the same manner. Thyra stared at her, eyes wide and breathing hard.

"Where are they coming from? They can't all be Asger!" the commander yelled.

"They're not," Thyra confirmed.

Kari threw her a sharp look.

"You all right, warrior?"

Thyra flashed her a quick smile in return.

"Yes, Commander. Fine."

Kari's gaze softened.

"Be careful, Thyr."

"You too. Stay close to me, all right?"

But before Kari could even reply, Thyra spotted one of the invading fighters. He had grabbed a woman by the hair, thrown her to the ground, and was raising his sword to kill her. She flung herself at him, fell on top of him with her knife drawn. She sank it into the side of his neck and twisted a couple of times. There. Done. When she looked back, her lover had disappeared, replaced instead by a wall of advancing fighters. Thyra had no time to think, no time to worry. For what felt to her like days, all she did for the next hours was fight to stay alive and protect the weaker members of the clan. It all became a blur. The screaming and the blood; the relentless surge of fighters coming at her; the growing fatigue that made it so hard to keep going, and the terrifying, debilitating sense that this was never going to end...

When it did eventually, Thyra stood in the middle of the village and stared at the scene of total devastation that greeted her. She herself had come through it all pretty much unscathed, with just a few harmless bruises and light cuts on her body. But everywhere else that she looked, dead or slowly dying men littered the ground. Thyra saw women amongst them, and lots of children as well, lying too still in a pool of their own blood. Most of the buildings had burned down to the ground. The stench of charred human flesh and so much blood that hung heavily in the air was nauseating. It seemed ludicrous, and even almost like an insult that the sun was sill shining so brightly, and that the sky was such a serene, vibrant blue. A sudden wave of dizziness washed over Thyra. She dropped onto one knee, rested her left forearm on her thigh, and lowered her head. She closed her eyes and breathed out. In and out like this for a few seconds. She had never known such exhaustion in her entire life.

Kari...

The abrupt recollection that she had lost sight of her lover during the fight was like a strike of lightning through her heart. Thyra instantly jumped back to her feet. *What the hell am I doing?* This was no time to rest! With her bloody sword still securely in her hand, she started walking.

"Kari!" she yelled. "Kari, can you hear me?"

She spotted some of the other Volsung warriors on the way. A few of them nodded or even raised a hand when they saw her. She pretty much ignored them all. *Where is Hrorek?* A slow, simmering fear started to make its presence known at the back of her mind.

"Kari!" she screamed. "Answer me! Kari!"

She started jogging. She went looking into buildings, peered under fallen debris, and checked the dead bodies on the ground. *This cannot be happening!*

She kept on running, calling, and searching frantically for her lover, feeling all the while that she was in real danger of losing grip on her own sanity. This was just too much. *Tait was first, and now…* Where the hell was her Kari? And would this abominable day ever come to an end eventually? How much more heartache and disaster would it throw at them all? This was pure torture, but still, Thyra kept going. She had to find her lover. She simply had to, there was no other way. She knew that she would keep going until she did, no matter what it took.

"KARI!" she yelled at the top of her lungs.

It was not too much later on when she eventually managed to track her down. Unfortunately, Thyra's instant relief at doing so did not last for very long.

"Kari?" she called.

The commander did not respond immediately. She was leaning against the side of a damaged building, still standing but with her eyes closed, and looking like she was struggling to stay on her feet. She glanced up with a startled look on her face when she sensed someone approaching her fast, but then, a look of total happiness flashed through her eyes at the reassuring sight of her lover. Thyra looked strong and full of life still, despite all the blood that she was covered in, and her obvious fatigue after so many long hours of fighting. Kari forced herself to smile.

"Thyra… There you are. I was worried…"

"Are you all right?" Thyra exclaimed in reply. "I lost sight of you earlier, and then I had to…"

Her words instantly died on her lips as soon as she noticed the careful way that Kari was holding onto her side, and the steady trickle of blood that seeped through her fingers. Their gazes met. Kari gave a soft shake of the head. Thyra's eyes filled with tears.

"No…" she murmured. "Kari, no…"

CHAPTER TWELVE

"It's all right, Thyr."

Kari's voice was soft and gentle, and full of much-needed reassurance as always. Nevertheless, the solemn look in her eyes also betrayed something dark about the situation which Thyra absolutely did not want to be true. It felt too big to handle, especially right now… She was also keenly aware that Kari needed her help, and so, she pushed the fear out of her mind, reached for her lover's wrist, and draped her arm around her own neck. She took up most of her weight, and she felt Kari sink against her with a relieved sigh.

"Okay, I've got you," Thyra murmured. "Let's take you inside and get you warm now."

There was a barn nearby which seemed to have been mostly spared by their attackers. A bunch of traumatised villagers were huddled together in there, and a team of able-bodied warriors were busy bringing in more of their wounded people together. Someone had built a warming fire in the corner, and this was where Thyra immediately led Kari. She was glad to also spot Hrorek standing in the middle of the room, talking to a bunch of his men, giving sharp orders to secure the compound. As soon as he caught sight of them walking in, he rushed over. He looked happy to see Thyra in one piece, but his face dropped at the sight of the wounded commander.

"I'll get Sigyn over here right away," he volunteered.

Kari shot him a tired, knowing glance. She shook her head.

"No. Let her help the ones who really need it."

"But what about you?" he protested.

"Thyra will stay with me. I will be fine."

For the first time, Hrorek noticed the growing bloodstain on her lower back. Kari's tunic was soaked in blood. He realised what this meant, and why she did not want Sigyn wasting her efforts on her. Shocked, he instantly knelt down by her side, and rested his hand over her shoulder. She spotted tears shining in his eyes. She was pretty sure that she had never seen him cry before about anything or anyone.

"Kari. I… I don't know what to say…"

She gave him a warm smile and squeezed his hand.

"It's all right," she murmured. "No need for anymore. Look after yourself, Hrorek, my beloved friend; and keep an eye on this one for me. Will you?"

Hrorek cast a quick glance toward the young warrior who appeared so heartbroken and was obviously fighting the battle of her life not to give in to her grief. To be able to do the right thing for the woman she loved right until the very end. Just to be there for her in all the ways that Kari needed her to be. He gave a sharp nod.

"Yes, I will. You have my word on that."

"Thank you. Now please, go and help the others."

She saw him hesitate. Of course, he would do that.

"Go, Hrorek," she repeated gently. "I've got Thyra with me, and your men and our people need you."

It was kind of an excuse, and they both knew it. But he was deeply grateful to her for making it easier. They had known each other and been friends for so many years… He hated the idea of waiting there to watch her die. He glanced toward Thyra again.

He was certain that this same thought had never even crossed her mind once, and he sighed. Yes, she would need all the help he could give her after this horror, for sure. And he would stand by his promise. Hrorek exchanged one last smile with Kari, a squeeze of the hand. And then, he stood up again on trembling, unsteady legs. He went back to his duties, back to what he knew how to do best, all the while blinking back tears of bitter sorrow he did not want his men to see.

"Does it hurt?" Thyra enquired once they were alone once more. "Are you cold? What else can I do?"

"No… It doesn't hurt anymore," Kari replied with a gentle smile. "And I'm not cold when you hold me like this. This is all I need, my love."

Thyra gave a tight nod, knowing that this was probably not the entire truth. But there was no need to argue at this time. She held her dying lover in her arms, made sure that she received most of the heat from the fire, and that she kept her feeling safe, protected in her embrace. It was all that she could do now. Kari looked at her.

"Talk to me, Thyr," she whispered.

Thyra met her gaze. The urge to blurt out things like '*I don't want you to go*', and '*Please, don't leave me!*' was pretty acute at this point. But she knew it would achieve nothing, and this was not about her now. It was all about Kari. She brushed a gentle kiss over her lips and caressed her cheek. She ran her fingers through her hair in a soothing gesture, and she felt her lover relax against her a little more. She managed a true, brilliant smile for her.

"I love you, Kari," she said. "I never imagined that I would meet someone like you, so beautiful and kind. So tender and strong. Thank you for trusting me enough to teach me the important things. And for loving me. You are the greatest gift."

She left out the part where she wanted to beg her not to die. She did not give in to the need to apologise for not being able to protect her, even though she knew that she had failed. But again, this was not about her now. Not about seeking solace for herself. So, Thyra spoke simply and honestly. She put as much feeling and emotion into her words as she possibly could, without going too far, and falling apart. Kari watched her intently, hanging on to her every word. She looked deathly pale, and her breathing had grown a little laboured. But she kept her eyes on Thyra's face, aware of the effort those loving words she spoke must require of her. To be this strong and this controlled when she felt so broken inside, simply because she loved her so much... Now this, Kari knew, really was the greatest gift.

"You will always be my *Shining One*," Thyra promised her, struggling to keep smiling and hold back her tears. "Always. And I am going to be the strongest broken link you have ever seen."

Kari gave her an exhausted, yet firmly approving nod. She rested her open hand over Thyra's chest, pressed her palm just above her heart, and felt its reassuring beat. She never once took her eyes off her. She could feel time beginning to run out, and she did not want to go without saying what she needed to.

"I will be with you, Thyr," she said. "All right?"

Thyra forced another brave smile of her own.

"Yes," she promised. "Don't worry about me, Kari."

Kari could feel her shaking now. This was so hard, but she carried on anyway. She had to see this through properly for both of their sake.

"Look inside your heart, and you will find me there. Live a full and happy life. Love, and be loved in return. There will be others. That's all right. Remember, this is not goodbye. We will see each other again."

She drew on the precious few fragments of energy that she had left to give her lover a genuine, reassuring smile. She did not think that Thyra could take much more of this. It was not fair to ask her for more. And Kari was feeling so tired now too, and so cold. It was time to let go. Time to let her go.

"Please, hold me, Thyr," she murmured.

Thyra instantly responded, and Kari rested her face against her shoulder. She managed to open her eyes one last time. There was one final look exchanged between them. And then, Thyra smiled that beautiful smile of hers.

"Sleep now, my *Shining One*," she whispered. "I will keep you warm."

∞

Hrorek saw her stumble out of the barn, alone. *So, it's over now. Oh, Kari…* He bit hard onto his lower lip. *Farewell, my friend.*

And now, where was the young warrior going on her own like this? He kept watching her intently, as she walked fast across the deserted square, out through the front entrance, and toward the forest. Something made him decide to follow her. He did not want to intrude if being all alone was what she really wanted, and he was careful to keep a respectful distance away. But not so far that he would completely lose sight of her. These were highly dangerous times, and he was worried. Thyra did not glance behind her even once. She seemed totally oblivious of his presence. When she was further away from the settlement, she started to run, and when she arrived at the edge of the woods, she headed straight for the nearest tree. She leaned against it and rested both hands against the thick, knotted black trunk. She lowered her head, and Hrorek watched her take several heavy, difficult breaths. She was sobbing. He stared down at the ground, wondering whether to go to her or not, leaning toward the former. He could hear Kari's voice in his ear, urging him to do it.

She really should not be on her own right now...

But before he could even move, Thyra let out the hardest, rawest, most wounded cry he had ever heard from man, woman or beast. Hrorek froze. And then, she started punching the tree with her fists. There was enough force and aggression loaded into each one of those strikes to knock out twenty men all at once. Over and over she did this, hitting at the tree as if she was hoping to bring it down. Hrorek was forced to watch her in reluctant silence. He did not enjoy witnessing her pain. He did not like to see her hurting herself in this way, and he truly ached for her inside. He was immensely glad, and relieved when Thyra delivered what he hoped was one final blow. She cried out when her knuckles broke over the unforgiving tree, sending a painful shockwave burning into her arm and shoulder. She leaned against the tree, panting, clearly exhausted. He thought it was all over then, but unfortunately not. After only a brief pause, she started hitting against the wood again, with renewed vigour and determination that was clearly borne out of rage, grief, and deep despair. It was heart-wrenching to watch it happen. Hrorek shook his head in frustration, and he clenched his own fists. He realised that she had to get the emotion and the pain of that horrible, devastating day out of her system, and so, he would not intervene. He was convinced that she would not be able to keep at it with such intensity for very long anyway, and he was right. After a while, Thyra stumbled, almost fell. She was running out of steam. Eventually, she collapsed on the ground and drew her knees up against her chest. She folded her arms over her legs and lowered her head. She started to cry again.

Hrorek turned his back on her, and he looked up toward the night sky. Silent tears were running down his face. He had lost some good friends today. He had lost Kari, too. He gave them both a few more minutes of private time before he walked over to her.

"Viking. What are you doing, uh?"

He was not even sure that she had heard him. Her knuckles were swollen, badly bruised, and bleeding. He winced at the sight of her left hand. It was broken in more than one place, he could tell that after just one glance at it. He thought that she was breathing a little funny too... And it was so damn cold outside in this snow. She did not look well. He had to bring her in, and quickly too.

"Thyra?" he repeated. "Can you hear me?"

He knelt in front of her and lifted her head up. She stared right through him. She had that vacant look in her eyes now, the one warriors got after they had seen too much and experienced too many horrors.

"Hey," he said. "You okay?"

"It's my fault," she mumbled. "It's all my fault..."

"Don't say those things," he replied fiercely, almost angrily.

He wrapped his arms around her waist and pulled her to her feet. He had been almost prepared for her to try to fight him, to push him back, but when she fainted against him instead, he was not entirely surprised. At last, this dreadful day was over. He gathered her up into his arms and started toward what was left of home.

THYRA'S PROMISE

NATALIE DEBRABANDERE

PART TWO: LEARNING TO LIVE

CHAPTER THIRTEEN

- Four Months Later -

"I'm leaving."

Hrorek slowly looked up from his breakfast and stared at her impassively. It had been a harsh and challenging few months for the surviving Volsung people, and that was putting it mildly. But now at last, all the snow was gone and spring was on its way. It was a time of rebirth and renewal. Change was in the air. Perhaps it was no wonder then, that she felt ready to move on too...

Every person in the village had worked extremely hard for weeks on end to rebuild and restore the settlement to its original condition. Thyra had thrown herself into all that work almost to the point of madness. More often than not, Hrorek would leave her working on a job when he went off to bed, late at night. When he woke up, at the break of dawn the next morning, and went to check on her, sometimes she would still be at it. He wondered if or when she ever slept for more than three or four hours at a time. And so, there she was now. Standing in front of him looking slightly pissed off, already in a combative mood it seemed. And uttering the one statement he had been expecting from her all along, although really not looking forward to at all...

He sighed and pointed to the stool opposite him.

"Sit," he instructed.

She looked impatient, but she did take the seat he offered, and leaned her forearms over the wooden table. Waiting for him to try to change her mind about going, probably. Or something else equally irritating in her view. He almost smiled. Her hands had healed well. He was not sure about the rest, but physically, she looked fine. The first five days following the deadly battle and the deaths of Tait and Kari had been the most difficult. She refused to eat. She spent most of her time asleep, or lying on her cot staring at the ceiling, as if in a deep trance. On day six of this charade, Hrorek had lost his patience with her. He had simply dragged her outside, given her a hammer and nails, and directed her to the nearest task to be finished. He did this even though her hands were still covered in bandages and she could barely even hold a spoon in her fingers at the time. But he was after a breakthrough, and he figured that this would cause one of two things to happen; either she would snap out of her crippling depression, right there and then, or she would punch him in the face and leave, never to be seen again. He was glad that she had chosen to get to work instead. He pushed a bowl of food in front of her. It was oats with a little honey added to the mixture.

"Eat."

Thyra stared at the food as if it were a disease. She had lost weight, although strangely enough, it did not seem to affect her strength or fighting abilities very much. A few weeks previously, she had become embroiled in an argument with another warrior. The dispute involved him refusing to carry out a simple task she wanted him to complete. It was building-work-related. Thyra's request was appropriate and delivered in the correct manner. But he resented taking orders from her. He told her the reason why; because he was annoyed that she was *'not even one of us'*.

Thyra shrugged, unconcerned, and just repeated her request. He told her to get lost in no uncertain terms, and as soon as she turned away from him, to carry out the task herself, he swung a heavy punch that was aimed at the back of her head. But Thyra had been expecting something of the sort from him for a while, and she was paying attention. She dodged the blow, whipped around, and dropped him easily with a well-aimed kick to the chest. After this, not many men refused to help her anymore. Hrorek watched her now, as she toyed with her spoon and her plate of food, all the while wearing such an unhappy frown on her face.

"Not hungry?" he asked. "It's good porridge."

She gave a loud exhale and threw him another aggrieved look.

"Did you hear what I said?" she snapped. "I want to..."

"I heard you, yes," he interrupted. "And where will you be going, Thyra?"

"East."

He raised an interested, thoughtful eyebrow.

"East is a pretty big place," he remarked.

She just shrugged, as he had suspected that she would. He knew that Thyra liked to keep to herself. She did not enjoy explaining her reasons. Yeah, well; he could understand that. He observed her carefully, as she continued to stare at her food. She was still wearing the torc that her lover had given her. As far as he was aware, she had not taken it off even once since that day. But Thyra never mentioned Kari's name, and not even her own brother's for that matter. She avoided personal conversations at all cost, and whenever he tried to find out how she was doing, and if she was feeling okay, she would shrug dismissively and just walk away. After a while, Hrorek got the message and he stopped asking. At least that crazy vacant look was gone from her eyes. All the same, she looked angry these days. It was a low, simmering tension that was quite easy to spot, and seemed to be building up.

"Hey, take it easy," he told her now, with an added shrug of his own. "I'm just curious, you know? Just asking because I care. I'm your friend, remember?"

Her shoulders finally dropped at the gentle reminder, and her features relaxed. She swallowed a mouthful of the food and met his gaze. One corner of her mouth twitched, which was as far as smiles went with her these days.

"Yes. I know," she said.

Hrorek nodded, feeling a little more satisfied.

"All right, then. So, east it is. Are you intending to follow the trade routes?"

"I guess so, yeah."

"Travelling by boat?"

"Yes... Partly."

It still felt like pulling teeth. He wondered if it was because she really had no clear idea of where she wanted to go, or if she simply did not want to share her plans with him for some unknown and unexplained reason. Hrorek hoped that this was not the case. She was a genuine friend. He really did care about her, and he hoped that she had not forgotten this, and that he could be trusted. Also, there was the promise he had made to Kari. *Keep an eye on this one for me...* Unfortunately, he would not be able to keep doing this for much longer if she wanted to leave. Maybe it was all right. Maybe not... It was hard to decide. Hrorek sighed, lost in a bunch of contradicting and worrying thoughts over promises made and difficult friendships. But then, all of a sudden, Thyra leaned forward over the table and made him jump. Her eyes sparkled with sudden excitement.

"Constantinople, that's on a trade route, right?" she said.

He chuckled, reassured. All right, then. She really was just trying to figure it all out inside of her own head. He was being paranoid for no reason at all.

"Aha," he smiled. "I see you're not just talking about a short trip down to the Rhine region. Yes, Constantinople is on a trade route. Actually, it's on more than one."

Thyra looked interested.

"What do you mean?"

"It's a major centre. There are lots of ways to get to it. You could travel by boat, over land if you wanted to, or do a mixture of both."

"Really?" she exclaimed. "Great!"

"Yes, although it might take you a bit longer depending on which option you choose. At sea, it also depends on the winds and the weather. It's hard to be sure. You will need to do a bit of both, I'd say."

"All right. I'll be looking for the most direct route."

"Good for you. I've only ever gone as far as the Rhyne."

"All the way down the river?"

"Yes, all the way down."

She nodded eagerly. She had a lot more colour in her face now, and with her crystal-clear blue eyes burning bright, he was reminded of the old Thyra. He had not seen her looking so alive since the day of the attack, and he happily shared more details of all the lands he had travelled through. Hrorek had lost many friends besides Kari on that brutal day, and he was not looking forward to her leaving. But it was good to see that she still had fire in her heart.

"Follow me," he invited.

He led her to the newly reconstructed barn, and to a section at the back where they kept tools, grooming equipment, and grains for their horses. Hrorek brushed a bunch of hay from off the floor and uncovered a hidden wooden trapdoor sealed with a metal chain. He lifted it up and motioned for Thyra to follow him down the set of stairs.

"Only I am allowed down here now," he said.

Thyra nodded silently. *Now that Kari is gone* was what he meant, and she swallowed hard at the reminder. Unconsciously, she brushed her fingers against her necklace, for much-needed reassurance and to ground herself as well. At night, she would often lie in bed and hold on to the precious torc, remembering her lover. She would think about the wonderful few days they had shared together during the storm, all alone in Kari's quarters before the world had turned insane. She would replay their first encounter in her mind, and the first time they had made love. She would just do this, over and over and all-night long. Remembering her lover's voice, her brilliant smile, and the amazing feeling of falling asleep in her arms knowing that she was safe, loved, and protected...

"Hey."

Thyra looked up, startled. Hrorek had stopped talking, and he was standing with his hand firmly over her shoulder, looking concerned.

"Are you with me?" he asked.

"Yeah. Sure, I'm with you."

"All right. So, look at this."

Thyra eyed the wooden chest that he had opened up, which was literally filled to the brim with jewels and pieces of gold. She did not feel any emotion or excitement at the sight, just mere curiosity.

"That's a lot," she commented.

"All from trade, I can assure you. No looting or anything of the sort."

"And why are you showing me this?"

"Because," he replied impatiently, "travel isn't cheap."

"Well, I know, but I don't have any money."

He smiled at her naivete.

"Of course, you do, Thyra," he murmured.

She watched in sudden grateful understanding, as he filled several leather pouches with gold coins. He handed her one and slid the others inside the pocket on his belt.

"I will go with you as far as the North Sea and arrange safe passage for you on a Volsung boat," he announced. "We'll leave in the morning."

Thyra's mouth dropped open in surprise, and she stared at him with her eyes wide. Her face was a picture of wonder and amazement. He grinned at her and clapped his hand over her shoulder again in a friendly gesture.

"What's the matter, Viking?" he enquired with an amused chuckle. "Did you think I was just going to try to stop you from going?"

She returned his smile.

"Well, not stop me, but... Maybe. I don't know."

Her heart was pounding hard inside her chest. *We will leave in the morning...* At last, her dream to go travel the world was about to come true! For the past several weeks, she had felt the urge to go away build inside of her until it was overwhelming, all-consuming, and completely impossible to ignore. It was a weird mixture of the old wanderlust that she used to experience so often before, and a new, intense awareness that it was time to leave. Not that she did not feel like she belonged with them, of course. The stupid guy who had argued with her over a simple job was the only one who had ever dared to suggest otherwise. All the other Volsung warriors fully accepted her. After all, anyone who would risk their life the way she had and fight so hard against their own kind just to defend their new friends' families and homes was one of theirs, no questions about it. She had also earned the right to wear their deceased, beloved chief's family torc around her neck, which commanded a lot of genuine respect too. Thyra worked really hard, she did everything she always could to help everyone else around her, and as a result, she was extremely popular throughout the village. Hrorek truly was like a brother to her, and he never missed an opportunity to make her feel more valued and included. Despite all this, which was wonderful and made it so tempting to stay, something deep and primal inside Thyra kept telling her that it was time to move on out of there, and that she had to keep going.

"Well, in case you're wondering, I will miss having you around," Hrorek informed her now, as if he had been reading her thoughts. "And not just because you are such a good worker. I am not making it easy for you to leave just because I want to get rid of you. You understand that, right?"

She nodded, eyes bright.

"I know. But thanks for saying it."

He saw her hesitate. She began to move, hesitated again, and then she shocked the hell out of him by throwing her arms around his neck and hugging him really tightly for several long seconds.

"I'll miss you too, Hrorek."

She looked much more settled when she pulled back, and like a massive weight had been lifted off her shoulders. She even managed another bright smile for him, and a small joke.

"Not just because you keep feeding me up," she added.

He laughed at that. Yes, he reflected, and felt better himself all of a sudden. *In time, she'll be just fine, Kari...*

"So, let me ask you then; what makes you want to go to *Miklagard,* Constantinople, of all places? What's so special to you about that place?" he enquired.

She gave him one of her trademark *'as if it's not obvious'* shrugs, which she had learned from Tait. Although this time, she kept her smile firmly in place as she replied.

"Because it's east," she declared. "Different. And hot."

He chuckled at her disarmingly uncomplicated answer.

"Seems to me as good a reason as any. Different, hot, and great for trade," he added with a smiling glance at her. "From what I've heard about the place, I think that you'll love it. The city is an open portal onto the Far Eastern regions and all the many untold riches of the south."

"Like what?" she pressed him.

Her eyes were still riveted onto his face, and she was visibly boiling with excitement. Not really looking where she was going either, and he grabbed onto her arm and pulled her to the side to save her from walking straight into a wall.

"Well, let's see," he replied. "There are things like Arabic silver, rare spices, and expensive silk. As well as good furs and precious amber stones; delicious exotic fruits, and wine so sweet it will make you weep tears of delight."

Thyra rolled her eyes at him, genuinely amused.

"Hey, I had no idea you were such a poet," she observed. "Tait would be impre…"

She froze at the unconscious mention of her brother's name, and the rest of her sentence just died on her lips. She looked positively stricken. Hrorek instantly passed his arm over her shoulders. He gave her a strong, firm squeeze, and carried on walking as if nothing had happened.

"It's okay to talk about him, you know. It's all right to let him be a part of your life still, even now. Especially now, Thyra. And with Kari, too…"

He felt her immediately stiffen against him, and he glanced at her.

"Are you okay?"

He watched her in silence, as intense emotion slowly spread across her face, making her cheeks colour darkly. She bit onto her lower lip so hard that she drew blood. He noticed how she struggled to take a proper breath.

"You know, sometimes I miss him so much that it stops me breathing," she gasped. "And when I think about Kari, it's even worse than that. It's like… I just feel like…"

She shook her head. She had no words to describe it, how horrible it all was. Turns out she did not really need to put it into words for him.

"Feels like dying a hundred times," Hrorek muttered.

A single tear rolled down the side of Thyra's cheek.

"Yeah," she murmured. "Just like that."

CHAPTER FOURTEEN

It rained extremely hard and pretty much incessantly for the first five days of her voyage, but it was fine with her. Thyra was quite content to remain lying down under cover, waiting patiently for the weather to improve. She spent most of this idle time resting, reflecting on things, and allowing the murky weather to lull her into a state of quiet melancholy. In a way, it matched her mood absolutely perfectly. It had been extremely hard to say goodbye to Hrorek, much harder than she had anticipated initially. When they arrived at the boat, heavy goods were being loaded onto it. Would-be passengers argued loudly with the captain and the crew about pricing and other inane things to do with travel. In the middle of this crazy cauldron of human activity, Thyra and Hrorek found a little quiet spot to have a private chat.

"So, here we are," he grunted.

"Yeah. Here we are," she replied in the same tone.

Neither of them felt particularly at ease at that moment. Hrorek made her promise to look after herself and be careful. Thyra extracted the same promise from him. He gave her all the rest of the gold coins he had brought along with him, and extra fresh food, *'just in case you need it'*. She teased him about it.

"Still trying to fatten me up, uh?"

"'Course. Any chance I get."

She laughed, and he pulled her into his arms for a goodbye hug that neither of them had expected would turn so emotional and make them both shed a few tears eventually.

"Thank you, Hrorek," Thyra murmured when he released her. "For everything. And I'm sorry…"

He gave her a thoughtful smile.

"Don't be, Thyra. The Gods have their ways. You may have been a catalyst in all this, but it was certainly not your fault. Take it from me. Trust in the higher purpose. And be happy."

He told her that he was looking forward to seeing her again soon, but she suspected they both knew the truth that she might never come back. She certainly had no intention of ever setting foot back in the Highlands of Scotland again. There were just too many bad memories there. Too many ghosts.

"When you get to the river Rhine," he reminded her, "all along the way and every time the boat stops, it will be at villages and settlements that Kari and I visited. And where we traded often over the years. You will find friends there."

"All right," she murmured. "Be safe, Hrorek."

He squeezed her shoulder.

"You too. Now go."

She climbed onto the boat just as they were casting off, and quickly found her balance. When she turned to look at him, Hrorek was sitting on his horse, looking solemn and grave as he watched them sailing off. He raised his open hand in a farewell gesture to her, and Thyra did the same thing. Her heart was pounding with barely restrained emotion and sadness. Hrorek slowly turned his horse around and started on the ride home. Thyra kept her eyes on him until he disappeared over the horizon. After that last wave, he did not turn to look her way again. And she was grateful to him for that, because letting go of the only friend she had left on the planet was pretty horrendous.

It seriously tested her resolve to leave. The impulse to jump off the boat and run back to him, and to everything else that was familiar and safe was there all right. It was really strong, too. Thyra felt terribly alone and desperately empty. But then again, it was not for the first time. She forced herself to stand at the front of the boat, gritting her teeth until she could no longer see land. Until it was too late to go back. Killing all of her weakest options, leaving herself with no way out but through. And then, she took a deep breath to steady herself, and focused all her attention on her new temporary home. *Ignore everything else. Just focus. And keep going.*

The boat was one of those long and sturdy Viking ones that was equipped with three large linen sails, a dry covered area useful for sleeping under, and plenty of room for travellers and cargo. They carried wool and leather in this case, to be traded later on for cases of good wine. There was a small crew made up of five hard-working, experienced, and able men who were there to help with the sailing and ensure the safety of all passengers and goods along the way. The ship's captain was named Arvid. A small, compact man with massive shoulders and the neck of a bull, he had known Hrorek and Kari for many years, and was a strong Volsung ally. Arvid was appalled and incensed at the news of her violent death.

"I have had dealings with this Bjarke of Asger of which you speak," he exclaimed. "He and his kind are not welcome on my boat."

Thyra tensed slightly at those words, but she did not allow her emotions to show. She was a Volsung now anyway, through and through. She had earned her allegiance with blood and tears. She decided to let Hrorek handle most of the conversation on her behalf, and she remained silent. She had nothing whatsoever to say on the subject of her violent older brother.

Thyra often wondered what had happened to Bjarke after the battle. They had not found his body amongst the dead, and she was not entirely sure what that meant. It made her feel uneasy and terribly anxious at times. Had he even fought amongst his men at all? Had he been wounded? Most likely, he had crawled off somewhere to die and just never been found… At least, this was Hrorek's take on it. There had been so many casualties, and on both sides. Whichever way he had perished, Bjarke was gone now, and nobody would miss him.

"We'll be two to three days at sea, depending on the winds and the weather," Arvid confirmed when Hrorek asked him. "Then, on to the river for fifteen or twenty more."

He glanced toward Thyra.

"Ever sailed on a boat before?" he wondered.

"No. First time," Thyra replied.

He was obviously quite curious about her, although he did not ask any unwanted questions about how come his new passenger, this tall woman who dressed and looked so much like a warrior, and wore a chief's torc around her neck to boot, was travelling on her own to such a distant land as Constantinople. He simply welcomed her on board, was grateful for the payment she offered him, and promised Hrorek that he would get her safely down the Rhine and to the mountains.

"Good man, Arvid," Hrorek thanked him.

The captain nodded and shook his hand.

"All right, all aboard! Let's go, let's go!" he shouted.

Once they were on their way, he had the good sense to leave Thyra alone most of the time. It was obviously what this quiet and thoughtful Viking warrior wanted, and that was fine by him. Then, it was a series of short and uneventful sailing days along the west coast of England, all the way to the jumping-off point where they would cross over to the main continent. Thyra was looking forward to finally catching the river Rhyne she had heard so much about and continue on down into Switzerland. The motley crew of passengers who hopped on and off the boat at different loading points throughout England was entertaining, and they also tended to keep to themselves for the most part, which she appreciated greatly. A certain level of curiosity and engagement amongst fellow travellers was to be expected on such a small vessel, of course, and she was polite and respectful to everyone, as they were to her back in return. She was friendly with the captain and the crew as well. But she was very keen to avoid deeper engagements, and any probing questions, which nobody seemed to find a problem.

Except for one person.

The lone male merchant who embarked shortly before the main crossing proved himself to be a bit of a nuisance. He spent his entire first afternoon trying to strike up a conversation with her. And on that very same night, Thyra observed him in lethal silence, as he afforded himself a good long look at her body under cover of darkness. Not that there was much for him to see, dressed as she was in her usual boots and trousers, long-sleeved tunic, leather protective vest, and warm woollen cloak. He must have thought that she was fast asleep, and he moved even closer. She remained completely still while his eyes hovered all over her with disturbing, predatory-like intensity. Thyra had dealt with men like him her entire life. Right now, he was only looking, but he was not the type who would stop there. One day, soon, he would want to take what he felt was his just right to possess, by force if necessary. Just like Bjarke. Seething anger was keeping Thyra warm and alert that night. She did not move a muscle when his gaze lingered over the well-maintained sword that she wore attached to her belt. The weapon was a statement all on its own, and it would give anyone pause. But he really was a fool, and something else more important quickly got his attention. Thyra heard his breathing quicken when he inspected her gold necklace, which he had noticed before and even remarked on.

"Nice. How much for it?"

"It's not for sale."

He laughed a little too loud.

"Everything's for sale."

"Not this one, it isn't."

The necklace was obviously of significant interest to him still, despite her unequivocal previous answer, and he leaned even nearer to her. He reached for the torc. He was badly startled when his eyes drifted toward her face at the same time, and he finally realised that her eyes were wide open. And that she was watching him intently. He jumped.

"Oh, hi…" he muttered, and instantly stopped moving.

He noticed the unwavering way that she returned his gaze, and the slight ironic lift of her left eyebrow, that signified exactly how much she did not appreciate being stared at in this way. Stupidly, he took it to mean that she was amused. He grinned at her.

"Hey, how you doing, girl?" he murmured.

He touched the side of her neck with his finger. Before he could do anything else with it, she leaped forward and wrapped her right hand around his throat. Damn, she was so strong! He was unable to make a single sound, and quite powerless to free himself. He started to suffocate as she crushed his larynx. Her message to him was quite simple.

"My torc is not for sale. Neither am I. Touch me again, and I'll kill you. Is that clear?"

He nodded, mouth open wide and gasping for air, even as he felt the blood drain from his brain and tears start pouring out of his eyes. He clawed at her hand, but it only made her squeeze harder in response. His eyes rolled up into his head. He was clearly finished. With a grimace of disgust, Thyra dropped him onto the deck.

"Keep breathing," she advised him coolly.

He lay there heaving and coughing for rather a long while, and she had to take herself away from him, otherwise she might have done something that she would regret later. She went to sit alone at the back of the boat to cool off. They had anchored for the night in a sheltered cove, and she could just about make out the outline of the coast in the distance, in the thin moonlight that pierced through the clouds here and there. Thyra took a few deep breaths. She counted to ten inside her head. And again. She thought about Kari.

"Warrior. Tomorrow, we are crossing," Arvid announced from the shadows.

He was leaning against the main mast, smoking his pipe and watching her with interest. Thyra had known he was there all along. She just nodded. She was not in the mood for conversation.

"He's getting off at the first stop," the captain added.

She glanced at him and spotted the wry smile on his lips.

"Good," she replied.

"I think he'll be relieved too."

Arvid walked away on that comment, chuckling to himself. Thyra leaned against the side of the boat, and she looked up toward the sky. She finally allowed herself a small smile.

CHAPTER FIFTEEN

The rest of the river journey unfolded peacefully and without further incidents. Thyra felt rather tremendously bored in her passive role as a paying passenger though, and over the twenty days that it took for them to reach Switzerland, she actually transformed herself into a valuable member of the crew. She went hunting or fishing whenever they stopped along the way, either to unload goods or take on more cargo and passengers, and she generally brought enough food back to feed everyone on board. She was really good at cooking it, too. Her efforts were appreciated by all, especially since she did not ask for anything in return. She learned how to handle the boat, and the basics of river navigation. She started to connect with those around her, take part in conversations, and smile a little more often. As the weather improved, and the days lengthened into summertime, the heavy blanket of sadness that had felt to her at first like it would never lift from her shoulders began to grow lighter. She still thought about Kari often. She dreamt of her all the time. Sometimes, just before she fell asleep at night, she could feel her presence incredible strongly. A couple of times, she even sat bolt upright and looked around, peering through the darkness with her heart pounding hard, certain that her lover must have materialised out there out of nothing...

I am always with you, Thyr...

Yes, Kari was making her presence felt all right. In the days and weeks that followed her death, Thyra had been unable to connect with her spirit, trapped as she was in a vast ocean of depression and destructive emotions. She was feeling guilty, for one. She was terribly angry, too. And she felt utterly lost, and like she should never have survived that atrocious battle. But now, at long last, she could feel that Kari had settled inside her heart, just as she had promised, and that she was there to stay. Thyra still felt extremely alone, but perhaps not so completely destroyed. Every day, her soul grew a little stronger. She was also absolutely convinced now that she had made the correct decision in leaving home. Maybe there was something good waiting for her out there in the Far East after all. She was beginning to get a sense of a bigger purpose, and something more that she should be aiming for. She had no idea what it could possibly be, but the calling was there, no doubt about it. And she was happy to respond to it, whatever it may eventually turn out to be.

"Hey, warrior."

Thyra looked up at the sound of Arvid approaching. He had never once called her by her real name. She was not too keen on the title of warrior anymore, but she let it go.

"So. You ready for the mountains?" he asked.

She smiled and gave an enthusiastic nod.

"Yes, I am. Absolutely."

The very next morning, they would be reaching the end of the line as far as travelling over this particular river went. The next leg of Thyra's journey was about to start. It would be long, hard, and involve travelling up and over the Alps, down onto the Venetian coast. From there onward, she would find another boat to cross the Adriatic Sea and get herself over into Greece.

"What will you do when you get to Constantinople?" Arvid enquired.

She threw him an impatient look. He shrugged. He must only have asked her the same question about a hundred times before, and the answer that she gave him was always a variation on the exact same theme.

"I don't know yet. I haven't really thought about it."

He shook his head, watching her with the usual perplexed and wondering expression showing on his face. As she relaxed, and he got to know her better, Arvid had quizzed her endlessly about the real purpose of her journey. At first, he was fully convinced that she was being overly secretive, and that she must have an excellent reason for going to Constantinople in the first place. He believed her ultimate goal was probably to make a lot of money and acquire significant riches in some way or other. She must have a plan, one that was so good and guaranteed of success that she did not want to share it with him. But it must be worth it, otherwise, what would be the point of travelling such a long way? After a few conversations with Thyra though, he quickly realised that she was being completely genuine. She really had no idea. But she did not strike him as being an aimless drifter either. The woman was driven and committed, for sure. And so, the real purpose of her travels, he suspected, the end goal of it all, was still being hidden even from her.

"I should have known that you would say something along these lines," he muttered with another light shrug. "Anyway, here's for you."

And he dropped several heavy gold coins into her hand.

"What's that for?" she asked, surprised.

"Crew pay. You more than earned it."

"Thanks, Arvid. That's kind of you."

"Now, about what happens next."

She instantly looked up, interested. Much more interested in what he had to say now, it seemed to him, than if even a mountain of gold coins had suddenly appeared in front of her.

"Yes? What is it?" she prompted.

He grinned, amused at her reaction.

"Well, it should take you about a month to get over the mountains from where we'll dock tomorrow morning, maybe a little less, depending on how fast you walk. There is a famous boat captain in Calis named Mattia Gabriele. He runs a fleet of ships across the Adriatic and the Greek islands. You will find him easily in one of the many taverns where he conducts his business. Tell him I sent you. He is a good friend of mine, and he will see you through. Fair prices, no questions asked, no funny business."

Thyra filed away the precious name for future reference, and she offered Arvid a warm, grateful smile in return. This was priceless information to her at this point.

"All right. Sounds good. I'll find him."

"Anything you want me to tell Hrorek when I see him?"

He saw an instant flash of pure emotion burn through her eyes at the mention of her friend.

"Tell him I'm doing fine, and that I'm happy. Tell him I miss him. And if you wouldn't mind, give this to him also, please."

Thyra casually handed back the few gold coins that Arvid had just offered to her. He raised a bewildered eyebrow and stared at the money she had just put back in his hand. It was not an insignificant amount… And yet, she was giving it all away so easily. What a strange, puzzling woman this was.

"Are you sure?"

"Yes, I'm sure."

"Well, up to you, warrior."

With one last mystified shrug, and a firm promise to pass on the coins and deliver her message to her friend, the captain walked away to get his head down and grab some well-earned rest. Thyra herself could barely sleep for the rest of that night. She spent most of it waiting impatiently for morning to come so that they could start moving again. Until at last, a pale new dawn crept up over the land. A few hours later, armed with the good luck wishes of the rest of the crew, she disembarked for the last time.

"Safe travels and all the best to you, my friend," Arvid told her, as he waved her an enthusiastic goodbye. "Hope you find what you're looking for."

∞

Thyra was eager to get going. She did not want to linger too much around the local settlement, but she did take the time to locate some stables and acquire a small horse that she figured she could always sell on when she arrived in Calis. She also bought a warm woollen blanket, which would be useful in the mountains at night, a brand-new knife, and some food. It was simply bread, meat, and some hard cheese that would keep her going for another few days. And then, she started walking straight away, even though it was already late afternoon by then. But no matter. By nightfall, she had reached a reasonable location and gained some altitude. She had also put some good distance in between herself and the last farmstead that she had encountered along the way. It felt safe to her to stop, then. She built a warming fire by the side of a small brook. She ate some of her food, and then, she lay under the blanket, glad to finally be able to get some rest at last. It had been a long and tiring day.

She was also beginning to realise that she really was not keen on goodbyes. Thyra ran her fingers over her necklace, and she looked up toward the stars. Her thoughts turned to Kari, as always, and she gave a weak smile when a beautiful shooting star instantly streaked across the heavens, as if on cue. *Good night, my love...*

"Good night," she murmured. "I love you, Kari."

She could have sworn that somebody was there with her then. She felt a faint breath of air against her cheek, like a woman's sigh drifting teasingly over her skin. Thyra shivered with a mixture of deep sadness, reluctant hope, and acute, unfulfilled wanting. With a shake of the head, she threw some more wood onto the fire and snuggled deeper under the blanket. She closed her eyes, gave a tired sigh, and drifted off to sleep with her lover on her mind.

For the next five weeks, it was exactly the same routine for her. Get up at the break of dawn, have something small to eat, and start riding. From time to time, she would stop at farms and small dwellings when she came upon them, to rest for a bit and buy more food from the farmers. She hunted too, on and off along the way. Thankfully, finding enough water was never a problem in the mountains. The nights were usually clear and cold, the days mostly bright and sunny. Only one afternoon, she noticed a bunch of black clouds accumulating fast around the peaks. The temperature suddenly dropped, and it became almost too dark to see. Thyra found a tiny cave for herself and her horse to shelter in, as a storm of biblical proportions unleashed over the area. She made a small fire and huddled next to it with her blanket wrapped around her shoulders. She watched the rain fall and listened to the thunder roll. It was nice and dry in the cave, and so, she spent the rest of the night there. In the morning, the sun was back again, and she got going early.

The five weeks went quickly like this. She lost track of time. She relished the simplicity of the journey, and once or twice, she even considered stopping for good. She could live this life all right, all alone in the mountains. She could stay away from people forever, with just her own thoughts and memories for company. But something kept her going. *Maybe,* she mused. *Maybe there is something out there, waiting for me...* She kept walking.

CHAPTER SIXTEEN

The morbid whistle of a whip slashing through the air brought an instant chill between Thyra's shoulder blades. After spending so much time on her own, arriving at the busy port town of Calis on the shores of the Adriatic Sea was a shock to the system all right. There were only three words to describe the place: loud, frantic, overpopulated.

The first thing that Thyra did when she got there was find a place to sell her horse. She was pleased to get a good price for him. Then, she treated herself to a solid meal at a nearby tavern. Once her stomach was full, she wandered outside to explore a little bit more of the rest of the town. It was not what she had expected to find or was looking forward to experiencing. There, in the middle of the harbour, in plain sight of an eager crowd of onlookers, several people were being beaten. And hard, too. Thyra stood watching for a while, to try to understand what was happening, and why, as each poor victim was dragged to a sturdy post, tied down to it, and had their tunic ripped off their back. Then, they were whipped. There was a small queue of prisoners waiting in line for their turn. They had all been made to kneel down and were guarded by men who were all dressed the same and carried long spears. In contrast, the prisoners had much darker skins, and seemed not to understand a lot of what was being communicated to them. *They must be slaves*, Thyra suddenly realised with a jolt of reluctance. She remembered how Bjarke had talked so much about slaves. He had said there was a flourishing trade going on. *'Those guys have got it made!'* he roared one day, referring to the slave traders. Thyra remembered how he thought there was great money to be made for even easier work, and how he had announced then that he would definitely become involved in the slave trade. *Yes*, she reflected darkly, *Bjarke would have fitted in perfectly with these guys.*

She carried on observing the scene with growing horror, as the next slave in line for a whipping was pushed forward and shuffled up to his tormentor. He was just a child, ten at the most, and appearing even younger. When the slave master tied him down to the post, he started to cry. He looked terrified. Some spectators had the gall to laugh at him then. They were pointing at the kid and chuckling at his tears. Thyra pursed her lips in disgust at their behaviour. Instinctively, she tightened her hand around the handle of her sword. She was extremely tempted to jump forward and do something, anything to help this child. But a quick glance around the place confirmed that there were too many slave traders keeping watch. And the crowd would not be on her side either. Even though it felt quite outrageous to her to simply walk away from this situation, she realised there was nothing she could realistically do about it. And so, it would probably be best for her to move on now and get going with her real purpose. Thyra decided to go in search of the boat captain Arvid had recommended to her.

As she made her way through a maze of people busy selling hardware, all kinds of food, or loading goods onto the waiting ships, she stopped a few times to stare at those in open wonder. These were no tiny river boats, for sure. They were much bigger, more imposing, and magnificent-looking in every way. Thyra felt her heart truly lift at the sight of them. And then, there was all the rest of this incredible live scene, which was completely fascinating to her. She found it riveting to observe the activity of the busy Mediterranean harbour, unfolding so vividly before her eyes.

There were fishermen selling their catch straight off the boats, and the smell of freshly caught fish hanging in the air. It was mixed in with the sweet salty odour of the sea, which was carried on the light warm breeze. A hint of mysterious spice floating through as well, maybe? It made Thyra think about all the foreign lands further east which she had yet to reach and discover. She loved to hear the hard cry of the seagulls flying overhead. Best of all was watching all the people, who looked terribly busy and did not pay a single bit of attention to her. It was mesmerising, and Thyra enjoyed that last part very much. Normally, just the simple fact that she was a female travelling on her own tended to attract unwelcome company. It was nice to feel anonymous for once… Wandering around with her eyes wide open, trying not to bump into anyone, she made her way to the other end of the bustling harbour. When she got there, she spotted a tavern that looked promising. She walked straight in and enquired at the counter.

"Mattia Gabriele?" she asked. "Boat captain?"

The bartender examined her briefly yet thoroughly, and then he nodded, apparently satisfied. He pointed to a spot right behind her back. Thyra glanced toward it, and she smiled. All right, then. That man looked just as she had always imagined a successful boat owner would do. He was big in every way, tall, balding; with bushy eyebrows set over a pair of inquisitive black eyes which immediately spotted and settled on Thyra. The man's gaze focused on her torc.

127

"Volsung," he exclaimed. "Am I right?"

He looked pleased with his insight when she confirmed that indeed, she was one of them.

"Arvid sends his greetings," she added.

"Ah. Yes. He told you to come see me, uh?"

He laughed in satisfaction, and even as he did so, his eyes were in constant motion. Drifting all over her, taking in the torc again, her sword, and the way that she was standing in front of him looking so relaxed, strong, and confident. For her part, Thyra was well aware that he was assessing her, figuring out her worth to him, and how much money he could possibly attempt to squeeze out of her. She was not surprised by that, since it was the way business was normally conducted. And so…

"Arvid said you ask for fair prices, and no funny business," she informed him.

She figured it would not hurt to throw that one in there. He smirked, leaned back in his chair, and reached for his drink. She took the seat opposite him.

"Arvid is right. Now, where you going, Viking?"

"Greece, first. And then, on to Constantinople."

He nodded. This was a fairly standard request for him.

"All right, then I suggest you sail to Oroska first. Cross over land to the Aegean Sea. Once you get there, you'll have no problem finding yourself another boat."

Thyra did not have to think about it for long.

"All right," she agreed. "I'm happy with that."

"Good." He looked pleased as well. "Average sailing time to Oroska is five days. Price to you will be five gold coins. I have a ship that leaves in a couple of hours. Will that do, warrior?"

Thyra was delighted at the news. Two hours! And only five days' time! For some reason, she had expected that it would take her much longer to get across to Greece… This was just perfect.

She paid him his money, and he accompanied her to the ship she was to travel on. It was one of the ones she had noticed before and even stopped to admire. Thyra was growing quietly excited at the thought of spending time on it.

"It's really beautiful," she remarked.

Mattia seemed happy with the comment.

"Yes, one of the best I have," he agreed in a proud voice.

He introduced her to his captain, who was a tall, sinewy man with leathery skin turned almost black by years of constant exposure to the sun and sea air. He kept his long white hair tied at the back of his head in a low ponytail and appeared the usual mixture of deeply interested and slightly taken aback when he was introduced to her.

"This is Thyra, of the Volsung clan," Mattia explained to him. "She's on her way to Oroska. Thyra, this is Domenico. He's a great captain who can read the winds better than anyone. He'll get you there in no time."

Thyra nodded her hello, and she shook hands with him. She thanked Mattia for his help, said goodbye, and stepped on deck. She was pleased to see that the ship was spotless, in perfect condition, and smelled nicely of freshly applied tar and resin. Arvid's recommendation was turning out to be a brilliant one. Tilting her head back, Thyra squinted up the mast at the heavy canvas sails, neatly folded in for the time being. She could not wait to see those unfurled and blown full of wind. Smiling at the thought of what a magnificent sight it would be, feeling light and free for a change, she was taken aback when she noticed a small line of slaves being pushed on board the ship. She exhaled sharply. *Not those bloody traders again!* It was just five prisoners this time, accompanied by two armed men. Obviously, it was some of the same people that she had seen being beaten earlier on, and Thyra shook her head in profound sympathy.

Her heart really went out to those poor people. And she was itching to help. She could see that two of the slaves were in a serious condition. They could barely walk from their recent injuries, and they had to lean onto the others, who did not look in much better shape themselves. Thyra kept her eyes on them, gritting her teeth in helpless frustration. Then, she noticed something else that she had really not expected to see. At the back of the line, not tied to the men, stood a young woman. Thyra froze in place at the sight of her. She narrowed her eyes. For a split second there, as she looked, the air around the prisoner seemed to shimmer and shift. Thyra even grew a little dizzy with it. She grabbed onto the railing to steady herself, shook her head to clear her vision, and recovered quickly. *What the hell was that?* she wondered. She looked toward the prisoner again.

She had no idea how someone dressed in such dirty rags, with a rough, heavy rope tied around her neck, and her wrists bound in the same manner could exude such an aura of control and calm. But somehow, this woman managed to do it. Thyra continued to stare at her in total surprise, as the male slaves shuffled past in silence. They were led down below deck by one of the guards. Then, it was the woman's turn to go. This one held her head high. She did not drag her feet. When she walked past Thyra, their eyes met only briefly. Intense, burning black orbs plunged into sparkling blue ones. The combination of raw anger and fierce pride that Thyra spotted simmering through the slave woman's gaze almost took her breath away.

"Hey, warrior."

Thyra was startled when she heard the captain chuckle next to her. She glanced at him. She had not noticed him standing there, watching her a little more intently than she appreciated. She did not enjoy being caught off guard.

"Yeah?" she said.

"Don't worry, my friend," he assured her, having mistaken her thoughtful expression for one of annoyance. "These beasts will be kept locked down below for the duration of the crossing. You won't have to keep looking at them all the time."

Thyra struggled to control her rising temper at his hateful words.

"Right," she muttered.

She caught a last glimpse of the woman's back as she was being led away. Her skin was lighter than the men's, a gleaming bronze colour. She had short black hair and a slender, fluid body that unfortunately also bore marks of a recent whipping. The sight of her was at once mesmerising and tragic. And even though Thyra knew better, she could not help herself. She had to find out more about her.

"Where did this one come from?" she enquired.

"Egypt, from what the manifest says. The story goes that her owner wanted to keep her here originally, but now he's decided to send her to his brother over in Greece."

The captain turned to look at her. Thyra felt his busy little eyes scrutinising her face. It made her skin crawl, and she suppressed a shiver.

"She's nice, uh?" he smirked. "You like her?"

She met his gaze straight-on. He looked excited, as he waited for her to comment further. She did not. She did not reply at all. It was a huge effort to maintain her composure, and not shove him back violently the way she really wanted to do. Her stomach was churning. What in the world did this man believe she must think was '*nice*' about seeing a woman tied up and humiliated on the end of a leash like that? Thyra's head was spinning with outrage at the very idea of it. But she was not stupid, and so, she gritted her teeth and kept on smiling.

"Just wondering," she said.

Mattia had introduced her to the captain, and she knew that it was not the norm. So, that guy now probably just thought she was an important passenger, and he was treating her as such. Maybe, hopefully, there would be something in it for him later. As for her, Thyra was very much aware that she was totally on her own here, and that she would be a passenger on this man's ship for the next five days. She knew she had everything to gain by keeping him on side. But as they started on their way, and she went to find a quiet spot to stand alone, it took a long time for her hands to actually stop shaking. All of a sudden, she could not have cared less about this ship, the upcoming sea voyage, or Constantinople for that matter. She barely noticed the sails coming down, the loud clanking of the rigging, and the sharp crack of the linen, as the sails caught the breeze and filled up to their full size. All that she could think about were those dark, proud, blazing black eyes, and the intense look that the woman had given her. As the coast quickly receded in the background, and the ship found its true rhythm, Thyra only knew one thing for sure. She needed to find a way to help her.

CHAPTER SEVENTEEN

She went to lie down for a few hours after sunset, but she did not fall sleep. Instead, she paid undivided attention to the crew's movements.

At night, most of them vanished off to their quarters down below deck, and only a few rotated on-duty, to keep an eye on things and maintain the ship on its correct bearing. At all times, the entrance to the lower levels was left open and unattended. Thyra had chosen to bed down pretty much right next to it. The two armed guards who had come on board with the slaves were sleeping on deck as well. She had watched them carefully all afternoon and well into the evening. No one had been down even once to check on the prisoners, or to bring them any food and water, and she had a nasty feeling that no one would bother to do so now. After all, it was only five days at sea, right? Who cared if a bunch of slaves lost a little bit of weight or got thirsty? As far as Thyra was concerned, the way that these people were treated was revolting, although, in a sense, it would also make it easier for her to do what she was planning on doing now. And so, she pretended to be fast asleep, and she waited patiently. She held back for several long hours, until the darkest part of the night; and then she got up and headed silently toward the steps that led below. No one noticed her disappearing down there.

The first level housed the captain's and the crew's quarters. The reason Thyra knew this was because she had asked Domenico to give her a tour of the entire ship earlier on that afternoon. He had seemed pleased that she would show such keen interest in it and answered every single question she could come up with. He was incredibly talkative, open, and tremendously helpful to his '*important*' passenger. Now, thanks to him, Thyra kept going quickly toward her intended destination, as silent as a ghost drifting through. When she reached the second level, she was struck again by how hot and stuffy it was down there. This was where the slaves were kept, and Domenico had only allowed her a quick peek inside of it.

"It stinks in there," he commented. "No air."

Indeed, the stifling atmosphere had made a rather powerful impression on Thyra. She would have hated to be forced to spend any time at all in that room, let alone restrained and without any water. The slave men were held inside of another closed-off area at the back, tightly locked. It must have been even worse for them in there. The woman herself, Domenico explained, was kept separately tied up to a sturdy post inside the main room. Thyra had been unable to catch a glimpse of her earlier on because it was too dark. And once again, she had to wait several long seconds for her eyes to adjust. A single porthole on the side allowed a tiny sliver of moonlight to shine through. Not much, though. Not enough. And Domenico was right, it was hard to breathe down there. Regardless, Thyra focused her mind on her mission. *All right, let's do this thing,* she decided. She could just make out the outline of a woman's body. The prisoner was lying face down on the hard-wooden floor. She appeared fast asleep. Or maybe unconscious? Thyra slowly crept over to her. She came extremely close. And unconsciously, the woman must have felt her presence through her uneasy slumber.

She stirred suddenly. When she opened her eyes and discovered a stranger leaning so close to her, she was immediately startled. She gasped, and a scream would surely have followed if Thyra had not instantly clamped her hand down over her face. She had anticipated this might happen. She was keen to reassure the woman as quickly as she possibly could that she had absolutely nothing to fear from her.

"Sshhh," she murmured. "Don't be scared. I am not going to hurt you."

She pulled out a handful of food from the folds of her dark cloak and showed it to her.

"This is for you. Okay?"

It was everything that Thyra had managed to save up, and which should have constituted her own dinner that evening. Bread stuffed with vegetables, drizzled in olive oil, and pieces of fresh white fish; along with a flask of cold water taken from the ship's ample supply. All paying passengers had free access to that, and Thyra was taking full advantage of the opportunity. She watched in careful silence as the prisoner's eyes instantly widened at the sight of the food. Thyra relaxed a bit more when her expression turned from surprise and panic to incredulous delight. This was more like it. Only then did she slowly remove her hand from over the woman's mouth. The prisoner stared at her in open wonder. Up close like this, and without the attitude that she had projected earlier, she appeared much smaller, certainly a lot thinner, and extremely pale despite her naturally tanned skin. Thyra flashed her a gentle, friendly smile, and she sat down right next to her.

"I brought you some things. Here."

She handed her the flask of water first, and the woman reached for it with trembling hands. She was too weak though, and she almost dropped it twice.

"Wait," Thyra whispered.

She took the flask back from her, opened it, and held it in the correct position for the exhausted prisoner to be able to drink from it. The woman laced her fingers around her wrist as she did so. Her hands felt almost too hot on her skin, burning, and Thyra could sense utter desperation in the way that she gripped on to her so tightly.

"All right, just take your time," she encouraged. "It's okay."

Overhead, there was a sudden creaking and shifting of the wood, as someone walked around the crew area. A muffled buzz of voices followed. Thyra looked up in alarm, heart pounding. Every muscle in her body tensed up, and she held her breath for a few anxious seconds. But the voices soon died down, and all that could be heard again in the sudden silence was the sound of the waves hitting gently against the hull. Just the crew going about their business. Nothing to worry about. Thyra exhaled, relieved. She met the woman's gaze, and saw the same feeling reflected in her eyes.

"Phew," she grinned.

And then, she stayed with her that night until the woman had finished all the food, every last crumb, and drained every drop of the water too. Thyra knew that she had to leave then. She could not afford to stay down there for very much longer. But she still allowed herself to make eye contact with the woman one final time. She nodded. Those dark eyes stared back at her with heart-breaking intensity.

"Okay," Thyra murmured. "I have to go now."

She turned to leave, but the woman held fast onto her wrist.

"What... What is your name?" she whispered.

Thyra blinked, elated. It had not even crossed her mind that this woman might speak her language, but now, she felt a hot surge of excitement and possibility at the realisation that she did.

How ignorant of her to assume that she would not, just because she happened to be in chains...

"My name is Thyra. What is yours?"

"Thyra, I am Merit."

"Merit. That's nice."

Thyra flashed her another brief smile. She was moved when the woman also forced a courageous one for her in return. This all made Thyra want to leave her behind even less, but there was no other choice. Unless she wanted to get found out, of course, and end up sharing a set of shackles down there with Merit on a much more permanent basis. The promise to come back and see her as soon as she could do so was out of her mouth and on her lips before she even realised that she had said it out loud.

"I'll bring you some more food and water. Tomorrow night. Okay?"

"Yes," the woman murmured.

She spoke in an urgent, low whisper that was loaded with gratitude, and tremendous emotion.

"Thank you..."

Thyra nodded, and she quickly made her way back up the ladder in the dark, praying that she would not be spotted at this point. But luck was definitely on her side, and no one noticed her going past the crew quarters or coming out of the darkened entrance way. She glanced once toward the two slave traders, and found them still nicely fast asleep, snoring loudly on the other side. The crew were going about their normal work, as per usual, and the ship felt reassuringly steady on its way. *All right, then...* She had made it. Thyra was feeling a little too wired to go to sleep after her daring adventure though, and she went to lean over the side of the boat. She took several deep breaths to calm her racing heart, all the while thinking about her new Egyptian friend, who, sadly, did not enjoy the privilege of fresh night air...

Thyra wished that she could help her in this way too. She had got away with it this time, after all... Now that she had started, she had absolutely no intention of stopping. It struck her as a little bit mad, and she wondered what Kari would have thought about it all.

"Do you think I'm crazy?" she murmured into the wind.

As if in response, an image shot through her mind of her lover, standing on the shores of the lake that morning, on the day of their first encounter. Smiling brightly, the way Kari so often did. It was a memory of happier times. And a blessing, maybe? Thyra was sure that the brave and generous Volsung commander would have whole-heartedly approved of her risky actions this evening. To help another woman who needed it so badly, just because she could... This was great. And she had not needed to hurt anyone else in the process either, which felt good too. It was the way of *The Shining One*. Thyra had definitely not forgotten about that, or the promise that she had made to Kari. *I'll be the strongest broken link...* She let out a small sigh of frustration as she thought of the male slaves. She would have liked to do something for them as well, but she could not get into that locked room without a key. And then, there was only so much food she could carry down there at any one time. It was infuriating, and Thyra knew that it would most likely drive her insane if she kept thinking about it.

"Let it go," she murmured to herself.

She was doing the absolute best that she could do with the limited resources at her disposal, and she would continue to do so. No more, but certainly no less. She would go down to see the woman prisoner again, for sure. She would bring her more food, water, and she would talk to her. And when they finally got to Greece, and the ship docked in Oroska... *What will I do to help her then?*

The thought was totally unexpected, and it startled her. There was nothing she *could* do, nothing that she *should* do, and Thyra knew it perfectly well. The woman was a slave, under the guard of two heavily armed men. There would be a lot more of them waiting in port. And it was one thing sharing a bit of food with her when no one was really paying attention, but to even think of doing something more… Now, that was crazy. Still, the idea kept gnawing at the back of her mind throughout the rest of the night. Thyra only managed a couple of hours of sleep after that, until dawn peaked brightly over the horizon. She woke up with a headache and literally starving, which was not surprising since her last meal had actually been at the tavern back in Calis. At breakfast, she wolfed down two big servings of thick, honey-sweetened porridge. But she kept the bread and cooked meat for later, hidden away inside her belt pocket. Domenico was up and about too; roaming all over the ship, talking loudly to his crew, and eager to catch up with her as well, it appeared. As soon as he spotted her, sat alone on one side eating her meal, he came over to talk to her.

"So, how was your first night on board, my friend?" he enquired.

For one single and terrifying moment, Thyra thought this might well be a trick question, and that he was only asking her because he had found out what she had been up to during the night. But she was quick to push the worrying thought out of her mind, and she flashed him an easy smile around a mouthful of oats.

"Great," she replied. "Slept like a baby."

"Glad to hear that," he approved. "The last passenger Arvid introduced to me started throwing up as soon as the sails went up, and he was sick all the way to Greece."

"Uh-uh," Thyra commented.

"I had to keep an eye on him the entire way, just to make sure that he didn't faint, or fall over board and drown himself; or something like that."

"You won't have that same problem with me," she assured him.

"Yeah, I guess I can see that now," the captain chuckled.

He smiled at her, as she continued to shovel big spoonful of porridge into her mouth.

"Being out at sea makes you double-hungry, uh!"

Thyra nodded. *Yeah, you have no idea.* She suddenly realised that the man was just being friendly with her, nothing more, and she relaxed. And then, as he clapped his hand over her shoulder and left it there a little longer than required, it also dawned on her the reason why. Did he *like* her? She cringed at the very notion. But perhaps she could use that to her advantage as well. So, instead of grabbing onto his hand and breaking all his fingers, the way that she would normally have been inclined to respond, she forced herself to return his smile, and raised a hopeful eyebrow toward him.

"So, I was wondering. Any chance of getting some more meat?" she asked.

He laughed at the request.

"Sure! We got plenty!"

CHAPTER EIGHTEEN

"Thyra, will you help me escape?"

The burning question came on the fourth night, and it was hardly surprising. Thyra wondered why she had been so naïve as to think that Merit would not ask her. After all, she carried a sword on her belt. Everything about her, from her well-muscled body, to the weathered leather vest and the arm bracers that she wore screamed *fighter*. It was no wonder Merit wanted to know. Over the past several days at sea, Thyra had been true to her word. She had gone down every single night to give the woman food and water, to spend time with her, and to talk to her. Only twice had the slave traders actually been below to bring Merit and the slave men anything to drink, and nothing else. Over time, Thyra discovered that her new friend was only a few years older than she was, and extremely accomplished in her own right. During the many hours that they spent together, Merit explained to Thyra that she was a practitioner of the ancient arts of energy healing, a teacher as well, and that she could speak seven languages fluently. She came from a once thriving community of highly educated people which at one time had included priests, astronomers, royal scribes, writers, and educators from many other disciplines; her village was situated in upper Egypt on the banks of the river Nile.

"You should see Egypt, Thyra," she enthused. "It is a special place. It has light and energy like nowhere else I've been. The land is rich, ripe, and plentiful. You would love it there."

And then, her voice gradually grew more tense when she related how one day, without any warning, an army of white men had swept through the village like wildfire. There were too many of them to fight back, and they were too well-armed. They burned the houses. They tried to bring the local temple down. The invaders butchered all of the young men and most of the old people. They captured the women and children. Merit herself was snatched from the temple and taken as a slave. She was loaded onto a ship and sold to a rich Venetian merchant. In a split second on that fateful day, everything had changed for her. Her life had been nothing but hardship and misery ever since.

"Will you help me?" she repeated urgently.

Thyra shook her head.

"I don't think I can…"

"Please!"

"Merit, there is nothing I can do," Thyra repeated.

She exhaled sharply, blowing air out in total frustration. She had been thinking about nothing else, day and night for the past three days, and racking her brain to find a solution. Yes, she could probably kill the two armed guards in their sleep and throw them overboard. It would be an easy thing for her to do. But what would that achieve? Not much. They would still be stuck on the boat. Also, it would be cold-blooded murder, pure and simple. *Never to attack… Never to retaliate…* The Volsung commander's words of wisdom still echoed loudly at the back of her mind. Thyra would never betray her lover's rule. But she wondered how else she could really help Merit if she did not take bloody action. *What would you do, Kari? What can I do to help her?*

Thyra had gone over so many different scenarios in her head... There was the other option of trying to escape with Merit through Greece, of course. Once they arrived there, and when the slaves were taken off the ship, there would be a single opportunity for her to do something. But again, there were bound to be other slave traders waiting in port, just like there had been in Calis. Thyra was on her own, after all. How would they manage to escape and avoid recapture? It all felt totally impossible to her. Thyra had been tossing and turning in her sleep and all waking hours, struggling to find a solution to these tormenting questions for hours at a time. She could not figure it out. In the end, it seemed as if it really was just as she had said. There was no way out of this. There was nothing she could do.

"I'm sorry," she murmured. "Merit, I..."

She spotted hot, disappointed tears welling up in Merit's eyes before the woman broke eye contact with her and dropped her head. Thyra was seething in irritation. She was feeling angry and discouraged. She watched as Merit pulled helplessly at the length of rope that was tied around her neck. It was heavy and uncomfortable, and Thyra knew for sure that it was painful. She ached to use her own knife to cut through it, but again, that would be a sure sign that someone had been down there. And she burned to be off this ship too, which had started to feel increasingly like a floating prison to her as well. On the river journey down the Rhyne, she had been able to get off the boat and move about when she wanted to. She could go hunting whenever she felt like it, and spend her time doing useful things for herself and the other people. This sea voyage just felt like a long idle wait to her, and a complete waste of time. In fact, she had recently decided that when she arrived in Greece, she would buy herself a brand-new horse and travel the rest of her way to Constantinople over land, not sea...

"Gods," Thyra murmured bitterly.

She glanced toward Merit again. It felt obscene and even shameful to her to be thinking about all this travelling stuff, and to be looking forward to it, when the beautiful, kind, intelligent woman that she had grown to know and like so much was condemned to a life of slavery and abuse. Thyra took a single hard breath. She felt like she was going to throw up suddenly.

"I don't want to let you go," she murmured. "But..."

In response, Merit threw herself into her arms. Her wrists were tied to the side of the ship, only allowing her limited movement, and she was not able to hold onto Thyra very well. But she leaned into her all the same and pressed herself against her. Thyra's pulse skyrocketed in reaction. There was nothing at all a suave, long-haired boat captain could ever do to make her breathe faster, but this woman's instinctive reaction, and her obvious need for protection and reassurance certainly achieved that. Without even thinking, Thyra wrapped her arms around Merit's shoulders. She pulled her close against her own body. She took another trembling breath. The situation was hopeless. There was nothing that she could say or do to make it any better for Merit. And Thyra knew full well that she should not be reacting to her in this way. It was only making things worse for the woman. She reflected that perhaps it had been a mistake to come down and bring her food every night. Maybe it had actually been wrong to form a friendship with a woman that she could never hope to rescue. Yes, she had made her voyage a little easier over the short term. But now, false hopes were being cruelly destroyed. Thyra was responsible for giving Merit hope in the first place. She was to blame for this. She would have gladly punched her fist through the side of the boat in fury and disappointment at the unfairness of it all. She was fuming inside, and part of her also just wanted to cry now.

"I'm sorry, Merit," she repeated. "I wish I…"

"It's okay. You don't need to say any more."

"I just don't know what to do," Thyra raged on.

Merit was the first to pull back from their embrace. She met Thyra's gaze, and she nodded tightly, swallowing back burning tears that she felt she had no right to inflict upon her. She had also spent endless hours thinking of all the ways that she might be able to escape. But she could not figure out any real option to deal with the problem that would not also put Thyra at risk of ending up with a rope around her neck. She could never and would never ask this of her.

"It's okay," she said, a little more firmly this time. "I thank you for what you've done for me so far. I will never forget you, Thyra."

Thyra felt her heart sink at her words.

"Merit, I'll do my best to…"

A loud booming noise interrupted her, just as Thyra was about to say that she would try to come back one more time. Her heart was beating out of her chest in sudden dread. *How can I let her go? How can I leave her here?* she wondered. A growing sense of urgency flooded through her. Suddenly, none of her earlier logic made sense anymore. *What the hell is wrong with me?* Thyra thought. *I can't. I simply cannot do this and walk away!* She looked up sharply, her decision made at last. She reached for the knife on her belt. She would free the woman up right now. She would cut that ugly rope, take it off her friend's neck, and to hell with the consequences. If she had to fight to protect Merit, she would. If she had to kill, then she would do it too. And if she had to die… *Well.*

"Merit, listen to me," she started. "I…"

But in the next second, the entire hull of the ship creaked. It vibrated and shook violently. Loud screams erupted from above.

What the hell is happening? Thyra jumped to her feet and ran to the ladder. She looked up and froze at the sight of the cloud of smoke that she could see swirling and billowing above the entranceway at the top. *A fire?*

"I'll be right back," she shouted over her shoulder.

And with one last reassuring glance toward the helpless woman still shackled to the floor, she grabbed onto the ladder and started climbing fast. Five seconds later, she was back on deck. Her mouth dropped open at the awful sight that greeted her. Another ship had slammed into the side of them. Men were jumping on board and attacking the crew with machetes and swords. Domenico ran up to her. He was livid, his face a mask of raw terror.

"What's happening?" Thyra shouted.

"Pirates!" he yelled. "Draw your sword, warrior!"

Thyra did not have time to reply. She spotted one of the invading men advancing toward them with his weapon raised. He had his eyes fixed onto the captain and preparing to slice Domenico's head off clean from his body.

"Move!" she screamed.

She grabbed onto the man's shoulder and shoved him out of the way. She took one small step forward and sank her sword into the attacking man's throat. All she really had to do was raise her blade. He was coming at them with so much speed that he pretty much just impaled himself on top of it. She pushed back off him, withdrew her weapon from his body. He dropped at her feet, dead. Thyra quickly raised her eyes to look around. She was breathing hard from the adrenaline pulsing through her veins. She had no idea how things could have turned so bad so quickly. The pirates were lobbing burning torches onto the ship's deck. A couple of those caught the sails, which instantly ignited into flames with a loud *wooshing* sound. Thyra felt the heat increase ten-fold as the mast then caught on fire next. There was no way to stop any of this from happening, and she suddenly spotted more pirates jumping on board. *Where are they all coming from?* Crew members were fighting for their lives, using anything they could get their hands on as improvised weapons. This was about personal survival now, no longer to save the ship or any of the cargo. And then, Thyra heard a terrifying cry from one of the crew.

"Captain! We've got a hole in her! She's going to sink!"

As if on cue, the ship suddenly started to turn over onto its side with a sinister accompanying creaking sound. Domenico was still standing by, motionless. He appeared frozen in shock, uncomprehending, as his precious ship was about to go down. Another shout was heard.

"Captain, we're taking on water over here too!"

Unfortunately, Thyra could see that this was indeed the case. And not from just a single side either. One entire portion of the ship was already dipping way below the water line. On the lower levels below deck, the water must be high up already, and rising fast. *Merit...* Thyra grabbed onto Domenico's shoulder again, as the man attempted to crawl away from her in order to go hide under a pierce of tarp. She yanked him back roughly and shook him to get his attention.

"Where do you think you're going?" she snarled.

His eyes had grown wide and empty. He was trembling in abject fear.

"Domenico, listen to me," she urged him. "Hey! We have to free the slaves; do you understand me? Otherwise, they are going to drown! Give me your keys to the back cell. Come on, where are the keys?"

He attempted to push her off him and free himself. When he could not do it, his face suddenly contorted in rage and anger.

Gone was the friendly captain from early days. Now that his life was on the line, he was finally showing his true colours, and it was not a pretty sight.

"Forget about the bloody slaves!" he yelled. "Fight for my ship!"

Thyra punched him in the face. She was done talking, and there was no time for his crazy rantings. She rifled through his pockets, desperately looking for the keys that she knew he must be carrying somewhere on his person. Finally, she found them dangling from his neck on a thin leather cord. She tore it off him and prepared to run back downstairs on her own. By then, the ship was listing dangerously, and the fight between the crew and the invaders was still dragging on. But Thyra had no time for any of that either. She headed toward the entrance way, slashing her way through the melee with her sword. She only found one lone pirate standing between her and her final goal. He grinned wildly at the sight of her approaching so fast. Or rather, at the sight of the heavy gold torc that he spotted around her neck.

"You want it?" she said. "Come and get it then!"

He launched himself at her just as the ship shuddered and shifted on its side a little more. It was bad timing for Thyra. She lost her balance and fell. His blade sliced through her upper arm, but thankfully, his aim was off, and it was not a crippling blow. His second strike was a much better one. It would undoubtedly have severed her arm off at the wrist, if not for the solid protective bracer that she wore. Thyra did not give him a third opportunity to get it right. When he raised his hand again, she was much quicker than him, and she thrust her blade into his stomach. A quick push, a single twist, and he was no longer a threat. Then, there was no one standing between her and the steps anymore. And no one would follow her down there either, she was sure of it. It would have been suicidal, a fact that she realised as soon as she reached the second level. The water was all the way up to her hips already, and in the manner that Merit was tied down, she was struggling desperately to keep her head above water. Her eyes lit up in instant hope when she spotted Thyra.

"Help!" she screamed. "Thyra!"

Thyra glanced toward the locked room at the back, but she still went to free Merit first. She used her knife to slice through the rope collar, and then, she had to dip underwater to take care of the heavy restraints around her wrists. It took her two attempts to cut through those, and Merit was gasping for air by the time she managed to get it done. As soon as she was free, she threw her arms around Thyra.

"Thank you," she cried in pure relief. "I knew you would come back for me!"

Thyra nodded.

"Go to the ladder now," she instructed, "and wait for me over there. It's not safe up on deck."

"Where are you going?"

"To let the others out."

Merit seemed delighted and also terrified at the same time.

"Please, hurry!" she pleaded. "I could hear them screaming in there when the water began to rise!"

"I'll get them out," Thyra promised. "Just make sure that you stay safe, all right?"

She quickly made her way toward the holding cell. The water was rising fast, way too fast for her liking. When she reached the cell, she realised that it was even deeper over there. It was a dangerous place to be, and once again, Thyra had to go underwater to fit the key into the lock. She struggled to turn it. This was proving a lot harder than she had expected it would be.

Suddenly out of breath, she had to resurface for a brief moment. The men inside were banging hard against the door now. Thyra could hear them yelling at the top of their lungs, shouting to be let out. The water was up to her chest. She risked a quick glance over her shoulder, and spotted Merit holding onto the ladder as instructed, watching her intently. She looked worried, anxious, but she shouted strong words of encouragement.

"You can do it, Thyra," she yelled. "I know you can!"

Yes, I can do it, Thyra thought. *And either I will succeed, or I'll die trying.* As she returned her attention to the task at hand, she was very conscious that either way, she would be happy with the result.

CHAPTER NINETEEN

As a battle of epic proportions kept raging on above her head, Thyra filled her lungs with another deep mouthful of air. She disappeared under the surface one more time. It was hard to see what she was doing down there, and there were lots of bits of wood floating around that kept getting in her way. The key was ill-fitting, and she struggled with it for several long seconds. Eventually, to her great relief, the rusty lock simply broke in her hands. She pulled on the door, helped by the men who were pushing against it from the other side. Two of them then stumbled out, fighting against the weight of the water that held them back. The other two, the unlucky ones who had gone in already carrying more serious injuries, had not survived. Their bloated corpses floated by. Thyra made sure that she stayed well away, and she did not allow herself to look at them again past the initial glance. There was no time to mourn for these people now.

"That way," she shouted to the survivors.

She pointed toward the front of the room. The men stared in that direction, looking lost. They glanced back at each other, hesitating. They remained rooted in place, as if in a daze.

"Go!" Thyra repeated urgently. "Get over there now, come on!"

They finally seemed to grasp what she wanted them to do, but they were physically weak from their ordeal, extremely so, and they needed a huge amount of help to get going. By then, the water was rapidly headed toward the ceiling, and everybody was swimming. The men struggled to stay afloat. Thyra did her best to keep them both on the surface, but she was finding it difficult as well. She could barely touch the floor now. She slipped when her right foot caught over something dragging underwater. She failed to catch herself, slumped forward, and swallowed a big mouthful of water.

"Merit," she gasped.

But Merit had spotted her getting into trouble, and she was already swimming out toward them to help. She grabbed onto the first man's arm and said something to him in a language that Thyra did not understand. Whatever she said, it must have been right on the money though, because the man yelled something incomprehensible to her back in reply, and instantly redoubled his efforts. Merit screamed the same words at the second guy, and tears instantly came up to his eyes. He nodded frantically and went harder at it too. Merit continued to urge them both on in the same foreign language, sounding like a harsh drill commander.

"What are you saying to them?" Thyra shouted.

Merit threw her a sharp glance back over her shoulder. She even flashed her a brilliant smile at the same time. In that single instant, she appeared as fierce and as determined as any warrior Thyra had ever trained or fought alongside with. It was great to see.

"I told them that if they survive this, freedom awaits on the other side! No more shackles! No more whip! Not EVER!"

Thyra felt an electrifying shiver run down her spine at the savage expression in the woman's eyes when she said that. She knew how relevant her own words were to herself as well. She vowed to help her reach that goal.

"All right," she instructed, as soon as they reached the foot of the ladder. "Merit, get up there. I want you to be first. Let's go."

Merit hesitated. She even looked for an instant as if she might argue about it, but then obviously decided not to. She hated leaving Thyra behind on her own, but someone had to go first, and there was just no time for discussion of any kind.

"All right," she replied. "Be careful."

She tore her gaze from Thyra's after one last grateful smile and disappeared up the ladder at lightning speed. Thyra sent the more able of the two men up straight after her, and she waited behind to help the last remaining one. He was heavy, struggling like hell with his legs, and she had to support most of his weight onto her shoulders. He crawled painfully upward, breathing hard all the while, agonisingly slowly as far as Thyra was concerned.

"Merit?" she shouted. "Merit, are you up there yet?"

There was no response from her. Just the roar of the sea, and some vague, distant shouting. Thyra gritted her teeth and she carried on upward. She pushed harder with her legs. She urged the man on in the only language that she knew, but the burning intensity in her voice was unmistakable and easy to understand. He yelled something in reply and heaved himself up at the same time. But then, without warning, his feet slipped off the wet ladder and he fell back on top of her. It was almost enough to cause her to lose her grip, but not quite. Thyra steadied him with a strong hand. She looked into his eyes.

"It's okay," she said. "You're fine."

But the reassurance was lost on him. He was completely spent now, and sobbing as he looked toward the exit, which must have appeared like a million miles away in his current state of exhaustion. He glanced at Thyra and shook his head. She saw defeat flash through his eyes, and he gestured weakly for her to go on up ahead of him. If she did that, he would never come out, and they both knew it.

"No," she snapped. "I won't."

She kept a firm hold onto him, and then gave it every ounce of strength she had left in her body. When they finally reached the exit, together, the man tumbled out of it ahead of her. Satisfied, Thyra took two seconds to catch her breath. Her wounded arm suddenly began to throb painfully. She told herself to just ignore it. The fight was not over yet, and this was no time to rest. *One last push, Thyr. Come on, keep going!* Thyra reached for the sides of the entrance, gripped hard onto the wooden railing, and pulled herself out. In the clearer light of dawn, she could see that one half of the ship had disappeared under water completely. The rest was on fire and breaking up into pieces. She blinked hard and stared all around her. She wondered how far they were from the coast of Greece now. Close enough to swim to shore? *And where is the crew? Where the hell has everyone gone?*

"Merit, where are y…" she began to ask.

But Thyra did not see the powerful wave rising up behind her. In the next second, a solid wall of water slammed into her body, knocked the breath out of her once more, and dragged her off across the splintered deck.

"Thyra! Over here!"

Thyra heard the call, and she spotted Merit, holding on to one piece of the broken mast with the two men they had rescued next to her. She was waving frantically to get Thyra's attention.

"Thyra!" she screamed again.

As if things were not bad enough already, the weather had turned on them as well. Heavy black clouds charged across the sky, illuminated now and again by a strike of brilliant lightning. After a particularly blinding one streaked across the horizon, a deafening boom of thunder made it feel as if the heavens had cracked open. A sense of impending doom and even worse disaster was suddenly oddly palpable through the air. The sea was behaving accordingly, smashing across what was left of the ship's deck in a voracious attempt at swallowing it whole. Thyra had no time to think. Before she could even turn around or respond to Merit, her entire world got swept away under a mountain of liquid hell. Another wave, much bigger than the last one, and so powerful that she could do nothing to resist its violent pull took her down hard. The rest of that section of deck got sucked under the surface as well. Merit witnessed it all happen in a sickening flash.

"No!" she gasped. "Thyra..."

She stared at the boiling, angry sea, desperate to see her reappear. It seemed like a very long time before she could spot broken bits of wood come floating back up in places. But no Thyra. Merit clenched her teeth. She leaned forward a little more and scanned the surface anxiously. *Gone?* she wondered, feeling stunned at the very thought of it. Thyra was gone? No, this was unthinkable. *Not like this, not now!* It was not something that Merit was in any way prepared to accept without a fight. She simply would not, could not allow it to happen. Period. And so, when she could find no sign of Thyra anywhere on top of the water, Merit threw herself into the churning sea, and went after her friend.

∞

Thyra never even saw her coming. When the wave dragged her under, she became tied in with some ropes and bits of sail that were still attached to the boat. She reached for the knife on her belt to cut herself free, but she had lost it. Her sword was gone, too. She struggled against the heavy weight of the rope but realised with a growing sense of desperation that it was futile. She was fast running out of air, and everything suddenly started to hurt. Her chest, her throat, and the inside of her lungs. She screamed underwater and pushed against the debris that kept her down and sinking deeper now. She swallowed some water, and her body spasmed. She tried to angle her face toward the surface. Everything was turning black. *It hurts.* Nothing in the entire world had ever felt so painful to her, not even when Bjarke had used his whip to slice through the flesh across her back. In retrospect, that had been nothing. This was a hell of a lot worse. Thyra had never experienced such intense torment as when the entire sea tried to force itself inside her body and into her lungs. She fought hard for her life. She sure did not go easy. But then, suddenly, it all became extremely quiet inside her mind, and the pain disappeared. In a flash of dazzling white light through the water, Thyra spotted her lover, standing watching her in the distance.

"*Kari!*"

All at once, the water was gone and she was back in the mountains once more. It did not even feel a little bit strange. Thyra instantly recognised the lake. The air was full of a sweet fragrance, and vibrantly clear. It was warm in the sunshine, and it made perfect sense to be there. Up ahead, Kari's face broke into a brilliant smile.

"*Thyra,*" she called. "*What are you doing here? Come to me, my love.*"

At the exact same time that Thyra fell into her lover's arms, Merit caught up with her unconscious friend. She used the sharp knife that she had picked up from a dead sailor's chest earlier and started slicing through the ropes that were tangled around Thyra's legs. She had no idea of what was going on in her world at that particular moment. All she knew was that she had to cut her loose.

"I have to go soon," Kari said gently.

Her embrace felt strong, safe, and just like pure oxygen to Thyra. Right there in Kari's arms was where she desperately wanted to stay. With Kari was the only way that she could even think of wanting to exist in this world.

"Go where?" she exclaimed. *"I'll come with you."*

Over the glittering-blue waters of the highland lake, past the mountain peaks that Thyra loved so much, the light was getting brighter, shifting and changing in the wind. It was now calling for its *Shining One* to return home. It was time.

"Listen to me, baby," Kari whispered. *"Look at me, Thyr."*

Thyra pulled back just a little bit to be able to gaze into her lover's deep green eyes. Kari traced a soft finger over her cheek. She kissed her, just the way that she used to. She gave her a tender smile.

"This is not your time," she murmured. *"Not yet."*

"But I want to stay with you!"

"I'm sorry. You can't."

Merit finally won her battle against the rope, just as she was beginning to seriously run out of air herself. She wrapped her arms around Thyra's waist, kicked hard with both legs, and started swimming toward the surface. She was feeling extremely weak now, dangerously so. She needed to get back up. She was not sure she could do it.

"But Kari, I don't want to leave," Thyra argued. *"Please, I…"*

Kari rested a gentle finger over her lips to stop her protest. Thyra's eyes filled with tears in anticipation of another cruel goodbye she did not want to have to concede.

"Please, Kari," she repeated. *"Let me stay with you."*

"Sshhh…" her lover replied, brushing at her tears. *"Don't be sad, my darling. You know I love you, now and forever. I will always be with you. But now, you must go and live."*

And then, in the blink of an eye, before Thyra could even say anything else to her or realise what was happening, Kari vanished in a cloud of bright, sparkling, and powerful light. In contrast, everything turned absolutely pitch black on Thyra's own side once again. A terrifying feeling of falling fast down into a deep and dark abyss suddenly seized her. She could not breathe down there.

Kari, I can't… It's too hard… Please, don't leave me…

In Merit's world, things reflected a similar nightmare.

"Thyra, breathe!" she shouted. "Come on, breathe!"

She had just barely managed to drag her unconscious body onto a larger piece of drifting wood, one that had obviously been part of the main deck at some point. It seemed solid enough for the both of them. And now, she was kneeling by her side and pounding on Thyra's chest with every bit of strength that she still possessed. She was terribly scared at the idea that she might very well die right there. She had spent such a long time under water, and it was a real possibility… But Merit was tough, and she would not give up on her. She carried on fighting to bring her back.

"Wake up!" she yelled. "I am begging you, Thyra, wake up!"

She blew more air into her mouth and hit her even harder. Thyra remained unresponsive. Eyes closed, face ghostly pale, her body heavy and totally limp.

"Thyra!"

Merit slapped her hand over her cheeks a few times, hard enough to hurt, but unsuccessfully. She screamed her name out loud, and she pushed her over onto her side. She hit her on the back between her shoulder blades. She tried to get her to start breathing, any which way she could think of. She really did not know what else she could do to bring her back to life.

"Please," she cried.

They were out of sight of the sunken ship now and drifting off into a thick blanket of fog. The worst of the storm was over, thankfully, and the pirates' frigate was nowhere near. All of a sudden, there was no one else around, be it enemy or friend. The slave men were gone too, probably dead... Merit shivered violently at the thought. It felt to her as if she may well have shifted into a parallel world, one that was eerily quiet and shockingly empty. She felt desperately alone and frightened to find herself out there all on her own.

"Thyra, I need you to come back," she pleaded.

She wrapped her arms around her shoulders. She closed her eyes for a brief moment and held tightly onto the woman whose presence and strength she had come to depend on so much.

"I need you," she murmured. "Please, don't leave me."

CHAPTER TWENTY

It was that earnest plea sounding somewhere at the back of her mind and a sharp return of the pain inside her chest that finally brought Thyra back to some sort of full, if somewhat confused consciousness. She jerked awake in Merit's arms, and instantly started to struggle. She reached around and felt blindly for her sword, convinced beyond a shadow of a doubt that she was still in the middle of a battle, and that people were trying to pin her down to kill her.

"Be still, Thyra," Merit exclaimed in sudden alarm.

If they were not careful, they would both fall off the float.

"Get off me!" Thyra screamed. "Get off me, now!"

Lost in a fight to the death that was only taking place inside her mind, she seized onto Merit's right wrist, and pushed her down. She twisted her arm with such brutal force that it brought instant tears to the woman's eyes.

"Thyra, stop!" Merit cried. "Stop it, please, you're hurting me!"

Enraged and unyielding, Thyra raised her fist to hit her. Stunned by her reaction, Merit stared back at her in wide-eyed horror. If Thyra struck her as hard as she seemed capable of doing, she might well kill her without even realising it.

"Don't!" she gasped. "Thyra, it's me, Merit!"

This seemed to do the trick. Thyra suddenly hesitated. She faltered. She blinked hard a couple of times, as she started to recognise her friend, but could not make any sense out of the situation. *What am I doing to her?*

"Merit?" she murmured, frowning in bewilderment.

Merit let out a huge sigh of relief when she noticed Thyra slowly beginning to calm down and lowering her fist. She still appeared a little unsure and uncertain about it. But she looked slightly more in control. Definitely a good sign.

"Yes, it's me, Thyra," she replied. "Please let go, it hurts…"

Thyra shook her head, looking deeply disturbed when she finally realised who the person was that she was holding in a death grip beneath her. It really was only poor Merit, who was sobbing by now with the sharp pain that she was inflicting on her. Horrified at her own behaviour, Thyra immediately let go of her wrist.

"Merit, I'm sorry…" she started to say. "I don't…"

But instead of the fuller apology she wanted to give voice to, Thyra ended up twisting over instead, and vomiting what felt like the entire Adriatic Sea back into it. She dropped onto the deck, face down and gasping for air. It was not over. Her vision blurred again. Everything started to spin all around her, at incredible speed, and she held harder onto the piece of floating wood.

"Oh, Gods," she groaned.

Merit was still breathing a little hard too, mainly from the fear and residual shock of what had just taken place between them. She would have liked a few seconds of respite, but something else was even more important to her at that particular moment, and it was their overall safety. She rested a calming hand on Thyra's shoulder and leaned over her to speak urgent words of reassurance into her ear.

"Take it easy, okay?" she advised. "Take some deep breaths for me. Be still."

She was extremely conscious of their precarious position on top of the raft, and she knew that Thyra had not realised yet quite how dangerous it still was for them. They could capsize at any moment, and Merit was worried about not being able to get back on again. As her world slowly began to return to normal, Thyra gave her a small nod in response. She appreciated those wise words of advice, and she wanted to say something too. She had questions. Lots of them. But all she could really do at first was grunt rather weakly. Her throat was on fire. It burned as if somebody had been rubbing stinging nettles all over the inside for hours on end, and her voice came out hoarse and painfully dry when she first attempted to speak again. She coughed a few times, which only made the tightness in her lungs grow more acute. She clutched at her chest, and squeezed her eyes tightly shut.

"Don't worry," Merit murmured. "I know it's bad now, but it won't last, I promise."

She rubbed her hand in a soothing gesture all over Thyra's shoulders. She massaged the tense, quivering muscles in her back, and she attempted to get her to calm down enough to recover a bit better than she was doing now. Getting frustrated and angry about the situation would not help.

"You're doing well," she approved. "Just give yourself a few more minutes before you try to sit up. It's all right, there's no hurry."

Thyra threw a tired glance at her.

"The… the attackers…" she croaked.

"The pirates are gone. Nobody's after us."

"What about the two men?" Thyra insisted. "The ones we got out, where have they gone?"

162

Merit shook her head in genuine sadness and regret at the thought of them. It was the cruellest thing as far as she was concerned. To come this far, this close to freedom, and to suffer so much for it, only to not be able to see it through to the end was the worst thing she could imagine.

"I don't know what happened to them both," she confessed. "They were with me when we first walked out on deck. But I went straight in after you when you got dragged under the water, and then, I..."

In spite of herself, she jumped in fright when Thyra reacted unexpectedly by slamming an angry, frustrated fist against the deck.

"Please, don't be like this," Merit murmured, as fresh tears suddenly welled up in her eyes. She was truly exhausted, and this was not helpful behaviour. "You must stay still, Thyra," she repeated tiredly. "We have to be careful what we do on this thing, all right? And you need to get some rest."

Thyra had absolutely zero intention of lying on her back for any length of time. Doing nothing and taking it easy the way that Merit kept repeating she should do struck her as extremely foolish. She could not afford to relax in the situation they found themselves in. She had to find the best way to get back to shore, and quickly too. She needed to figure out a solution to this problem, something that would keep both of them safe, and alive. But even though her mind wanted to keep going, her body had other ideas, and it chose that moment to let her know. All of a sudden, Thyra found that she could barely keep her eyes open. It took every ounce of energy she possessed to just carry on talking. And pulling her thoughts together to make any kind of sense was growing harder with every passing second too.

"All right, just for a minute then," she muttered reluctantly.

"Great. Just a minute," Merit agreed with a knowing smile.

She was tired beyond words, but she suspected that Thyra was about to crash in quite spectacular fashion. She decided to remain awake for a while longer, however long it took really, and make sure that her friend was okay as she slept. She had just literally drowned, after all. No wonder she needed to recover from it. She watched her carefully, as Thyra stretched out onto the wet wooden raft and dropped her head onto her folded arms. She noticed her eyes flutter closed again. Satisfied, Merit continued with her gentle touch. Thyra breathed out eventually, and she relaxed into it.

∞

She was not even aware of having drifted off into a deep, healing sleep, but the next time that she stirred, it felt like several hours had passed. The sun was out once more, shining high in a pure and cloudless sky. It was scorching hot on the surface of the water, and Thyra discovered that she was indeed lying on her back. *Yeah. So much for taking action...* she reflected drowsily. She was still not fully awake yet, just hovering around the delicate boundary that comes just before full and total awareness. She stared at the immensity of azure blue above her head for a few comforting, lingering seconds. *Kari, my love... Where are you now?* Thyra could remember being back with her lover again. It could not have been anything other than a dream, and yet it had felt so real, even more real than when she was awake in a normal way. She thought about holding her, and the amazing sensation of her lips brushing against hers once more. She was confused. What had happened to her? Why was she back now? Kari had told her that she could not stay, and the memory of this hurt very badly. After that, there had been a sense of falling, and then... *Oh, no!*

Everything suddenly came back to her in a horrifying flash. The pirates' attack, and the ship sinking. Rushing below deck to free the slaves. Drowning in the water, and Merit crying and yelling for her to wake up. Thyra hurting her. She had acted violently toward Merit. Made her cry and caused her pain. The memory of that was like a hard punch to the face for Thyra, and it caused her to wake up in a panic. She sat bolt upright and spun around, almost causing the delicate platform to flip over with her sudden movement.

"Merit!" she yelled.

The response came instantly.

"Thyra. I'm here. It's okay..."

Thyra felt immediate relief flood through her when she spotted Merit, sitting there right behind her. For a split second before she caught sight of her, Thyra had feared that she would be gone, fallen overboard while she herself had been resting so selfishly.

"Sorry," she apologised. "I forgot where we were. Are you all right?"

Merit flashed her a gentle smile. She got up onto her knees and shuffled a little closer.

"That's probably because you have been out cold for half a day," she remarked. "I'm pleased you managed to sleep. And your arm has stopped bleeding. Yes, I'm all right. How are you feeling?"

Thyra glanced at the length of fabric that the woman had neatly wrapped around her upper left arm. She had forgotten all about that injury too. Then, her eyes fell over her own tunic. She noticed that a good chunk of it was missing on the side, and she grinned. Merit was turning out to be a sharply enterprising and efficient woman. Thyra liked that in people.

"Thanks for doing this. Are you sure you're okay?"

"Yes, I'm fine," Merit replied, perhaps a little too quickly.

She did not look fine, far from it. She was too pale, for a start. And looking frazzled with it too, although that was to be expected, of course… But all the same, it was easy to see that she was not being truthful about how she really felt. Thyra hesitated, wondering why that should be. Surely, there should be no reason to hold back between them at this stage… Something was definitely not right here, and she wanted to know what it was. Her eyes drifted searchingly over Merit's face, over her body, looking for any sign of an injury. Eventually, she spotted her wrist. She was appalled. The woman's skin was all black and blue there, and a vivid bruise ran all the way up and around her forearm. It was badly swollen. Thyra immediately paled at the sight of it.

"Did I do this?" she murmured. "I did, didn't I?"

She was clearly devastated at the realisation, and Merit attempted to make light of it. She knew for a fact that Thyra would never try to hurt her intentionally; of course, she would not. Even more than that, she owed the woman her freedom and her very life, nothing less. Her debt to her was immense and could never, ever be repaid. She certainly did not want her to feel bad about some stupid bruise.

"It's okay, Thyra, don't wor…"

"Is it broken?" Thyra interrupted. "Let me see."

Merit knew it was not necessary to make a fuss about it, but she still allowed Thyra a closer look, hoping that it would help to make her feel better.

"It's not broken," she assured her. "Just strained. It'll heal. I can still move my fingers just fine, see? It's nothing, don't worry about it."

But Thyra looked deeply affected.

"I'm sorry," she murmured.

Somewhere at the back of her mind, she could hear Bjarke laughing. *See, you really are no different than me! You weren't there to save your lover. You allowed your brother to die. And you're crazy enough to hurt your friend. Well done, Thyra!* It was a good while before she could chase those dark and confusing thoughts from her mind, and even so, not completely. Feeling at a loss, and desperate to make it up to Merit in some way, she offered to keep an eye on her while she got some sleep. Merit accepted the suggestion quickly and gratefully. Thyra was relieved when she did, and as she realised that Merit still trusted her enough to take care of her. This was important to her. Over the next few hours, Thyra did everything in her power to help her friend rest and recover. And over the following days, they kept up the very same routine, taking turns watching over each other so that both could sleep, and not worry about falling off the deck whilst they did.

On the morning of their third day at sea, Thyra tried to fish. She used one of her leather bootlaces and the twisted tip of her belt buckle as an improvised hook. They had no bait. The likelihood of catching anything with that method was remote to say the least. But never mind that. At least, she was doing something useful. Unfortunately, even though she was at it for the entire day, she was unsuccessful in her attempts. In the end, she became enraged and frustrated with her lack of results. Merit suggested quietly to her that it might be best to simply stop and conserve her energy. Thyra did not like it one bit, but she agreed eventually. She knew full well that food was not their most pressing concern, anyway. Lack of water was a much more important problem, and already beginning to take its toll. She had a headache which was pretty much constant now. Her skin hurt from way too much sun. And even though Merit was not complaining, it did not look like she was faring much better.

Thyra dropped her bits of fishing gear on the side, and she stretched out onto her back once more. She raised her arms and crossed them over her face to protect herself from the merciless sun. She let out a heavy, weary sigh. *How much longer can we really last like this?* she wondered. She knew that they were fast approaching their limits. Maybe another day... Perhaps two.... Probably no more than that before they lost consciousness for good, and never woke up again. The days were long, and the nights even worse. She was losing track of time. It felt to her as if they had been drifting for years on that piece of wood instead of just a few days. And there was absolutely nothing she could do about it. It was becoming harder to move, and harder to stay awake. She sighed again in heartfelt frustration, and Merit glanced in her direction.

"Thyra?" she murmured.

"Hmm... What?"

"Who is Kari?"

CHAPTER TWENTY-ONE

Thyra registered the question perfectly, but she did not instantly reply. Instead, she went extremely still and silent. As she waited for her to say something, Merit spotted a tiny muscle on the side of her jaw tighten and clench a few times in rapid succession. It made her realise that her question, although completely innocent of course, might well remain unanswered. And she vowed not to ask it again, since something about it was obviously disturbing to her friend. After a few seconds, Thyra finally sat up and met her gaze. Her eyes were searching. She looked anxious and unusually tense.

"Sorry," Merit murmured. "It's none of my business."

But Thyra just shook her head, looking both impatient and slightly rattled. She was not one to avoid answering questions, no matter how personal or difficult the subject might be.

"Kari's the woman who gave me this," she said, pointing to her torc. "And that's fine, you can ask. I'm just surprised because I never told you about her before. So, how do you know to ask about Kari?"

Merit gave her a gentle, understanding look in reply. Thyra may well think otherwise, but she had actually mentioned Kari several times previously.

"You've been saying her name in your sleep a lot…"

It was the last thing Thyra would have expected to hear. Taken aback, she stared at Merit for an instant before dropping her gaze again. A wave of something that felt very much akin to panic washed over her.

"Really?" she muttered.

Apart from with Hrorek, and even then, only just once, she had never discussed Kari with anyone else. And now, it was Merit of all people who had brought her up. Thyra could not help but feel extremely uneasy about that, although she was not completely sure why it should feel so wrong to her either. After all, Merit was a friend by now, was she not? Thyra gave another bewildered shake of the head. In spite of the apprehension that she felt about it, and not for the first time either, she found herself wanting to open up to the young Egyptian woman. She reflected that perhaps it was this steadily growing urge to do so, more than anything else, that was really the issue...

"Thyra, are you okay?" Merit insisted. "Look, I'm sorry for mentioning this. It's just that every time you call for her, you start to cry as well. Is there anything I can do?"

Thyra grew instantly irritated. To her, this was just another frightening example of not being in control of her own damned mind. What else had she been blabbing about in her sleep? Why was this happening to her all of a sudden? She was feeling upset and seriously flustered. When she looked up, she found that Merit was still watching her intently. Her expression was simply a mixture of curiosity, respect, and deep, heartfelt sympathy. Like this crying-in-your-sleep business was no problem at all, and nothing to worry about. Thyra was somewhat reassured by her lack of a more negative judgemental reaction; once again, she felt herself being pulled in by those kind, intelligent black eyes. There was a certain energy coming from Merit at times that she found extremely difficult not to respond to.

"Kari is dead," she murmured with a reluctant shrug. "I miss her, that's all."

Part of her did not want to talk about Kari; even though her lover had been dead for going on nine months now, it still felt too raw and recent to Thyra to be discussing her with someone else. Another part of her was also pretty desperate to explain it all to Merit. She sighed. She was growing increasingly confused about her own volatile and conflicting emotions, and she hated feeling this way. Her head was pounding now as well, even harder than before. And so, when Merit came a little closer to her, Thyra did not move. When the woman took her hand in hers, with such great compassion showing in her eyes, Thyra shot her a quick, startled glance. Suddenly, she found herself fighting tears.

"It's okay," Merit murmured.

Thyra understood something else in that moment that was quite puzzling to her, if not shocking. It made her realise how much she had missed all this. Just to be able to feel another woman's touch. Simply to be close to another woman in a more intimate way. It was nowhere near the level of intensity she had ever felt with Kari. This was not about falling in love with Merit. But there was something there all the same. Thyra may not have liked the idea very much, and it may even have scared her a little. But it allowed her to drop the persona of the tough-as-nails warrior for just a moment, and there was tremendous relief to be found in that.

"What happened to you and Kari?" Merit enquired.

"Well..."

Haltingly, Thyra started to tell her. Merit had mentioned her own family to her, and she had talked about the life that she had led before being captured. She had done so freely and more than once during those furtive moments together on the ship.

But Thyra had been reluctant to share much of her own personal stuff with her at the time. No more so now, and she began to relate the events that had led to her being on that sea journey in the first place. She talked about Bjarke, and the horrible so-called hunting day in the forest when he had almost killed her. She showed Merit the still striking marks that his whip had left on her back. She mentioned Tait; what a wonderful human being he had been, and how much she still loved him. And then, she spent a long time talking about Kari. She described their first encounter at the lake, and Merit laughed when Thyra repeated Kari's ultimatum to her on that day. *'Sword or clothes, take your pick.'*

"Sounds like a pretty confident woman, uh?" she smiled.

"Yes," Thyra replied, eyes burning at the memory. "She was..."

She told Merit about their immediate physical attraction, and the all-consuming relationship that followed. She did not go into great details with that, but just the intensity in her voice when she mentioned it only briefly was enough to make Merit blush. Thyra concluded with a description of the terrible battle it had all ended with.

"I was supposed to be right there for her on that day, you know," she murmured. "I was supposed to protect her and keep her safe. That was my job as a warrior. But just like with Tait, I failed."

From the look of fierce regret and self-loathing that flashed across her eyes, Merit suspected it would not do much good to try to argue with her about the validity of that statement. But there was something else she could say that would probably be even more helpful.

"Kari must love you very much, Thyra," she remarked.

Thyra flashed her a sad, slightly puzzled smile in response.

"What makes you say that?" she asked. "And you're right, she did love me, but now…"

"If she comes to visit you in your dreams, she must love you very much still," Merit assured her with a gentle, confident smile. "In my culture, we say that there is not much separation between the worlds of the living and the dead…"

"Enough to keep us apart," Thyra reflected, her tone bitter.

"But when you miss her this much," Merit insisted, "when you feel the separation as if it were an abyss of distance between you, it actually means that she is right there by your side. What you interpret and experience as such painful loss is actually the strength of her love for you coming through the veil. So close. You really need to understand this, Thyra. That's why I say that she must love you very much to be willing to shine so brightly for you."

Merit smiled at Thyra's startled expression.

"What?" she asked. "You seem surprised."

"Well. Kari was… She is known as *The Shining One*…"

Merit gave her fingers another gentle squeeze.

"You see," she smiled. "Not much separation."

"I just never thought of it quite like that before," Thyra replied. "I do feel her with me from time to time, and very strongly too, you're right. I understand that, but the way you explain it is a little different."

"Well. Does it make sense?"

"Yes. It does make sense."

"And does it help you?"

Thyra nodded pensively. It was actually the wisest and most reassuring thing she had heard in a very long time. It even sounded like something that Kari herself might have said. She went on to relate her experience of almost drowning under the ship to Merit, and meeting with Kari as it happened.

"It felt like so much more than just a dream to me then," she exclaimed. "When I held her in my arms, and when she kissed me, it all felt so incredibly real. And I felt so alive! I know I was just hallucinating, but…"

"No, I don't think you were at all," Merit interrupted. "I'm sure it was real. And she was right there with you then too, don't think that you just made that up."

"But how? And how do you know?"

Thyra appeared desperate to be given definite answers she could trust, and maybe even a way to access a lot more. Merit rested a soothing hand over her shoulder. She realised that she had to be a little careful here. She could not ever undo or change what had happened to Thyra. Now, it was just about living with it as best as one could.

"I don't know how," she admitted. "But this experience you speak of is not unique. The priests at my temple knew of those things."

"Really?" Thyra exclaimed. "What about you?"

Merit shook her head. She gave a small smile.

"I know some things," she replied. "When you are dying, as you were, sometimes, the doors to other levels of perception can open up for you. But there is a limit to how far we can go when it is not our time. Just like you found out for yourself. I wish that I could tell you more, Thyra. I wish things were different. For you, for your friend… And for me too…"

Merit suddenly went quiet, and she stared far off into the distance with a stricken look on her face. Thyra realised that she must be thinking of her own people then. Of her family. Of all the ones that she had lost, and of the life that had been so cruelly stolen from her. But now, she was free once more, and Thyra was determined to help her. *If only I could figure out a way to get us off this stupid piece of drifting wood and back onto dry land…*

Thyra spotted Merit brush a few tears from her own eyes, and throw a quick, somewhat embarrassed glance in her direction. She appeared frustrated with it too.

"I'm sorry, Thyra," she murmured. "I can see that you're hurting. I wish I could do more to help..."

CHAPTER TWENTY-TWO

Without worrying about how the movement might be received, or even pausing to think about it, Thyra leaned toward Merit, and she gently scooped a single tear off her cheek with a folded knuckle. It was an impulsive act, simply borne out of a strong desire to make her feel better. Thyra wanted Merit to realise that she was not alone with her pain, certainly not as long as she was around. She did not mean anything else by that small touch, just a show of friendship and support, and she only became aware of how else it might be perceived when Merit bit onto her lower lip, looked down, and blushed furiously. All in one single, highly revealing reaction. Thyra froze, and she frowned in sudden dismay. It dawned on her that perhaps she should not have acted so instinctively. But it was too late to take the gesture back.

"Well, no need to apologise," she said roughly and with a quick, rather nervous smile. "I dumped all this stuff on you, and it's not fair. Thank you for listening. I know you're hurting too, and I wish that I could comfort you the same way you comfort me."

Merit seemed touched by her words. Even though her tone was brisk, and her manner the same, it was obvious that Thyra really meant what she said.

"Oh, but you do comfort me," she replied. "You really do, Thyra."

Once again, Thyra noticed the eagerness in her expression, and the shy, unmistakably hopeful smile that crept up all over her lips. Merit obviously tried to hide it from her, but she failed. Just the fact that she did not want to let it show spoke volumes about her true state of mind, and Thyra immediately tensed up. This was wrong. It was not what she wanted to happen between them. Not at all the message that she wanted to send out.

"Merit," she started. "Look, I, uh…"

She drew in a hard breath to speak up and apologise to her. But before she could say anything on the subject, Merit asked her something else which gave Thyra absolutely nowhere to run. It was a devastating question.

"Do you wish that you were dead now?" Merit murmured.

Thyra went still once more. She stared into Merit's eyes for as long as she could maintain her composure, but then, she had to look away once more. She dropped her gaze, the same way that she had done before, and she struggled with her emotions. *I don't want to be here,* was the answer. *I really don't want to be here anymore,* was the only thing that came up in response to Merit's question. And Thyra did not want to say it out loud. It would feel like too big an admission of defeat. Something that could hurt her if she even said the words. She cleared her throat. She blinked furiously a few times. And she remained totally silent. Merit did not touch her. She did not even move. She just waited patiently for an answer that never came. Instead, Thyra muttered something vague about trying to catch some fish. She reached for her bits and pieces of gear. She was visibly shaking. And as night came, not a single other word was spoken between them.

∞

Dawn found Thyra lying on her back in her usual position. Eyes wide open, staring unseeingly up at the stars that still sparkled in the early-morning sky.

Fishing the night before had been wildly unsuccessful. She had spent another night fully awake. As Merit went to sleep, and she was left alone with her thoughts, Thyra started wondering why she even bothered to try to make anything better. The situation was what it was. Hopeless. The sea was never-ending. And they had nothing. They were going to die, simple as that. Why was she fighting it so hard? After all, she did not want to be there, right? *Right,* Thyra realised. Her heart beat faster at the thought. It was scary to realise that it was going to happen this way. Having time to think about dying was strange. But she could be okay with it. She could just let go and find refuge and solace in sleep. *Will I wake up again if I drift off?* she wondered. *Or will that be it this time?* She was so tired. And dying always felt so painful. She almost laughed at the irony of it all. She wondered briefly if there was a single way of achieving death that might not be so difficult... Her headache had spread to just about every part of her brain now. She felt dizzy every time she moved. Even breathing was an effort. Her tongue was swollen. Her eyes hurt. *Why don't you just let go?* she thought to herself once again. *Just go to sleep...*

"Thyra."

Thyra glanced to her right, and she managed to get her eyes to blink just once. Even that little move of the head cost her. She found Merit sitting up next to her, holding on to her right arm and staring intently down at her face. She looked agitated, and deeply worried.

"What?" Thyra sighed.

"What are you doing?" Merit exclaimed.

What do you mean? Thyra wanted to ask her. But it felt like too much of an effort to speak the words, and the need to know did not even last for very long. *Don't worry about it... Just sleep...* She closed her eyes.

"Hey," Merit yelled at her. "Wake up!"

She shook Thyra even harder, in growing alarm at what was happening. Merit had been watching her friend for a little while, not exactly sure of what was going on with her. But she had noticed her growing increasingly detached and still. It was as if she were slipping into a deep trance. Thyra even stopped blinking at one point, and her eyes became fixed onto a single spot somewhere in the middle of the sky. Merit frowned then, and she instantly leaned forward.

"Thyra?" she asked.

But Thyra did not reply. She just gave a heavy sigh, and her breathing started to slow. Merit jumped in sudden shock, eyes wide in panic.

"Thyra!" she called again, louder.

But Thyra appeared not to hear her. It was at that moment that Merit realised what she was doing. Thyra was giving up. She was letting go, right there in front of her. Making the choice to die.

"No!" Merit shouted. "Don't you dare do this!"

She was feeling just as weak as Thyra was, perhaps even more so, but the fear of losing her gave her extra strength she did not know she had. She grabbed onto Thyra's shoulders and pulled her up into a sitting position. She took her face in both her hands, and she stared intently into her eyes. She found them frighteningly hazy and dull.

"Stay with me," she urged. "Don't drift off, all right?"

She gave her another firm shake, and Thyra looked startled, as if she had just woken up from a long and difficult dream. Her eyes finally regained some of their usual light. She took a deep breath. Oh yes, she had been drifting off all right. Thinking a whole lot of strange and scary thoughts... Not feeling very much attached to reality anymore.

"Yeah," she murmured. "All right, Merit..."

"Keep your eyes open. Keep talking to me."

Thyra looked at her, wondering why she was saying those things to her, and in such a loud and authoritative voice too. She was taken aback when she realised how positively terrified Merit also appeared. She looked almost on the verge of tears.

"What's wrong?" she asked her, confused. "You okay?"

Merit shook her head in deep frustration. No, she was not okay, far from it. And she was fast getting angry with Thyra's antics now as well.

"Thyra, what's going on here?" she asked. "Stop playing such stupid and dangerous games, all right? I thought that you were dead there for a second!"

Thyra felt instant guilt at her words. Merit was not joking about this, she could tell. The emotion in her voice was genuine. She sounded shaken to her very core, and this did hit home with Thyra.

"Sorry," she murmured. "I didn't mean to scare you like that. I guess I just fell asleep with my eyes open... I am kind of tired."

Merit stared at her in utter amazement. She knew this was a massive lie, just meant to reassure her. She supposed that was all right in a way... But Thyra had been playing with fire, and her comment was also most certainly designed to stop Merit from asking any more uncomfortable or challenging questions. This was really not okay, not for a second. And despite her crushing fatigue, Merit opened her mouth to let her know exactly how much she did not enjoy this pathetic attempt at manipulation. But then, a flash of sudden movement caught her attention.

"Wait..."

Thyra did not even reply. Merit paused; she waited; she looked again. There was a lone seagull flying in the sky out there, right above Thyra's left shoulder. There was a seagull flying. *But wait... A seagull can only mean one thing...* Merit held her breath. In the next second, she spotted something else that was even more exciting than the bird. She almost fainted with relief at the sight of it, but she instantly caught herself. She had to be sure about this before she said anything to Thyra out loud. After all, maybe it was just her overly tired mind playing tricks on her... She stared anxiously for another few breath-taking seconds, and as she did, all doubt soon completely disappeared. This was real. It was no hallucination. *We are going to live... WE ARE GOING TO LIVE!* Merit let out a piercing, triumphant yell which made Thyra jump out of her skin in fearful surprise at the sound of it.

"What now?" she snapped.

"Land!" Merit shouted in reply. "I can see land up ahead!"

Thyra whirled around, heart pounding with sudden hope.

"Where?" she exclaimed in a loud voice.

"Over there!" Merit screamed. She grabbed onto Thyra and turned her head toward the spot. "There!" she insisted.

Thyra stared hard in the direction that she pointed to.

"Can you see it?" Merit asked, almost crying. "Can you?"

Thyra narrowed her eyes. Yes. Yes, she could see it. Oh, yes! There was no possible doubt about it for her now either. Indeed, it was land. Instant tears came to her eyes, as she kept staring toward the patch of yellow beach in the distance.

"We're going to be okay..." she murmured.

___

_____

That sudden undeniable realisation was the sweetest feeling in the world for Thyra. Only a few minutes before this, she had been willing to die. Now, the urge to stay alive and fight for it had never been stronger. It made her breathe harder, deeper. It sent a rush of adrenaline coursing through her entire body. Merit threw her arms around her neck in exuberant fashion. She gave her the kind of silly crazy hug that almost made them both fall off the raft. Thyra burst out laughing. It hurt, but it felt bloody amazing.

"LAND!" she shouted.

"Do you think we can swim to it?" Merit asked her.

It was much too far to do this safely, and yet, Thyra was not worried about it. She grinned at the mixture of excitement, relief, and joy that she could hear in Merit's voice. She was feeling just the same. It was wonderful.

"No, we can't swim," she replied. "But we won't need to. Look."

She had spotted a small boat sailing in between them and the beach. She pointed toward it so that Merit could see it too, at the very same time that the boat began to make its way toward them.

"It's turning," Merit exclaimed in delight. "The boat's seen us!"

On board the small vessel was a lone and friendly fisherman who seemed quite puzzled at the sort of catch he had stumbled upon that day. They waved at him, and he waved happily back in reply. When he got within speaking distance, Merit greeted him in a language that they luckily both understood, and she quickly relayed their predicament to him with as few words as she could really spare.

"He says we can jump on board," she translated when he replied.

Thyra could barely feel her own legs, but she helped Merit to get on first, and then the man did the same for her. With her next breath, Merit asked him for some water. He smiled and instantly obliged.

"You first," Thyra said.

She waited patiently for her turn, smiling weakly as she watched Merit drink from the man's flask, with her eyes closed and a look of pure delight shining over her face. It was clear that they were not in a very good state, and the man did not ask a lot of questions after that. He was happy to share all the water he had with them. He even passed along some pastry biscuits filled with vegetables, herbs, and a kind of soft white cheese. Then, he turned the small boat around and headed straight back toward the shore. Thyra sat on the bottom, shoulder to shoulder with Merit. She sipped her water when it was her turn, and slowly ate some of the food as well. She glanced toward her companion and chuckled at the blazing smile that Merit instantly flashed her in return.

"Feeling better?" she asked.

Merit nodded vehemently. She giggled.

"Oh, yes!" she exclaimed. "So much better now!"

She looked about ten years younger all of a sudden, beaming with joy. And when she threw her arms around Thyra's neck once again, and pulled her close, Thyra simply returned the embrace. When Merit kissed her on the cheek as well, she just smiled and gave her a gentle squeeze.

"Are you okay?" Merit asked.

Her tone was slightly more serious when she asked that, and her voice definitely a lot lower. She was clearly concerned about her still. Thyra just gave her a reassuring nod.

"Stop worrying so much," she murmured.

"Well, just answer me then, please," Merit insisted.

Thyra took another big gulp of her water before she replied. It felt quite simply divine to her at that point. And then, it was kind of funny, really. Merit's arm resting around her shoulders suddenly did not feel anywhere near as frightening as it had before. And that light kiss on the cheek had been kind of all right too... Thyra could not make much sense out of any of it. It was weird how everything just kept changing inside her mind all the time. She wondered about it briefly. Maybe she really had spent too long underwater... She realised there was a real possibility that all of this was just a sign that she was losing her mind. She gave a small chuckle at that. *Oh well...* At least, she was alive.

"Yes," she promised. "I'm fine."

CHAPTER TWENTY-THREE

It was all desert, vast and empty as far as the eye could see. And hot with it, too.

Thyra was not upset in the least about landing on the shores of North Africa instead of her original destination. In a way, it was even better. She had left her home in the Scottish Highlands because she craved adventure after all, and one of her main goals had always been to see the desert... This one could not have been more breath-taking. And so, it was fine. Being thrown off course in such an unpredictable manner seemed good to her as well, almost like a rare and precious gift had been given. It felt like the actual clean break from her painful past, which she had been looking forward to all along, had finally occurred in her world. Thyra was very far away from home now, in every single way possible and imaginable. Everything was so incredibly new and fascinating to her. The climate, the food, the scenery, and certainly other people as well. Most of the times, she only had a vague idea of what the locals said to her, which, even though she wanted to learn more languages eventually, just like Merit, was exciting all the same. She had definitely hit on two of the main things she had told Hrorek she wanted to achieve: yes, it was hot; and, oh boy, was it different all right... To top it all, she could still make the third part of her dream come true. She could still head east and make it all the way to Constantinople eventually. The best thing about it was that she would be travelling over land now for the rest of her entire journey, as she had promised herself a while back. It might take her longer to reach her destination in this way, but she was determined that there would be no more messing about at sea for her now. She may be of Viking descent, and proud of it, but she was done with ships and sailing for the foreseeable future.

Every day, Thyra ventured out for a walk into the desert. She would climb up to the top of a sand dune, sit herself down, and simply breathe. She was convinced that she could have sat and stared at the immensity of the land that stretched out in front of her for days on end, and not become bored with it for even a single second. She relished those meditative sessions on her own because that was when she could access the silent, still part of herself where Kari would sometimes come and speak to her. The communication occurred through images, feelings, and quiet whispers at the back of her mind. Some people might have called it wishful thinking, of course... But Thyra had no doubt that her lover really was speaking to her, through her intuition and the deepest sense of herself and each other. Merit thought that was the case too, and it was enough for Thyra. She liked to sit and think, to be still, and to observe. At the same time, she still ached to know more. She was burning to see what was on the other side of this mysterious desert, to explore and discover more of the world out there and its people. Being able to drink plenty of water, eat enough food, and even just a single night of decent sleep had been enough to quell the dark ruminations which had started to take root inside her head whilst they were drifting out at sea. What Thyra was filled with now instead was a seemingly unquenchable thirst for more travel, discovery, and an ardent desire to keep moving forward. She was extremely relieved about it. It had been scary for her out there on the float, and not just because of the obvious. Those morbid thoughts she had experienced had made her feel like she was losing herself completely and getting out of touch with the deepest core of her identity. She had felt out of control in every way, unable to stabilise, and terrified that she might be turning into Bjarke; bitter, angry, carrying a dead heart inside of her. Now, she was completely reassured that this was not the case. Life was calling still. She was alive, still, rather unbelievably. And so, why not answer that call?

Of course, spending time with Merit also had a lot to do with her renewed enthusiasm, without a shadow of a doubt. After being rescued, the next logical thing to do had been to stick together for a while, and they accepted an invitation from the fisherman and his family to spend a few days at his village in order to rest. In the end, they ended up staying over three weeks there. Merit especially needed more time in order to recuperate fully. For her, malnutrition and abuse had been pretty constant features of the last six months of her captivity. Mentally, she was extremely strong, as she had demonstrated already a few times. But physically, she needed to give herself a bit longer to heal. And it never crossed Thyra's mind not to spend that recovery time with her. The fishing community was a nice place to be. Life was easy and comfortable there for the both of them for a while. And there were no more awkward moments between the two women either, which helped too. Thyra quickly put her earlier misgivings about Merit down to her brain not functioning properly at the time. Lack of water and food had certainly played a big part in that. Yes, Merit was a little more tactile than Thyra was perhaps really used to. But then again, she had not often enjoyed the company of many other women back home...

187

She had grown up with male warriors mostly, and she was not used to this softer side. Her budding friendship with Merit felt comfortable and really precious to her. She was not going to worry about a few hugs here and there, the odd teasing smile, and gentle touches which were always meant as a true reflection of support and genuine affection. Truth be told, Thyra enjoyed it very much. There had always been a sense of constant pressure within her, as far back as she could remember, a tension which she was never able to control very easily. But now, she found that two things really helped with that: her solitary walks in the desert, and Merit. Being with her felt just like hitting a reset button at times. It was nice, badly needed, and Thyra decided that it did not have to be made into anything more complicated than that. With Merit, she actually started to feel just like she had with Hrorek. It was a relief to have a buddy once more, a solid friend she knew she could really depend on. And so, they made the most out of those few weeks living on the edge of the great Sahara Desert. The village was close to a most beautiful, expansive beach. Thyra very much enjoyed spending thinking time on her own there too.

"I do like the sea," she told Merit once. "Just not being on it very much..."

The location was stunning, and there were other significant advantages to being in Africa. One of them was that it was so hot all the time that there was no need for elaborate shelter. Even at night, a few sheep skins spread out onto the ground to soften it, along with some light sheets to sleep under were more than enough to keep Thyra comfortable and happy. She loved to notice and highlight the differences.

"Where I come from, Merit, autumn will be starting soon, and then it will be full-on winter," she explained. "Plenty of snow and ice. Big storms, and freezing winds."

Merit shook her head, frowning at the thought.

"Doesn't sound that great," she remarked.

Thyra flashed her a brilliant smile.

"Oh, but then, there are the sunny days too. Sun shining on snow. Melting ice glittering off the trees. Everywhere you look, it is all perfectly clean white stuff, and it sparkles constantly. Being out in that always feels pretty magical."

Merit nodded, and she smiled.

"This would be better," she agreed.

She tried to picture it all in her mind. She enjoyed listening to Thyra talk about her home, especially since she looked so happy whenever she did it. Stories and anecdotes of growing up with Tait started to emerge. Whenever she remembered him, Thyra did so with a smile on her face. She laughed as she related some of the funnier things they had done when they were kids. Only occasionally did it make her feel sad. Merit was pleased with the slow but steady change that seemed to be taking place within her. Even though she did not mention it to Thyra, from listening to her story, it was pretty clear that she had not left Scotland at first because she wanted to travel. That may well have been the driving force before all the bad stuff had taken place. But when Thyra had left this time, Merit realised that it had been a case of simply needing to run away from too much pain. She was fine with that knowledge too. She knew that sometimes, there was nothing to be gained by hanging around. Now though, she was happy to see Thyra feeling so enthusiastic. She was asking questions, learning the language, and involving herself fully in her new environment. This was what made her travelling experience different and tremendously enriching. It was good, Merit decided, and she was pleased for her.

"Your world sounds intriguing," she commented.

Thyra chuckled. She smiled again a little thoughtfully.

"Yeah," she said. "The mountains there are beautiful."

They set up their own campsite a short distance away from the fisherman's main dwelling. His name was Ahmed. He was married and had four exuberant children all under the age of six. Thyra was surprised and amused to discover how much she actually enjoyed spending time with the little kids. She quickly became a sought-after baby-sitter, catering to the entire village. Ahmed's beautiful wife Djehma welcomed her and Merit with open arms, just like the rest of the people did. Thyra enjoyed making new friends. There was a tight sense of community there too that reminded her of the Volsung village.

"Feels just like home, sometimes," she declared happily.

Merit spent the first week that they were there simply eating a lot and sleeping the rest of the time. Getting better and stronger with every passing day. Thyra was pleased when she started to transform right before her very eyes. Soon, there was no longer any trace of the crushing tiredness that used to plague Merit. Now, that sense of pure energy and vitality which Thyra had been able to detect in her every once in a while, but only at odd moments, was pretty much always on, always in evidence. Merit smiled a lot, and she laughed often; she was full of joy, and she possessed a true zest for life. She never passed on an opportunity to tease Thyra about her more serious ways, but even though she kept that opinion for herself, she also enjoyed and appreciated the tremendous aura of power, strength, and overall sense of safety that came with it. It was obvious to her that Thyra was a natural protector, a provider, and with Merit, she fell back into that role easily. In return, her friend provided a fresh and easy perspective on life which kept Thyra in touch with her lighter side. It was a good balance between them, achieved effortlessly. It simply worked.

CHAPTER TWENTY-FOUR

Whenever she was not with Merit, in the desert, or looking after kids, Thyra spent most of her time wandering through the small village, looking for whatever ways she could find to help build or fix things around the place. No matter where she found herself in the world, helping out was her default setting. She had energy, great skills, and she liked to use both productively. This made her even more popular with the people. And for Thyra herself, who hated being idle at the best of times, it was an easy and simple way to give back to them in return for their hospitality and all-round generosity. It was a win-win situation for all involved, and it gave her options and opportunities too. On one such evening, she returned to their camp a little later than planned, starving, but looking extremely pleased with herself.

"Hey, check this out, Merit," she declared.

When Merit looked up, smiling in her usual way, Thyra pointed to the leather belt around her waist. On it was now secured a traditional Shamshir sword, with its original thick, curved blade, and a delicately carved wooden handle. It was obviously brand-new. As an object, it was beautiful, no doubt; if not for the much darker purpose associated with it, of course...

191

"So, do you like it?" Thyra enquired, grinning proudly.

Merit stared at the new weapon sitting on her friend's hip, her smile slowly fading off. She looked upset all of a sudden. Thyra's excitement instantly disappeared.

"What's wrong?" she asked, puzzled.

"What do you mean? Nothing's wrong!"

Merit followed that irritated and impatient statement with a quick half shrug. It was an attempt at brushing it all off and looking totally unconcerned, but her eyes when they met Thyra's were hard and unflinching. So, it was not nothing at all then, Thyra reflected. She opened her mouth to speak, but Merit beat her to it.

"What's this for?" she asked.

"Protection," Thyra replied.

"From what?" Merit countered sharply. "The kids?"

"Aha!"

Thyra chuckled in spite of herself. She could not help but feel amused at the sarcastic comment, even though she was also surprised with Merit's reaction. It was out of character for her to begin to lose her temper like this, and sound so annoyed. Thyra pondered that puzzling fact for a moment, and with growing concern, wondering how she was going to tackle the problem. Meanwhile, Merit handed her a piece of the flat bread she had just cooked on the fire, and a chunk of cheese to go with it. Her gestures were unusually brusque, impatient. And she was also purposely avoiding making further eye contact now. It was clear confirmation that something was not at all right. Thyra accepted the food, but her attention was on Merit.

"Thanks," she murmured.

She watched her attentively, as the woman sat across from her cleaning her cooking plate.

"You're not eating?" she remarked.

"I'm not hungry."

Well, this was like a fish pretending it could not swim. Merit was never *'not hungry'*. Thyra put her own food down, and she moved closer to her. She knew exactly what she was doing when she rested the top of her index finger underneath Merit's chin. She lifted her head up. Now, she was making it a lot harder for her to remain aloof, and Merit had no choice but to look at her. Thyra spotted tears shining in her eyes before she could lower her gaze.

"Don't," Merit snapped, and she pushed her hand off.

"All right, I won't. But what's the matter?" Thyra insisted.

Merit did not try to tell her once again that it was nothing, but she did attempt to get away from her. Thyra stuck to her like a magnet.

"Ignoring me like this is never going to work, you know," she pointed out, smiling gently. "Come on, Merit, talk to me. It's obviously something I've done or said to you, so tell me what it was."

Finally, Merit turned to her. She shook her head, and she stared toward the ground, thinking hard about it. Then, she took a sharp intake of breath and raised her eyes to Thyra once more. Her bottom lip quivered.

"Are you leaving?" she exclaimed.

Thyra sat back on her heels, dumbfounded.

"Well... Yeah," she replied. "I will be eventually. But you know that I..."

"That's fine. I just didn't think you would go so soon," Merit blurted out before she could even finish her sentence properly. "It's all right. Now, I understand better why you think you need protection. No need to carry on talking about it."

She reached out for a small clay pot on the side.

"Here, have some olives," she ordered, and looked away.

As she did, Thyra stared at her, frowning in wonder. *I didn't realise you would go so soon...* It suddenly dawned on her what the tears and Merit's reluctance were all about. She rolled her eyes, annoyed with herself at getting it so wrong.

"Listen to me," she started. "I'm..."

"I told you there's no need to talk about it," Merit argued.

She would have got to her feet and walked away if Thyra had not held her firmly back. Merit tried to twist free of her strong grip. She could not. She shot her a furious look.

"Let me go," she demanded.

Thyra obeyed, and Merit stood up.

"Wait a second," Thyra said loudly.

But Merit started walking fast away from her.

"Merit, wait! I am not leaving without you!" Thyra yelled.

Merit came to a sudden and abrupt stop. She glanced back over her shoulder. Thyra just stood there watching her. She was looking slightly worried by then, and thoroughly irritated as well. Merit hesitated.

"No?" she queried.

"No!" Thyra replied.

"But..." Merit began to say.

In a flash, Thyra caught up with her.

"Merit, look," she said urgently. "I am not leaving without you, all right? I just thought... Well, Egypt isn't very far from here. It's on my way east. And I figured maybe we could travel together for a while..."

She was getting flustered, thinking that perhaps she was only turning this thing into an even bigger problem than it was. After all, she was not sure of Merit's plans. The woman might not even want to stay with her. *How so very presumptuous of me to assume that she does...* Maybe Thyra was reading this situation all wrong, as per usual. She sighed in frustration.

194

"I don't know," she muttered. "I just thought maybe...."

But she should not have worried about it so much. Because in response, Merit simply flew into her arms with a little cry of joy.

∞

It was an extremely long time since she had allowed herself to feel any emotions like this. After being captured, for a long while, not a single day had gone by that she did not think about killing herself. And she probably would have done so, if only she had been able to. But she had become a slave, well and truly. She did not belong to herself anymore, and she was kept in such a way that even this fundamental right was out of her reach. When she tried to stop eating, they forced her to do it. They beat her savagely. Merit developed ways of shutting down instead, of making herself numb to the outside world. Her spirit shook and shrivelled. It retreated far away from her physical circumstances. For protection, she trained herself to stop feeling. She just became a living dead person. Nobody could hurt her, because nobody could reach her anymore. She stopped hoping that things would change, and she tried very hard to forget about the past, and the free, proud woman that she had been once before. Until that one night on board the ship of course, when out of the darkness and the pain, a woman with blazing blue eyes and hair the colour of moonlight appeared in her dream and smiled. When she had first laid eyes on Thyra, Merit had been convinced that she must be a figment of her imagination, a fabrication of her own traumatised mind. But the food was real, the water was fresh, and the woman, as it turned out, was genuine flesh and blood as well. And she kept on coming back. After her first visit, Merit fell into an infernal, hellish, yet quite irresistible routine.

She would spend every minute of every single day waiting for night-time to come. And when it finally did, she would sit in the darkness with her eyes open wide and her heart beating hard against her chest, waiting desperately for Thyra to appear. And not just because she was bringing sustenance with her. No, it went a lot deeper. Her presence alone through all those nights did more to keep Merit alive than all the best food and clean water in the entire world could have done. In fact, Thyra kept her very soul going. So, when the ship sank, and Merit saw her get swept off the deck, there was no question at all that she would follow. Whether or not she even survived if she did that had been of no concern to her then. If going after Thyra meant that she never got to live another single day as a free woman, then so be it too. She simply had to do it, and to hell with whatever happened next. Merit had no idea how or where she had found the strength to drag an unconscious Thyra all the way back to the surface, or how she had even managed to pull her up onto the float with her either. She was just grateful to the gods for giving her the necessary resources to do what needed to be done.

Over the long and difficult days that followed, from the way Thyra cried in her sleep, and especially thanks to that one striking conversation they had on the subject, Merit was shocked to realise how damaged and broken her friend really was. She would never have guessed it from her behaviour, and the way that her light shone so brightly... But actually, the woman who appeared so strong and invincible all the time was a mirror image of herself, crushed and fractured into a million pieces by the brutal harshness of her life experiences. Still, no matter how much she clearly struggled with the journey, and regardless of how many times she may have come close to doing it, Thyra had not given up. She was still there, and she was still fighting hard.

To Merit, who was struggling to keep going inside her own set of horrendous circumstances, this was such a precious shining example of how to be; of how to live one's life, no matter what horrible things it might throw at you. It only made her fall harder for Thyra.

And so now, she held really tightly onto her, and she allowed herself to experience emotion. She cried. She was aware that their friendship would probably be over in a flash if she expressed her true feelings for the Viking woman. She had a strong suspicion that it was not what Thyra wanted. And so, Merit had resolved to keep quiet about it. If friendship was all that she could have with Thyra, that is what she would settle for. But then, the woman had shown up carrying that brand-new sword, saying it was for protection. Merit feared it could only mean one thing; Thyra was leaving, carrying on with the rest of her journey. She was leaving her behind. All of a sudden, the dam that she had built so carefully to guard against her deepest emotions broke wide open inside Merit, and everything came flooding out.

"Hey, you dropped the olives," Thyra commented.

It was just the way that she said it. Quietly, seriously, like it was a really important issue. And yet, with a strong underlying current of wry amusement in her voice. Merit could not help but chuckle at the intentionally silly remark. She started to laugh. And once she started doing that, she could do absolutely nothing whatsoever to stop herself. She even got Thyra going with her as well. There they were, two grown women sat facing each other, shaking with uncontrollable laughter, with a bunch of olives scattered at their feet. This went on for a while. And it felt amazing. After Merit finally calmed down enough to catch her breath, Thyra kept her eyes on her for a few more seconds, smiling gently.

"Does that mean yes, then?" she asked. "You want to travel with me?"

Merit nodded intently. If she was not careful about this, she would start crying all over again. She felt relieved, excited, joyful, and shaken all at once.

"Yes," she replied. "Yes, I really do."

"Good," Thyra approved.

CHAPTER TWENTY-FIVE

Thyra did not let it show, but she was relieved at her answer too. After everything that they had been through together, it would have felt somehow really wrong to her to be without Merit. She did not attempt to figure out why. She chose not to ask her any embarrassing questions about the tears. And she did not probe as to what the reason for Merit's outburst may have been. She had a pretty good idea anyway, and she did not want to force her to discuss what was probably extremely personal stuff. If Merit wanted to talk, fine. If not, she was happy to just let it go. Thyra flashed her a bright, happy smile.

"Don't know about you, but I'm kind of fed up with tears and heartache," she said.

Merit returned the smile.

"Yes, me too," she agreed. "No more tears from now on."

Satisfied, Thyra handed her a small bag which she thought would go a long way to restore some warmth and happiness in her friend's heart.

"Here. I got something for you."

Curious, Merit accepted the bag. Inside were a bunch of clothes. Trousers, shirts, a long shawl that was typical of local dress, and shoes made of fine leather with good soles on them.

She looked up hesitantly.

"For me?" she asked. "Really?"

Thyra gave her another encouraging smile.

"Yes, go on," she prompted. "It's all yours, Merit."

Merit took the clothes out of the bag with growing elation. She tried the shoes on first. It had been so long since she had owned a pair of shoes! And Thyra had chosen well. They fit her perfectly. Eyes wide with pleasure and excitement, Merit carried on examining the rest of the bag's contents. She pulled the shirts out and held them out in front of her, shaking her head in amazement. These were made of the purest, softest Egyptian cotton, as were the trousers. The shawl was magnificent, with heavy threads of colourful silk woven delicately into the material. This was superior quality in every way. And the items were brand-new as well. They even smelled incredibly good, rich flavours of amber and cinnamon that reminded Merit of her early childhood.

"Thyra, those are so beautiful," she exclaimed. "I don't know what to say... Thank you, I..."

Merit shook her head again in open wonder. She had no words to describe how she really felt about this. She was stunned and exhilarated. Such an awesome gift was unexpected and hugely significant. It showed exactly how much Thyra really must care about her. Merit was aware of the fact that she had lost everything she owned in the ship wreck. All the money her friend Hrorek had given her, and everything else that she had been careful enough to save up for the longer term. Now, Thyra really had nothing to bargain with apart from her necklace, which Merit knew full well she would never trade up for anything, not even if her own life depended on it. The only other thing that she possessed of any value were her arm bracers, of course, and those were almost equally precious to her...

"Oh, Thyra," Merit murmured.

For the first time, she suddenly noticed that her forearms were bare. Her skin was a much paler shade there, where her arm bracers had once covered it. Merit met her gaze, biting onto her lower lip in obvious dismay. She knew what an extremely difficult sacrifice this must have been for her to make.

"What have you done?" she wondered.

But Thyra simply shrugged easily, as if this was no big deal to her.

"It's okay. You needed proper clothes, and I wanted a new weapon. So, it made sense to do it. I got some change from the trade, too. We'll be all right for a while."

The merchant had argued with her that he wanted both arm bracers in exchange for just the one sword, and nothing else added to the bargain. But Thyra was not stupid, and she knew the true worth of her equipment. The bracers were made of solid bronze, and the best Scottish leather. Not to mention the added value of expert craftsmanship that had gone into making them. They really were worth a small fortune, and Thyra made sure that she got what she wanted out of them. Then, she walked far out into the desert after the transaction had taken place and sat on her own in complete silence until the feeling of sickness fully disappeared. Yes, this was a big deal all right. But it served no purpose to drive herself crazy about it. No point remembering that morning back at the Volsung camp when Kari had given the bracers to her. No point dwelling on the reason why she had done it. Thyra knew that her lover would have approved of this trade, and so, the only thing she had to get over was her own troubled mind. The only obstacles she really had to face were her own insecurities. She still had the torc, which was the main thing. And on the plus side, she also felt a little more secure now that she had acquired a new sword.

"To tell you the truth, I'll be happy if I never have to fight anyone else ever again," she admitted with a small sigh. "But all the same, wearing that thing on my belt sends the right kind of message to anybody out there who might be tempted to mess with us along the way."

"Yes; it's just for protection, right?" Merit reminded her.

Thyra nodded, glad that she approved and understood.

"That's right," she agreed. "Just to be safe."

"All right then, in this case, I'm happy about it. Now please, turn around," Merit instructed in an excited voice. "And don't cheat, okay?"

Thyra laughed as she complied.

"All right, I'll do my best," she joked.

She turned to look the other way, as Merit quickly got rid of the rags she was wearing and threw them aside. They were so old, dirty, and ripped in places that they could not decently be described as clothes anymore. She slipped into her new, precious clean ones, wrapped herself in the shawl, and closed her eyes in pleasure at the sensation.

"Oh, this feels so good!" she exclaimed. "Okay, now you can look!"

Thyra turned around, and a lovely, thoughtful smile slowly spread across her lips. Just to be able to witness such a happy, joyful glint in Merit's deep dark eyes made it all worth it for her. To see her delight over the new clothes was worth trading her arm bracers a million times over. Yes, she was glad that she had done it. No regrets. She remained silent for a little longer, just watching her and thinking about it. Until she suddenly realised that Merit was still waiting for an answer and looking a little disconcerted by Thyra's unexpected silence now as well.

"Is it okay?" she murmured uncertainly.

Thyra flashed her a brilliant smile.

"Yeah, of course, it's okay," she replied. "Sorry, just got distracted... I think you look really great in these clothes, Merit. Very beautiful."

But then again you always are, no matter what you wear...

Thyra very nearly blurted those words out as well. It would have been a one-hundred percent true statement, genuine, and completely heartfelt. But thankfully, she managed to stop before she could get herself into a real sticky mess. She knew perfectly well why Merit had burst into tears earlier at the thought that she might leave without her. And something in Thyra definitely shifted at that moment too. Something big. What was it that Tait had told her once? Oh yes: *You know what, sister, people only ever see what they want to see, not the reality of what truly is...* Thyra had not thought about it much at the time, probably because Tait had been talking about Bjarke. But now, she realised that her brother had been correct. She had refused to face the truth about Bjarke, and in so doing, she had made it easy for him to almost kill her. In the end, her stubbornness to cling to her version of the reality she preferred had cost the lives of the two people she loved most on the planet. Then, with Merit, Thyra had headed down the exact same path once again. Blinders on, full speed ahead, and no questions asked. She had ignored every single sign, even though it was happening right in front of her own face, just because it felt too frightening to consider. *What a wimp I can be...* All of a sudden, Thyra was fuming at what she perceived to be her own cowardice. *How long am I going to keep doing this?* It was time to stop running and face the truth. It was time to wake up and start linking the dots. The situation was so obvious. Every time that Merit touched her, she lingered. Every time she looked at her, she struggled to take her eyes away. It suddenly occurred to Thyra that Merit was not like that with anybody else but her...

"Thyra?"

No, Thyra reflected intently, Merit was not *'tactile'*. No, she was not just *'being friendly'* or *'supportive'*. Thyra shook her head slowly, staring at the ground in growing amazement at her own powers of self-deception. She wondered how on earth she could have managed to ignore for so long the startling fact that Merit's feelings for her went a lot deeper than just mere friendship. Yes, it had kind of occurred to her once when they were on the float, but then, she had quickly convinced herself that she was losing her mind. How convenient. *I so did not want to see it...*

"Thyra?" Merit repeated.

But Thyra carried on not paying attention to her. If she had allowed herself to see it for what it was, she would have been forced to ask herself how she felt about Merit's attraction to her. Inevitably, she would have had to consider whether she might not be feeling the exact same way about her too. Just the thought of it now made Thyra breathe a little harder with stress. It made her start to sweat, and her head spin unpleasantly. But it also occurred to her at the same time how insensitive she had been to her friend's feelings, just to protect her own. No wonder Merit was crying now...

"Thyra?" Merit called for the third time. "Hey…"

CHAPTER TWENTY-SIX

As deeply lost as she had become in a whirlwind of challenging, bewildering thoughts that she struggled to handle all at once, Thyra had not noticed Merit coming to sit a little closer to her. When she suddenly did, she looked up, startled. She rested her eyes on her. Merit was still dressed in her new clothes, smelling wonderful and looking quite positively radiant. Everything about her suddenly felt a lot more intense, heightened, and it affected Thyra in an unusually powerful way. *What's changed?* she wondered in utter puzzlement.

"Thank you for being so kind to me, Thyra," Merit said.

She was speaking in a quiet, gentle tone, and yet there was also a fierceness there that Thyra was not really used to. The way Merit was looking at her now was definitely a lot more vivid and focused. Thyra exhaled slowly. *Oh... Okay.* Part of her just really wanted to laugh out loud and brush it all off. Maybe just say something along the lines of, *'Hey, it's just a bunch of clothes, don't worry about it'*. Walk away from here and go sit somewhere in the desert all by herself. But that would have been the old way of dealing with things. So, instead, she turned to meet Merit's strong gaze.

"You know, I'd be happy travelling on my own, but..."

She winced impatiently and in frustration at the inaccuracy and clumsiness of her own words. *Just get it out straight, Thyra!*

She tried again.

"What I mean is that it was never my intention to leave without you. Or at least not to ask you if you wanted to come with me. I wasn't sure what your plans were, but I am really happy that you want to travel with me."

She would have added 'a bit longer' to the end of that sentence, just to make it a little safer, but she forced herself to stop right there. Merit flashed her a relieved, grateful smile in response.

"Well, I'm sorry for the misunderstanding," she said. "I'm sorry about bursting into tears on you like that as well. I just have no idea what got into me, really..."

It was a blatant lie, and on some level, they both knew it. A brief moment of awkward silence followed her statement, and then Merit froze in surprise when Thyra suddenly reached out and took her hand in hers. Apart from grabbing on to her one day on board the raft, when Merit had almost rolled off the deck during her sleep, Thyra had never initiated any sort of physical contact between them before, not even once. So, when she did reach out to wrap her fingers around hers like that, so gently, Merit did not say anything, but her heart jumped inside her chest. She kept her eyes on her, as Thyra returned her gaze to the fire. She sat staring pensively into the flames, as if trying to figure out what to do, or even what to say next. Eventually, she just gave a light shake of the head, and she sighed.

"Hmm... can't believe I feel so tired..." she muttered, as if speaking to herself.

Merit instantly tensed at the admission. It was really quite strange for Thyra to blurt out something like this. She never complained, never admitted it when she was tired. Merit tightened her grip on her fingers, feeling both concerned and a little guilty at the same time.

"Thyra, it's okay," she started. "You don't need to...."

"No, no, just let me say this," Thyra interrupted.

Merit went quiet, and Thyra glanced at her. She spotted the worried look in her eyes, and she gave her a small, reassuring smile in return.

"I'm fine, don't worry."

"Are you sure?"

"Yes. Sure."

Merit did not look particularly convinced, but Thyra carried on anyway. She had to get that stuff out of her system. She had to do it now, right this second, before she could change her mind and convince herself once more that it did not matter. Because of course, it did.

"I'm just trying to explain that before I met you on board the ship," she said, "I had not been paying much attention to the outside world for a while. I had been travelling non-stop since Scotland and keeping to myself a lot. Crossing over the Alps was great in that way, you know? I was completely on my own for just over four weeks, and most of that time, I actually spent inside of my own head..."

She paused, frowning in wonder, as if she had suddenly realised something extremely important. Merit suspected that she knew exactly the reason for her sudden hesitation.

"Inside your head with Kari," she murmured. "Right?"

"Yeah, right," Thyra admitted eventually. "And my brother too..."

She said it had been great, but now in retrospect, she was not so sure of that. Most of that long gruelling walk through the mountains had been akin to a slow descent into madness for her, she could see it now. She had spent every waking moment talking out loud to a couple of ghosts essentially, obsessing about the signs she thought she received from them in return.

After a few days alone on the trail, everything became alive with crazy meaning. Every tweet from the birds, every puff of breeze blowing through the trees, and even the shape of the clouds in the sky above her head suddenly took on immense significance. Everything was a potential message from Tait or a link back to Kari. Madness, indeed… It was nothing at all like the gentle meditations that she now conducted in the desert from time to time. During those sessions, she invariably felt at peace, relaxed, and deeply grounded within herself. It was good, and useful. But back there in the mountains, she had just felt frantic and disconnected, the same way that she had become when drifting out at sea. Thyra sighed again, wondering why in the world such insight and clarity of mind had eluded her up until this very moment. When she looked at Merit again, this time, her gaze was laser-like in its intensity. Her grip on her fingers was relaxed, yet it was warm; gentle but unapologetic. And it was as if Merit also knew that something very important had just changed. She gave her a gentle squeeze to keep her going, and she rubbed her thumb over her fingers in an affectionate gesture. Thyra smiled instinctively in reaction.

"Do you remember that question you asked me when we were at sea?" she asked.

Merit nodded. It was not a moment she would ever forget.

"Yes," she murmured. "I remember it well…"

Thyra had not replied to her, but the look of utter despair in her eyes had said it all, really. It was the kind of expression that had made Merit worry about her. And wonder how long she would actually be able to hold out before she did something stupid to end it all. There had been a terrifying emptiness in Thyra's eyes back then, like she had exhausted every option and solution. But now, it seemed as if a powerful transformation had occurred.

"Well, the answer to your question is no," Thyra confirmed with strong, quiet confidence. "And I don't want to spend the rest of my life inside my head either. The thing is, I like being with you, Merit, but…"

"I like being with you too," Merit replied immediately.

She did not need to say it, although the *'but'* that Thyra had inserted into her sentence had made her instantly anxious. Thyra held her hand a little tighter, reassuringly. She kept her eyes firmly on her face. She noticed the faint blush that crept all over Merit's features. *I know you do,* she thought. *And I don't know why you would, but I don't care…* She had no idea what Merit found even remotely interesting or attractive about her, but all that mattered was that she did. And from the intense way she was looking at her now, Thyra got a sense that Merit probably wanted to say a lot more. It sent a little shiver down her spine, and in a good way. She took a deep breath in. It was time to be honest, open, and crystal clear.

"I'm sorry if I made it seem like I wanted out," she said. "I like you, Merit. I like you a lot. It's just that I didn't expect to be feeling this way again anytime soon, that's all. And probably not ever, actually…"

At first, her developing feelings toward the Egyptian woman had felt incredibly wrong to her, and like a monumental betrayal of her beautiful Kari; her amazing, brilliant, first, and only lover to date. But when she was out in the desert alone one evening, Kari's gentle whisper had echoed through her mind. *There will be others. That's all right.* Thyra remembered the awful night of her death as if it were yesterday. The clan chief had told her in no uncertain terms then that it would be okay to love and allow herself to be loved in return. Thyra would never forget those last words that Kari had spoken, and yet at the time, she had been convinced that it would never happen to her again.

After Kari, Thyra had been certain that she would never want to be close to anyone else. Let alone commit to a serious, intimate relationship with another woman. The best part of her also did not believe that she deserved to be loved again, period. She had let everyone down, had she not? And now, a solitary life would be the price that she would pay. She had got used to the idea and made her peace with it. So, when she realised how she was beginning to feel about Merit, she tried to fight it, to deny it. But in the end, the woman simply got under her skin in such a way that there was nothing Thyra could do about it. She simply had to tell her the truth of how she felt.

"Oh, Thyra…" Merit murmured.

The candid admission took her by surprise as well. It was one thing for Thyra to say that she liked being with her, and quite another to admit that she liked her *'a lot'*. For her to then confess that she was feeling *'this way again'*, was nothing short of astonishing. Merit would never have expected her to come out with something like this. But oh, how wonderful it felt to her to finally hear Thyra say it… At a loss for words, Merit impulsively threw both her arms around her neck, and she pressed herself against her body. This time, the response that she received from Thyra was thrilling. There was nothing restrained or reluctant about it. Nothing shy or hesitant. The way that Thyra held her made Merit feel like a big wall had suddenly come crashing down from in between them. The Viking woman kept one hand resting on the back of Merit's neck, warm and secure there, and the other one positioned flat against her lower back. It instantly made Merit breathe faster in reaction. This was a lover's confident touch. Focused, intense, not a friend's casual embrace anymore.

"Okay?" she murmured.

"Yep," Thyra nodded.

And so, Merit allowed herself to do what she had wanted to do for such a long time. She pulled back just so that she could look at Thyra. She smiled at her, and ran her fingers through her long, thick blond hair. Under the hot desert sun, it had grown even lighter. It was beautiful, and it felt wonderful to glide her fingers through it. Merit traced a light caress over her lips. She cupped her face in both her hands, and she stared into Thyra's sparkling blue eyes for several long seconds. She allowed herself to deeply feel everything that she had so far kept so carefully hidden from her. There was absolutely no need to say anything else on top of it, her expression was more than enough. Merit watched, mesmerised, as a slow rush of heat suffused Thyra's cheeks, and then, she thought of a question. Thyra did not need any translation. She gave a small smile in response and lowered her head slightly.

"Yes," she murmured.

CHAPTER TWENTY-SEVEN

The travelling days were long and hot; dusty, slow, and tiring. But Thyra was tremendously happy all the same. She actually spent most of those hard days trekking on the edge of the desert toward Egypt in a warm and blissful daze of sorts. Travelling was good for the soul, she already knew that. Travelling with Merit by her side was something else altogether. It dawned on Thyra after a couple of great weeks out on the trail with her that this first kiss they had shared at the fisherman's village represented another massive shift along her personal journey. With the deaths of Tait and Kari, it had felt as if all the pieces of her world had been blown apart by an evil wind and scattered to all wild sides of the universe. Nothing really made sense after that, not even the simplest things, and the world had been a dark, cold, and loveless place for Thyra then. Now though, light, warmth, and contentment once again filled her heart. It was like some magical being had managed to straighten up the broken pieces of her soul for her. And given her a gentle nudge along the path too. As far as Thyra was concerned, this felt very much like Kari's brilliant handiwork from the other side of the veil.

She had started to think of her lover as her spirit guide now. She still spoke to her often, in the silence of the night, and the quiet of her soul. Kari always answered back, proving time and time again that she was still Thyra's *Shining One*, and always would be, just as she had promised.

For Thyra now, being with Merit in this life that she had once perceived as a cruel death sentence to be endured until the bitter end was amazing. It was also very different from anything she had experienced in the past. Her relationship with Kari had been nothing short of magnificent in every way. There were even a few extra-special moments, like the days that they had spent alone as the storm raged outside, or their private summer afternoons together at the lake, when Thyra would have been delighted if time had simply stopped for them there forever. She had felt settled and deeply peaceful. But with Kari, she realised now that those feelings of being grounded never lasted for very long. What prevailed instead was a disturbing urgency, and the clear sense that this was a little too good to be true. Thyra had always feared that her time with Kari would not last but be abruptly taken away from her someday... Obviously, this had been a premonition of things to come. Also, the Volsung commander only ever had to glance her way once for Thyra to start to feel as if she would spontaneously combust. Being in a relationship with Merit was different. It felt like melting into an ocean of calm. There was no sense of danger with it, or the threat of impending disaster. Their first kiss was natural and true, full of quiet passion. And then, as the days went slowly by, they both developed into the relationship at the same kind of pace. Growing together like this, sharing the hardships and delights of a travelling life, made them tighter than Thyra had ever thought possible. It simply blew her mind. And she loved every second of it.

"Do you know how long I've actually been wanting to kiss you?" Merit murmured with her eyes half-closed, after doing it for the first time.

"Not really," Thyra replied with a sly grin. "A while?"

Merit burst out laughing, amused at her expression.

"Since the second night," she confessed, blushing.

"What, when we were drifting out on the float?"

"No, no, way earlier than that," Merit protested. "When we were on board the ship, and you came back to see me again. *That* second night!"

"Really?"

Thyra looked mystified at the admission, and even a little embarrassed to realise the truth. Touched by her reaction, Merit brushed another gentle kiss over her lips.

"Yes, really," she murmured. "Don't look so shocked."

She felt moved by this unconscious display of vulnerability. And then, she enjoyed watching the way that Thyra kept her eyes closed a little longer after she pulled back from the kiss, completely lost in the sensation. Merit loved to see the open look on her face, and the slow, lazy smile that crept over her gorgeous mouth as Thyra met her gaze once more.

"Why is that, then?" she asked.

Merit smiled at the question. She could not quite believe that Thyra needed to ask, really. As far as Merit was concerned, she was the most beautiful woman she had ever met, and with a heart and soul to match. She thought about it for a moment longer. During the raid on her village, she had lost people too. Family members and friends. She suspected that there were women out there right now, women she knew and loved, being held captive and used as slaves in various parts of the world. Every single night, she thought of them before falling asleep, and sent silent prayers of fortitude and strength toward them.

There were two women in particular who made her heart bleed whenever she thought of them. The first one was Ky, her cousin; the second was Hela, the young girl she had grown up with, who had not only been her best friend at the time, but also helped Merit understand who she truly was, during one very special night... Sometimes, she wondered whether both women might not be dead, and if that would not be better for them in a way. She suspected that she would never know, and she wondered about the life paths of all the people she knew. She thought about her own, too, all the twists and turns of life and death, and what it could all possibly mean in the bigger scheme of things. She could not speak for anyone else, but she knew that being taken as a slave had led to her eventually meeting Thyra. For Merit, being with her felt just like coming home. There was something about her that was inexplicably familiar, comforting, and reassuring. It was as if she had always known her.

"You know, just the simple fact that you have no idea how amazing you really are is one of the things I find so attractive about you," she murmured. "The other one is that you make me feel safe. I feel secure when I'm with you, Thyr. And absolutely complete."

Thyra flashed her a quick, pensive smile in response, and she raised a reflective eyebrow. It was a long time since anyone had called her that. Kari used to do it a lot. So did Tait. Bjarke himself had never called her anything but her full name, or simply 'girl'. It sounded awfully good to Thyra when Merit suddenly started to use the familiar nickname. And she could understand her feeling complete, because she was beginning to experience that too. The more she spent time with Merit, the more whole and filled-up she was beginning to feel. But safe was a lot harder for her to accept. Thyra had not felt strong within herself for quite a while. She told Merit that.

"I know," Merit replied, smiling gently. "But that is exactly what I mean, you see? Learning to live when you feel so broken inside, and you would rather not be here anymore… There lies true strength. And yours is shining bright, Thyra. Perhaps you cannot see it yet, but I certainly can. It's beautiful and warm, and stronger than steel. Just like you are, even if it does not always feel that way."

Yes, Thyra reflected, as they stopped for the night and she started a fire to cook their food. Being with Merit was good for the soul all right. She was also very much impressed by the land that she came from. Egypt was rich and beautiful, overflowing with resources, just as Merit had told her. They had reached the Nile river earlier on in the day, and suddenly, everything had turned lush, green, and tropical. There was an explosion of colour everywhere that Thyra looked; freshly-planted fields and gorgeous blooming flowers at every single turn. The river appeared busy. Commerce was prosperous in these parts, and the fishing was good. Egypt was a wonderful place indeed.

"And the best is yet to come," Merit promised.

As Thyra started to boil some water, and Merit laid out her cooking utensils next to her, she suggested heading for a small town where they could catch a boat the next day. Thyra frowned in instant distrust.

"What?" she exclaimed. "Did you say boat?"

Merit looked up from the fish she was preparing with a wide grin on her face. She had expected this sort of reaction from Thyra. After all, this was the woman who had involved herself in every activity when they were at the village; from babysitting wild kids to building houses, and planting row after row of boring seeds in the hard-beating sun. Thyra had done it all, apart from one thing: going out in a boat, despite Ahmed's repeated invitations for her to accompany him out on a fishing trip.

THYRA'S PROMISE

"Yes," Merit confirmed with a light chuckle. "I did say boat. You'll just have to get used to it, Thyr. On the river, it will take us only ten days to get there. If we walk, it'll be more like thirty. So..."

Thyra could tell when she was beaten. And there was no doubt that this was the case. She gave a resigned sigh, all the while secretly enjoying Merit's fiery attitude.

"So," she muttered. "Looks like it's the only choice, then."

"Yes," Merit concluded. "I'll get it all arranged. And don't you worry about it. There aren't any pirates around here, and Nile river boats don't sink. Or catch fire either."

Thyra gave a mischievous smile.

"What? Never?" she challenged.

"Never!" Merit asserted.

Thyra looked at her for a few seconds, smiling softly. And then, without saying anything else, she walked over and pulled her impulsively into her arms, knocking the frying pan and all the fish over in the process.

"Hey, I'm cooking here," Merit protested.

"I don't care," Thyra shot back.

Merit eyed her with a pretend annoyed expression on her face, but the delighted smile that she tried in vain to hide and suppress betrayed her real pleasure at Thyra's embrace.

"What do you want, Viking?" she asked.

"I just remembered something."

"Oh yeah?"

"Yeah," Thyra smiled, entertained by Merit's fake haughty tone, and how much she struggled to keep a straight look. "You know, when I saw you for the first time, back on the ship when they were leading you below; do you remember looking at me then, as you went past?"

"I do," Merit replied.

217

Her voice softened immediately. She stopped joking about it, pretending to be irritated, and she returned Thyra's smile, as she brushed a strand of hair from her brow at the same time.

"I noticed you, yeah."

Thyra traced a light finger over her lips.

"Well, I noticed you too," she murmured. "When I looked into your eyes that first time, it really took my breath away. And every now and then when I look at you again, Merit, I still find it a little hard to breathe. You are very beautiful. I thank the gods for you every day."

Merit was quite used to Thyra's unusual style by then. The woman could be quite infuriatingly silent for most of the day, lost in her own thoughts along the way. And then, suddenly, she would turn around and say the most beautiful things at the most unexpected of moments. Grab Merit for a passionate kiss, or a reassuring hug. Now, Merit sank her fingers into her hair, and she held onto a fistful of it, holding her back when Thyra tried to kiss her.

"What?" Thyra asked.

"Nothing. I just... Ah..."

Merit started to blush, and she suddenly broke eye contact. She tried to pull away, but Thyra tightened her grip around her waist.

"Wait," she whispered.

And when Merit looked back at her, Thyra simply smiled.

"I am in love with you, Merit."

The reason Merit had not been able to finish her sentence before was exactly because she wanted to tell her the same thing. But it felt so big, so binding, and she was concerned about going too fast and saying too much, too quickly. Thyra was obviously more than all right with this though. She was there with her all the way.

"I love you, Thyr," Merit replied intently.

"Even when I mess up your cooking?" Thyra teased her.

Merit chuckled, and she spared a single glance toward the abandoned fish that was spread out all over the sandy ground.

"Yes. Even when you ruin our supper," she replied.

"And when I wake you up before dawn to start walking?"

"Because you are a morning person, and I am not," Merit remarked, laughing easily now. "Yes, even when you do that awful thing. Thyra, there's not a single thing you could say that would make me answer 'no' to you. You understand that, right? I am in love with you. Have been for a long time."

Thyra nodded in reply. She looked deeply happy. She had not planned to say any of this to Merit, but it felt completely true to do it now, and absolutely perfect. She could feel the rightness of the moment pulsing from the deepest core of her being.

"So, this is it then, yes?" she grinned. "You and me, we are together now. For good?"

"For good, for the long run, and no matter what happens, yes," Merit promised. "I want to spend the rest of my life by your side, Thyra."

She held harder onto her and stared into her eyes. Thyra held her gaze intently, mesmerised. She could have lost herself forever in Merit's charcoal-black irises. They both exchanged a long, intense, smouldering look. Dinner was quickly forgotten, catching whatever boat they needed was no longer a concern, and the rest of the entire world ceased to exist for a few precious moments that belonged exclusively to them.

"I want to make love to you," Thyra whispered.

CHAPTER TWENTY-EIGHT

It only took them another eight days to make it to the place that had once been Merit's village, a little less than she had estimated at first. Although they were too late to embark on the earlier boat that she had planned to catch that morning, simply because Thyra overslept. It was a rare occurrence indeed for the high-energy woman who usually thrived on less than five hours each night.

"I never sleep that long!" she exclaimed, blinking hard in the warm sun that she was not used to finding shining in her face when she first woke up.

She looked astounded, and as if she had let herself down greatly by sleeping a little longer than normal somehow. Merit shot her a single glance, and instantly decided that Thyra looked devastatingly handsome in all of her splendid irritation.

"Don't worry about it," she laughed. "Who cares?"

She gave her a big hug and a reassuring kiss, all the while allowing herself a private smile of satisfaction. She thought it was really great that Thyra had felt so relaxed after their first night of passion that it had allowed her to rest for a lot longer than she normally did.

"Breakfast?" she offered. "We've got eggs."

Merit had been the first to wake up that morning, just after dawn. She had spent a long time gazing at her lover then, as Thyra slept on. Stretched out on her stomach with one arm folded above her head, and the other resting limply by her side. Hard muscles at rest for once. Tangled blond hair cascading all over her naked shoulders and back, with a single strand resting over her cheek. Full lips parted slightly open, and with such a peaceful look about her that all Merit had wanted to do was sit and stare at her adoringly for the rest of the entire day. Then, Thyra had woken up, screamed in indignation at finding herself already more than halfway through the morning, and ruined all her secret plans.

"I obviously did a little something to tire you out last night, uh," she remarked, as her lover reached for her clothes, and started to throw them on.

She was rewarded with a cute grin and an amused chuckle from her. Thyra buckled her belt into place and walked a little closer to steal another kiss.

"Yeah, I really enjoyed myself last night," she whispered in her partner's ear. "Very much so. And especially that one thing you did to me... You know what I'm talking about?"

"What do you mean?" Merit chuckled, blushing hard.

There were several things she had done the night before actually, which she would never have imagined that she would ever dare attempt with anyone. Thyra had taught her a few new ways to play as well. She had proved herself to be adventurous, inventive, and deliciously attentive in her love-making. Merit suspected that she might well start to shake uncontrollably if she allowed herself to think about it all for very long. Thyra shot her another devilish grin and moved a little closer.

"You're not sure?" she smiled. "Let me remind you."

They lost a bit more time there, of course, although it was hugely enjoyable for both of them. Breakfast eventually turned into an exceedingly late lunch. Thyra was no longer complaining by then, or even aware of the passage of time. It was only the next morning, in fact, when they finally managed to make it to the correct village and locate the right boat to travel on. At long last, they were on their way to Merit's beloved village. Although, truth be told, she was feeling extremely apprehensive about it.

∞

They had booked special passage at a cheaper price on a flat river-goods barge, and as it glided serenely along the river, snaking its way through luxurious scenery and quiet country scenes, Thyra watched her beautiful Merit grow progressively more nervous the closer they made it to their destination. The woman became strangely quiet and started playing with her food at meal times. And then, Thyra woke up with a start one night, to find that Merit was no longer lying by her side. Immediately on the alert, and full of concern, she jumped to her feet and went looking for her. She discovered her partner right where she had thought she would be, leaning over the railing toward the back end of the boat, staring out at the starry sky with an anxious look on her face.

"Hey," she murmured.

Merit glanced to the side, looking startled for just a second. But an instant smile flashed across her face when she recognised Thyra stepping out of the shadows.

"Hey, you," she replied.

Thyra came to take a spot right behind her. She rubbed her hands affectionately over her arms and kissed the top of her shoulder. She noticed then the almost imperceptible shiver that coursed through Merit's body, and the small unconscious sigh that she gave. She felt her lean back into her, instantly melting into her arms. Thyra marvelled that she would have this kind of effect on anyone. She was deeply touched to realise that Merit responded in this way to even the easiest and lightest of touches from her.

"Can't sleep?" she asked.

"No. I've been tossing and turning. I didn't want to wake you up."

"Next time, please do," Thyra murmured.

Merit held gratefully onto her as Thyra wrapped her arms around her waist from behind and pulled her a little tighter against her own body. This felt safe to her then, and like the best place to be in the entire world.

"Okay, I will. Thanks."

Thyra brushed a soft kiss over her cheek.

"We'll be there in just a few hours now. In the morning."

"Yes, we're almost there," Merit sighed. "I don't know why I feel so worried about it, you know? I mean, it's not as if I don't understand what we're going to find."

"What do you think that'll be?" Thyra asked.

"Well, it's been over a year now. Either some people will have moved back in, or the place will be totally empty. I think probably the latter. After what happened there, it would not be a good spot to dwell again. I guess I'm just anxious about seeing it. And meeting people I know…"

"Why?" Thyra exclaimed, surprised.

Merit gave her a shy, uncertain glance.

"Well, I'm… I survived, and… Well. Others haven't. And I found you as well. You're the love of my life, Thyr. I am so blessed. I'm just acutely aware that others have not been so lucky in the end…"

"Yes, I know what you mean," Thyra observed. "If you're talking about survivor's guilt, then I've got some experience of what that feels like."

She spoke in a thoughtful voice, in a self-deprecating tone that also held a slight trace of bitterness. Merit exhaled sharply, annoyed with herself for bringing up painful memories. Yes, she was lucky, incredibly so, and she would focus on being grateful. She took a deep breath of fragrant night air and stood a little straighter.

"It'll be fine," she decided. "Right?"

"That's right," Thyra approved with a tender smile. "And I'll be there with you, every step of the way."

Merit turned around to face her.

"Thank you, Thyra," she whispered intently. "I hope the temple is still standing. It is a very special place, and I would love for you to experience its energy."

"I'm sure it'll still be there," Thyra promised.

Merit was grateful for such unwavering confidence. She decided to share a little special gift with Thyra right there and then, an intimate practice that they could easily perform with their clothes on.

"All right, give me your hands," she invited.

Thyra held them out in front of her.

"Like this, palms open. Facing each other. Great."

"What are you doing?" Thyra enquired, intrigued.

"You'll see," Merit smiled. "Close your eyes, darling."

Thyra followed her instructions. She stood with her palms facing each other only a few inches apart, with her eyes closed and her head bent slightly forward in attention. Merit looked up at her.

"Now, what do you feel?" she whispered.

"Heat," Thyra replied. "Heat on the back of my hands."

"That's me. I've got my hands close to yours and gathering up my energy."

Thyra's smile widened instantly.

"Uh-uh. I think you've used that trick on me a few times before, haven't you?" she remarked. "We tend to lose big chunks of time whenever you do."

She heard Merit giggle at the memory, and she grinned as well. She could picture her lover's brilliant smile inside her head perfectly, even though she still had her eyes closed.

"Are you blushing, magic hands?" she asked.

"No," Merit said, and Thyra opened one eye to check.

"You liar," she laughed.

"Keep your eyes closed, Viking," Merit instructed.

She shook her head, amused. Thyra had started to use that nickname of 'magic hands' for her recently. It was because on more than one occasion, those gifted hands had done wonders to relax the tight knotted muscles in her shoulders and back, and even put her to sleep once or twice. Sometimes, Merit used her talents in totally unexpected, ingenious, and delightful ways. It was just as if she could turn the heat on and off in her fingers whenever she wanted to. It was great for massage and other equally relaxing activities.

"But it's not magic," she told Thyra now. "I'm just accessing the energy in the air. I can make the space around your head crackle with electricity, you know..."

In the next instant, Thyra felt a definite tingle right on top of her left ear. She jumped in surprise and immediately started laughing. She felt Merit move closer to her, and paid attention.

"Now, imagine a small ball of energy in the middle of your hands, swirling at incredible speed. See it become redder as it begins to heat up slowly. Feel that heat radiating all the way into your fingers. And then down into your wrists..."

Thyra frowned in concentration.

"Is it moving?" she asked after only a few seconds. "Are you doing anything?"

"Why? Tell me what's happening," Merit enquired.

"I feel something moving between my hands."

"Good. What else?"

"I feel hot," Thyra replied. "And not just my hands…"

Merit noticed a single bead of sweat sliding down the side of her temple. She nodded in quiet approval. Thyra was a complete natural at this, it seemed.

"Open your eyes, but don't lose your concentration," she instructed.

Thyra obeyed, looking serious and deeply absorbed in what she was experiencing. Merit showed her the inside of her right wrist to continue the lesson.

"I got bitten by a sand fly this morning, and now it's started to swell up. This energy you feel in both your hands is healing energy. All you need to add to it is intent, and then, let it flow."

"All right," Thyra nodded. "So, I'll just…"

She was totally focused. She did not finish her sentence, but instead simply applied her hands over the bite on Merit's skin. She closed her eyes, breathed deeply, and exhaled even longer. Merit watched her attentively and refrained from giving her any further instructions. Apparently, Thyra did not need any at all. Merit saw her cheeks start to colour, a little more sweat appear on her forehead, and she felt the palm of her hands start to heat up even more.

"Good," she whispered. "Keep going."

Thyra was using her breath in the right way, to keep herself grounded and connected, and Merit was impressed that she did not have to explain any of this to her. Some people were just naturally inclined to know such things. She loved that Thyra did.

"You cannot direct this energy," she just added, as Thyra continued to work. "It will go where it needs to go, and you don't need to worry about that. All you have to do is maintain your intent to heal. Keep breathing like you are. And use your entire body as an amplifier for the stream of life power to flow through you, and into your patient. Yes?"

Thyra gave a quick smile with her eyes still closed.

"Yes," she murmured. "Got it. It feels good…"

She squeezed her eyes a little more tightly shut. Instantly, Merit started to feel her own skin warm up, right over the spot where she needed it the most. It was tremendous relief over the insect bite. She could feel the heat flowing out of Thyra's hands, and from her entire body. It was like standing next to a powerful furnace. Merit felt a sudden jolt of pride and excitement at the realisation of how good her lover was at this. Not many people took to the energy so well. Not many had the gift that Thyra seemed to possess.

"Hey, are you all right?" she asked her after a few moments longer.

Thyra immediately opened her eyes wide and gave her a somewhat flabbergasted look. She let go of Merit's wrist and stared dumbfounded at her own hands.

"Yeah," she laughed. "I'm fine. Hey, I could see all kinds of weird colours swirling in front of my eyes. It was great. And I feel so hot… How did it feel to you?"

Merit smiled in approval.

"Great. I felt awesome relief."

Again, not many people could perceive the swirls of energy that were involved in the healing, as well as feel it in their hands. Although from some of Thyra's experiences with the other realms, Merit should not have expected much less than total perfection.

"So now, you just need to learn how to turn it off," she said. "Just do this."

And she wiped the palm of her hands three times on each side in quick succession, ending with a sharp gesture that was reminiscent of shaking water off the tips of her fingers. Thyra imitated her movements perfectly. As soon as she had done so, she started to feel herself cooling off.

"Wow," she murmured. "What was that?"

"Just a simple healing technique," Merit replied. "Look."

She raised her wrist again to show her. The reddening on her skin had definitely improved, and it even looked less swollen than before. Thyra shook her head, looking both pleased and a little puzzled at the same time.

"Really?" she wondered. "Am I hallucinating?"

"Nope," Merit exclaimed, laughing at her surprise. "You've just got a gift for it, that's all. I know that you were raised as a warrior, but perhaps being a healer is your true calling…"

Thyra stood looking at her hands, smiling at the thought of it. She wondered what her artistic brother Tait would have had to say about that. *Thyra the Healer…* A clear image of him smiling floated through her mind. Tait would have loved this.

"Yeah," she murmured. "I like it. And it felt really good to do it, especially when I was focusing on the intention. I really wanted to help you feel better, and…"

"It worked," Merit finished for her. "Thank you, my love."

She pulled Thyra into a warm embrace. She wrapped her arms around her upper body and rested her cheek against her chest.

"I don't feel so nervous anymore either," she realised. "And I am really glad that you can access the energy so well. When we are at the temple, it will definitely be useful to you to have a good experience."

Thyra felt quite enthralled by all this.

"In what way?" she asked. "What sort of experience?"

"Well," Merit replied with a mysterious smile, "this will not be known to either of us until we get there. That is what makes the temple such a special place."

CHAPTER TWENTY-NINE

Merit's old village was just an empty patch of dead ground, completely deserted, just as she had suspected. She walked through it in total silence, holding tightly onto Thyra's hand. She kept the fingers of her free one wrapped around her bicep for added reassurance. They did not slow down very much, as there was really nothing to look at. Here and there, remnants of the clay houses which had existed before could still be spotted, most of them now just showing the foundations of what had once been the happy homes of previous residents. The ground also bore traces of intense heat in some areas. Thyra glanced at those marks curiously as they passed through, wondering what sort of event could have caused those to stand out.

"They burnt people," Merit said to her in a whisper.

Thyra gave a sharp exhale, and she instantly winced at the thought. It was shocking to imagine people being capable of such things, and the horror of it all. It left a bitter and sour taste in her mouth when she tried to envision the scene.

"Right," she muttered. "Well, there's nothing more to see here, Merit. Do you agree? No one's still living here. And I don't think we should stay."

"You can feel it too?"

"Yeah. This place feels fearful," Thyra replied.

Merit shivered at such an accurate description. But yes, this was just the right word to describe it. What remained of her old village did not simply feel dead, but haunted too, and like Thyra had just remarked, a disturbing sense of fear was quite palpable in the air still.

Thyra stood with her left hand resting on the handle of her sword, which was a habit of hers whenever she was nervous. She remained rooted to the spot for a moment longer, taking in the ruined and empty scene in front of her and working hard to imagine what it would have looked like before the tragedy. There was so very little left of the village now that it was quite difficult to do so, and for some reason, it also made her think of her own people back at home. She was not sure why exactly, since after all, it was not the Asger settlement which had been destroyed by Bjarke's folly. She had never had to see her village in such a state of devastation, although the Volsung place had been all but annihilated in the battle, and her heart tightened at the memory of it. But back there, the Asger village probably looked exactly the same as before. Her people would still be there, of course, going about their daily lives just like they had always done. This was strangely reassuring to her somehow, and it made Thyra wonder how alone Merit really must feel. She was such a bright and positive person that it was hard to tell sometimes. Thyra thought about the Volsung, with Hrorek leading them. They were the family she had chosen for herself. She touched her fingers to her torc. All of a sudden, she was seized with an insane urge to find out how they were all doing. Had the two clans been in contact at all since she had left? Was her father still alive? And how was Hrorek? She was shocked to realise how much she really missed him.

"Thyra?"

Merit's gentle call brought her out of her reverie.

"Yes. Right here."

Thyra nodded and instantly flashed her a brilliant smile. Indeed, she was here now, with Merit. And she could not have been happier about that. Now, her job was to support her, not daydream about the past. She should be focusing on helping her lover get through this dreadful coming home of sorts. She passed her arm over her shoulders in a comforting gesture.

"Are you okay?" she asked. "I'm sorry this looks so bad."

Merit gave her a faint smile of her own. She did look a little shaken, but as always, she was not one to dwell on the darker side of things.

"I'm fine," she replied. "But you're right. I would like to leave now, go check if the temple is still standing. Is that okay?"

"Of course," Thyra agreed.

Merit sounded impatient to get moving, and so was she.

"Did you get what you wanted here though?" she enquired.

Thyra was keen to check on that and make well sure of it because once they left, she was not planning on coming back ever again. She was glad when Merit gave her a heartfelt 'yes' in response. Just walking through the dead remains of the once-thriving and beautiful village had brought her enough closure. There was nobody left there that she could help. And so, the best thing to do was to move on.

"Follow me, my love," she said.

She took Thyra by the hand. She led her away from the village on the riverside, and straight out into the hot desert. Once again, it was nothing but sand as far as the eye could see. But about half a mile into it, the scenery suddenly started to change. And there, in the middle of an oasis of vivid green, stood Merit's cherished temple. As soon as she saw it, she burst into tears of relief.

"It's still there," she exclaimed, delighted at the sight. "And it's not damaged too badly either… Oh, Thyra, I am so happy to see it again! It means so much to me…"

As Merit threw her arms around her neck and gave her a joyful hug, Thyra smiled in approval. She could see people in the distance. There were a few women standing in the water-stream, washing their clothes or simply cooling off, and a bunch of kids running around playing with each other. This was obviously a popular place to come and spend some time. The energy was so different from where they had come from. All of a sudden, they were surrounded by brilliant colour and exuberant life once more. Thyra felt instantly better about it, totally invigorated, and she was immensely pleased for Merit as well.

"That's great," she replied. "Yeah, it looks good."

Merit beamed at her, eyes sparkling in excitement.

"Let me show it to you!" she exclaimed.

The temple was a tall structure made of what looked like hard desert stone. It was simple in design yet looking just the way that Thyra enjoyed her buildings: safe, solid, and strong. Two columns framed the entrance, and on the side of one, she could clearly see that chunks of rock were missing. Someone had obviously tried to hack into the stone and not been very successful at it. She grinned in satisfaction at the disappointment they would have felt. Along the façade of the building, tall figures were carved into the surface. Thyra glanced up toward the roof, blinking in blinding sunshine. Up there along the entire length, she could see a string of further expert carvings. Everywhere that she looked, mysterious signs and symbols were etched delicately into the stone.

"It's beautiful," she said.

"And wait until you see the inside," Merit promised. "You won't believe your eyes."

She was right about that. Some clever design trick actually made the temple look way bigger inside than it should have been for its outside bulk. It was quite considerably cooler in there too, which was welcome in this heat. And again, statues adorned the sides of the walls, carved out in beautiful relief from the very mass of the rock. The floor was all smooth grey stones, perfectly aligned and ingeniously laid out. Yes, this really was a beautiful space, full of calm and a sense of peace. Thyra felt instantly at ease there. She wandered through, taking it all in. If nothing else, the place mattered to her because it was important to Merit. She kept going deeper into it. At the very back of the main room stood a huge statue carved out of solid granite, which she gravitated toward as if drawn to by a powerful magnet. She recognised the woman depicted in the statue from the ones that she had already seen at the entrance.

"Who's this, Merit?" she whispered.

"Our goddess Arkedis," Merit replied. "This temple was built specifically for her. She is a bearer of light and peace, fertility and healing, life and rebirth. She is a strong protector of families, children, learners, and all who fight with a pure heart. Like you, Thyra," she added, smiling gently.

At the feet of the goddess were offerings from the people. Food and flowers mainly, and some myriad other little things that went from a simple pink desert rock to beautiful drawings. Thyra jumped in surprise when she spotted a couple of long, thin snakes slither across the floor past the altar.

"All part of the scenery," Merit reassured her. "Snakes are always welcome in Egyptian temples. They are not what they seem, you know? And I wonder…"

She let her voice trail off. She had noticed the many candles and pots of incense that burned around the place. Normally, the priests would be putting those on, and so…

"Asim!" she suddenly exclaimed.

The man who had been sitting quietly in the far corner of the room looked up from his meditative trance, eyes wide, searching to see who had called out his name. His face lit up as soon as he spotted Merit walking quickly toward him, and he immediately jumped to his feet to receive her in his arms. Tears of pure joy streamed down his face as they embraced. Thyra stood aside, watching the reunion take place with a small smile on her lips. *So, then,* she reflected. *Not everyone has been lost here, thankfully...* A string of uninterrupted foreign words followed between Merit and the man, whose head was closely shaved and also tattooed. Thyra figured he was probably in his thirties. She noticed the two heavy black lines drawn in ash across his forehead, and she decided that he must be a priest too. He was barefoot, tall with a skinny build, a friendly face, and he was dressed in a long white robe of pure cotton. Thyra looked on, pleased to witness the happiness of the two friends. And then, Merit turned toward her excitedly.

"Thyr, come here, let me introduce you," she said.

More foreign words were rapidly exchanged, and then the man pressed both hands over his own chest and bowed deeply in front of Thyra. She laughed, surprised and taken aback at the gesture.

"No need for that," she exclaimed. "Merit, who did you tell him I was?"

"Just the truth, darling," Merit replied, laughing. "Thyra, this is one of the priests I told you about before. He's the only one who made it through and survived the massacre. But he's carried on looking after the temple since that day... And he says there is an older woman who comes here every day who I used to know. I can't wait to see her!"

"That's great, Merit," Thyra declared. "Brilliant news."

All three of them walked back out of the quiet temple and emerged into the dazzling afternoon sunlight to continue their conversation. Merit and Asim were walking slightly ahead in front of Thyra, still talking animatedly in that language she did not understand, and barely stopping to take a single breath. But she rather enjoyed watching them from behind, and especially witnessing her lover's overflowing joy as they conversed. Merit kept glancing back toward her from time to time, obviously a little embarrassed to leave her lover out of the conversation but looking so happy all the same. Radiant, and as far as Thyra was concerned, breath-takingly beautiful.

"Don't worry about me, Merit," she exclaimed after a while, laughing, as her partner shot her another guilty look. "You talk to your friend; I'll go for a wander and catch up with you later, all right?"

"Wait!" Merit exclaimed.

She ran back to Thyra and landed a spirited kiss over her lips. In peripheral vision, Thyra spotted Asim's eyes widen and a delighted smile spread all across his face. His reaction made her feel good.

"Are you sure?" Merit insisted.

"Absolutely. You two have a lot to talk about."

Merit held back for just a second, looking intently into her lover's eyes.

"I love you, Thyra," she murmured.

"I love you too. Now go. Have fun."

CHAPTER THIRTY

Giggling to herself, Merit hurried to get back to her friend. Thyra watched her go, smiling, and then she did just as she had said, and wandered off toward the stream to explore a bit more of the temple grounds. It was an open and friendly place. Inquisitive children immediately came up to say hello, and a few women as well. Thyra was extremely good at making new friends, even if she had no idea of what anyone was saying to her. But genuine smiles and a few inventive gestures were normally enough to get started. When Merit came to find her a bit later on, just as the sun started to go down, she found Thyra surrounded by a small crowd of eager and enthusiastic locals, engaged in sophisticated sign language conversation, and laughing easily with them. She looked around for familiar faces within the group but could not recognise anyone. She wondered where these people really all came from, and marvelled at how much had changed in such a short space of time...

"Hey, where's your friend?" Thyra enquired when she saw that Merit was alone.

"Back inside the temple, attending to his chores. He has invited us to spend the night there and share a meal together tonight. The old woman I told you about will be there too."

"Are you nervous?"

"Yes... How do you know?"

"Merit, you're shaking," Thyra replied.

She was looking a little pale too. Concerned, Thyra quickly stood up, bid her goodbyes to the people there, and wrapped her arm around her shoulders.

"Come on," she whispered. "Let's go somewhere quiet."

They found a solitary spot at the back of the temple, on the edge of the desert. Thyra offered Merit some fresh water, and a few pieces of fruit that she had kept from their morning meal. She knelt behind her, and gently massaged the tension out of her shoulders.

"Your hands are warm," Merit murmured with a sigh of appreciation.

"Yes," Thyra chuckled. "I am using my new skills."

She felt her lover smile and relax a little more.

"Why are you so tense?" she asked her in a gentle voice.

"Because being back home is both wonderful and really hard at the same time," Merit admitted. "It's a shock to realise it, but everything has changed for me now, and it would be a big mistake to try to recreate what once was. I don't think I belong here anymore."

Thyra was silent for a little while, giving her time to adjust to the realisation.

"What is on your mind?" Merit whispered eventually.

"Nothing much, just reflecting on what you said. On our way down here this morning, I was wondering if maybe you'd want to stop and stay longer. I mean, for good."

Merit turned around wildly to face her.

"What? Without you?" she exclaimed.

"No, of course not. But if you had wanted to stay, then..."

"Would you want to stay here?" Merit insisted.

Thyra gave a light shrug. She glanced all around her, although only briefly.

"No, I don't think so. Not for very long anyway."

"And we're headed for Constantinople, right?"

"Yeah. We are," Thyra murmured uncertainly.

It was a while since she had thought about that. She could barely remember her reason for wanting to go there in the first place. *Because it's different. And hot.* She chuckled to herself at the memory of saying that to Hrorek. It felt like a lifetime ago, and in many ways, it really was. With almost a full year away from Asger now, and months of constant travel under her belt, which included several high-adrenaline and life-threatening moments, Thyra had matured and transformed into a different person than she used to be. She felt a lot more measured now, less prone to knee-jerk emotional reactions. She still carried a sword, true, but she desperately did not want to have to use it. She was learning healing techniques and how to channel her energy into more helpful, positive ways. Most precious and surprising of all to her was the fact that she had fallen so completely head over heels in love with another woman... Not a day went by that she did not think about Kari or connect with her during some of her private meditation time. She was also beginning to get to grips with the deepening realisation that they had always been on two extremely different life tracks, and this from the very beginning of their unlikely relationship. Perhaps they had only been destined to meet briefly in this way after all; to enjoy, cherish, and adopt the very best that they each had to give to the other. And then, to carry on their separate ways, in different worlds. It made Thyra's heart ache to think about it in that way; it felt too cold, too cruel even... But it sure made a lot of sense too. And maybe, just maybe, there was an even more powerful, hidden purpose linked to all this.

Remember, this is not goodbye. We will see each other again...

Thyra sighed in barely suppressed longing at the memory of her precious *Shining One*. She remembered the sparkling blue waters of her favourite lake and the adored white mountains of her childhood, standing majestically in the pure light of a clear winter's morning. Now, the really big question was, where did she really belong? For the first time since leaving the Highlands, Thyra started to wonder if Constantinople really was the correct answer.

"Thyra?" Merit was watching her with a questioning look on her face. "Is everything all right, my love?"

Thyra shook herself. The images vanished, and she quickly got over her little moment of self-doubt. Perhaps it was just being here with Merit, in this strange land of forgotten temples and unfamiliar gods which brought it all up; and that disturbing feeling of homesickness with it as well.

"Yeah," she assured. "Everything's perfect."

∞

That night, they shared a simple dinner with Asim and his old female friend, whose name was Anet. She was indeed someone that Merit had known and liked before. The woman reminded Thyra of Sigyn, the ancient Volsung healer who had looked after her once upon a time. Anet appeared so old and wrinkled that it would have been impossible to guess at her age. And the really memorable thing about her was her wide, all-encompassing toothless smile, as well as the amazing warm light that shone from her eyes whenever she looked at people. She giggled often, loudly, and she liked dispensing surprisingly spirited bear hugs, which, considering her age and diminutive size, was quite a feat.

She embraced Merit for a long, long time, and then she did the same with Thyra, who for some reason was actually extremely happy to receive such unusual treatment from a complete stranger. To her utmost surprise, she even struggled not to cry. Merit almost did shed a tear herself when she noticed the moist look in her lover's bright eyes and guessed accurately the reason for it.

"It's like having a grandmother," she murmured. "Isn't it?"

Thyra gave a slightly embarrassed chuckle. She nodded.

"Yeah, well... I never had one, but I guess it would be nice to have someone like her. I like your friend, Merit. She's got spirit all right."

And then, she leaned over for a quick kiss when no one was paying attention to them, and she laced her fingers through her lover's, bringing her a little closer to her at the same time.

"I love you," she whispered. "Thank you."

"For what?" Merit enquired, surprised.

Thyra just gave a small shrug, watching as Anet and Asim prepared the food, bickering enjoyably about which spices to add to the meat, elbowing each other playfully out of the way, grinning and laughing at regular intervals.

"For being with me," she simply said. "For this moment."

It was a simple, heartfelt statement, and something about it rang really deep. Merit wrapped her arm affectionately around her partner's neck, and she kissed her on the cheek.

"You're welcome. And likewise."

Thyra shot her a little look, and Merit got a clear sense that she needed her close that evening. Since it was her favourite place to be, she took full advantage of it. She sat next to Thyra, shoulders touching, and throughout the meal, she made sure to always maintain physical contact with her. Through little warm touches, giving her hand a squeeze from time to time, or simply leaning more heavily against her body. She knew that Thyra enjoyed this, even if she did not say it in so many words. And it made Merit feel valued and appreciated to be able to provide the kind of support that her lover required, without Thyra ever having to ask. They were becoming really good at anticipating each other's unconscious needs.

"Beer?" Merit offered, as Asim passed her a full jug.

Thyra chuckled, and she raised her cup.

"Of course," she replied.

The dinner consisted of roasted goat meat, freshly baked bread sweetened with dates, and big juicy chunks of delicious melon to finish it all off. The light beer that Asim had managed to find to accompany their meal was delicious, and it gave Thyra a nice warm buzz she had not enjoyed in a long while. They all sat around a small fire, under an immense canopy of twinkling stars. Once again, Thyra did not understand a single word of the conversation, but she could pick up on the energy being shared, and it was beautiful. She and Merit stayed up to watch the stars together, long after the evening had ended and their friends had gone to sleep. Thyra drifted off in her partner's arms that night. But it was only a short while later when she woke up again, feeling instantly alert at the certain conviction that somebody had been calling her name. Thyra glanced toward Merit, who was still fast asleep. *Not her...* She looked around, frowning in concentration. Who was there?

Thyra...

This was not an outside voice, Thyra was sure of it. She left Merit to carry on sleeping, and she walked toward the temple. She quickly climbed the few steps that led to the entrance. Something made her walk all the way to the back, and the statue of the goddess Arkedis. Thyra looked up toward her beautifully carved face.

"Are you calling me?" she murmured.

A single beam of moonlight struck the statue in exactly the right place to make it appear as if the goddess were smiling. Thyra sat down on the warm tiled floor. She took a deep breath and closed her eyes.

"Hope you don't mind if I stay here a little while…"

In the next second, she started to feel even lighter than a feather. She looked up and felt herself rising fast toward the roof of the temple. She was pretty sure that she was dreaming, but she went with it all the same, going through the roof and flying faster and faster, all over the desert, some fields, the oceans, and endless forests of green. Until she finally recognised her home. She landed in the middle of a field of wild flowers. Her heart was beating wildly inside her chest. *What is this?* There were children laughing in the background. There! Tait flew right past her. He must have been all of ten years old, and as Thyra looked on, mesmerised, she recognised herself as a child too, running after him, pretending not to be able to catch up with him. She smiled. She used to love to let Tait win. Then, she felt someone touch her hand, and she turned to find that Merit was standing there.

"Hey," Thyra murmured.

It was wonderful to see her. Merit smiled, and she took her by the hand. All of a sudden, the scenery changed again. It was winter time now, in a different location but still on Volsung land. Sparkling snow, melting ice, just the way that Thyra had described it.

"Come with me, my love," Thyra invited.

She wanted to show Merit so much more. She wanted to take her to the lake and introduce her to the forest. She wanted to love her forever in this dream of white that was only theirs to share.

"I love you," she heard herself murmur.

But then, she spotted big rolling tears falling down her partner's face.

"What's wrong?" Thyra exclaimed.

Merit was pointing at the ground. She was crying silently, and with such great pain shining in her eyes that Thyra felt afraid to look down. But she did it anyway. And she gasped. There her friend Hrorek lay, bleeding heavily on top of a blanket of pristine white snow. Thyra felt her heart almost stop at the sight. She felt death in the air. She fell to her knees in front of him.

"Hrorek," she called. "Hrorek!"

He opened his eyes. Raised his hand toward her face.

"Thyra," he whispered. "Please... I need you back..."

THYRA'S PROMISE

NATALIE DEBRABANDERE

PART THREE: THE PROMISE

CHAPTER THIRTY-ONE

-Scotland -

Thyra stood watching the valley, smiling faintly. *I am home, at last...*

Long ribbons of early-morning mist stretched out across the land and above the dark-green forest, clinging to the top of some of the higher trees. The mountains were still lost in fog but would not be for very much longer. Already, Thyra could see tiny rays of autumn sunshine beginning to pierce through the clouds. She spotted an eagle flying majestically above the mist. Somewhere off to the side, she recognised the typical chuckling call of a red grouse looking for his mate. The rugged, dramatic mountain landscape was beautiful to observe, as was the local wildlife. And speaking of which... Thyra glanced back over her shoulder, her smile widening ever so slightly at the sight of Merit, who was still fast asleep, lost under a mountain of furs. It was just after dawn on their fifth day back in Scotland, and the temperature was quite comfortable for mid-autumn. Thyra thought it was actually really mild for the time of year, even though Merit was already wrapped up in everything she had.

The colder temperature here, coming from the Saharan climate that she was used to was quite an adjustment for her. But she enjoyed it all, and also wearing the new warmer clothes that she had acquired along the way. She was incredibly excited when Thyra told her that it would get much colder eventually, and as she described in great detail and much enthusiasm every kind of snow, ice, freezing fog, blizzard, and typical storm conditions that they were likely to face over the coming winter months.

"I can't wait to see the snow, Thyr," Merit declared. "It will be a first time for me, you know!"

It was an awesome pleasure to witness her going through her new experiences with such eagerness and delight. Thyra herself was feeling a mixture of apprehension and elation at being back home. After all, she had once firmly believed that she would never see the Highlands again... Fortunately, thanks to Merit's reassuring presence and her constant, unwavering support, happiness at being there once more really did prevail. Thyra suspected that she would be able to relax even more completely as soon as she was reunited with Hrorek. If the weather held, with any luck, it would be sometime that very afternoon. She was definitely excited about that. She turned around and walked back to check on the warming fire that she had started for Merit when she had first got up. She threw another log on it and went to lie down next to her. As soon as she did, her lover turned over and burrowed into her arms.

"Thyr..." she murmured.

"Yeah. Are you okay?"

"Now, yes," Merit smiled, with her eyes still closed.

Thyra gave a light chuckle. How she loved this wonderful woman... She drew the fur cover a little tighter around Merit's body and kissed the top of her head. She lay back against her and closed her eyes.

"Five more minutes?" Merit mumbled in a sleepy voice.

"Of course," Thyra replied. "There is no rush."

It had been a few weeks of intense travelling for the both of them. And it had all started in Egypt, that very night after their wonderful dinner with Asim and Anet. Thyra stumbled out of the temple in a kind of daze after the strange episode in front of the statue. She went straight to Merit to tell her all about it. She woke her up and described to her what she had seen in her dream, speaking fast and a little haltingly. Merit could tell that she was quite disturbed by it, and still very much lost in the event.

"Why did you go inside the temple?" she enquired softly.

Thyra reflected on it and gave a light shrug.

"I just thought I heard something. It woke me up. Like my name being called, although it also sounded like it was coming out of my own head... Like a voice, but not really. Anyway, I was drawn to the temple then."

Merit looked like this made perfect sense to her, and as if it was something that she had heard explained about a hundred times before. It certainly helped Thyra to feel a little bit calmer about the whole thing.

"I sat in front of the statue," she explained. "I was just going to be quiet within myself and meditate for a while. But then, I think I fell asleep. I'm not sure. Once again, what happened next didn't feel like just a dream. It was like I really did leave my body. The sensation was incredible! I felt as light as a feather... I had perfect vision, and I could hear really well too. I saw kids running, having fun. I realised that it was me and Tait when we were young."

Thyra shook her head in absolute wonder.

"And then, all of a sudden, I was in a different place," she said, "and you were there too, Merit. I was standing..."

249

"You were standing next to me, holding my hand. And you wanted me to come with you," Merit interrupted, eyes a little unfocused, as she connected with her own memory of the same event. "It was cold. There was a lot of snow on the ground, and your friend was lying there, injured. Hrorek? I think Hrorek was his name. I watched you go over to him. He reached out for you…"

Thyra stared at her lover, eyes wide and in total shock.

"How do you know all this?" she exclaimed, astonished.

It was then that Merit explained to her what she had meant by having an *'experience'* at the temple. Shared dreams, out-of-body experiences, lucid dreaming, precognitive flashes, and all kinds of weird and wonderful phenomena were pretty common-place there.

"Sometimes, things happen to people inside the temple that cannot really be explained. Like you feeling as if you travelled outside of your body; how you saw yourself and your brother as children; and then, when you jumped to a time much later on and which feels a lot more current…"

"Was it the future I went to?" Thyra exclaimed in sudden alarm. "When I saw Hrorek, do you think it was a premonition of things to come?"

"Not exactly," Merit replied in a reassuring tone. "Come on, let's go and find Asim. He is more experienced than I am, and I would like to hear his view."

They consulted with him in the privacy of his own room. It was full of snakes in there, but Thyra barely paid any attention to her surroundings this time. She was beside herself with worry about Hrorek, but like Merit, the priest was keen to reassure her.

"Asim says you had the experience of a different time in a possible future," Merit translated for her. "*'Possible'* but not *'inevitable'*. Do you understand?"

"No! What in the world does that mean?" Thyra enquired. She was feeling lost and upset about the dream.

"It means that the future is not set in stone, my love," Merit replied. "The world doesn't look very fluid from our physical perspective, I know; but in fact, it is a lot more malleable than we realise. Just like when you helped me with my insect bite, just with the power of your intent, Thyr."

Thyra still felt confused and only slightly reassured by the explanation.

"So, what you're saying is that what I saw in my dream is not necessarily going to come to pass," she replied.

Merit nodded in agreement.

"But then, why did I see it?" Thyra insisted, following her initial line of reasoning. "And if it is something bad and it can be changed... How would I do that?"

There was no answer to this, and Thyra shook her head in frustration. What was the point of knowing anything, then? And could she even trust any of her experience to be meaningful? Maybe she had simply enjoyed too much beer the night before... She sighed again. Yes, it would have been nice to blame Asim's silky smooth beverage for it, call the event a hallucination, and forget all about it. But unfortunately, Thyra suspected that she would only be kidding herself if she did.

"Hrorek said he needed me back," she reflected. "And you shared the same experience in your dream, Merit. What is that all about? And does it make it more likely to happen?"

Thyra looked anxiously to Asim whilst Merit translated her words to him once again. The man's expression softened as he observed the two women waiting expectantly in front of him. There was something very special about the combination of their individual energies. He spoke only a few short, intense sentences in response.

"Asim thinks we are lucky to be able to meet in our dreams like this," Merit translated. "Not everyone can do it. Our relationship is obviously meant to be, and perhaps even on some levels that we are not aware of…"

"I am sure that's the case," Thyra interrupted. "But what else can he tell us?"

"As for the rest of it," Merit finished, "he says that you should not worry too much about the meaning of your experience. We cannot control what will happen in the future, except for living our lives as authentically as possible in the present moment. If we need to know more, this will be revealed to us in due time, as and when we need it."

Thyra remained silent.

"I'm sorry, Thyr," Merit murmured. "I wish I could tell you more. But I don't know, and this is as much as Asim can really explain to us…"

Thyra felt grateful for the man's advice. She asked Merit to tell him so, and to thank him for her. She gave him a hug and a big smile, and he looked happy in return. But Thyra was also bitterly disappointed with the lack of definitive answers he could offer her. She went to sit out in the desert on her own for a while, just to calm down and reflect on a few things. Meanwhile, Merit started to pack up their few belongings. She was pretty sure of what Thyra's decision would be when she came back to her, and she was right about it. Thyra wanted to go straight home. She also had one single burning question for her partner.

"What about you, Merit?" she asked.

"Me?" Merit simply smiled. "I'll go where you go, Thyr."

Thyra was instantly unhappy with that statement, and it showed. She shook her head impatiently. This was no light matter as far as she was concerned, and yet, Merit had answered as if it were so easy.

"Look, this is not just up to me, all right?" she said.

"Of course not," Merit agreed. "I know that."

"I want you to be happy about where we're going," Thyra insisted. "Not to just follow me around because that's what I've decided. It has to be a mutual choice... For everything between us both. So, how do you really feel about travelling back home with me?"

She knew that Merit was not the type of woman to hold back and just tell her what she wanted to hear. But their relationship mattered too much to her for Thyra to let this go unchecked. Merit was quick to put her mind at rest.

"I feel wonderful about going home with you, Thyr," she reassured her gently. "And I do want our relationship to be one of shared decisions, you're right. The fact is that you have told me so much about your land, I would really love to see it now. I would be delighted to meet your friends. And those mountains of which you speak sound incredibly beautiful too..."

"They are," Thyra murmured with a brief, eager smile.

Merit could see how much she suddenly ached to go back.

"All right, my love, that is settled then," she decided. "Since we've been here, I know you've been asking yourself a lot of questions about where we're going, and your own path in life. Maybe Constantinople was not the end goal for you after all."

"Well, I don't know about that," Thyra replied with another worried shake of the head. "I don't like not finishing the things that I started."

"Sometimes, it is good to be flexible though, and recognise when a change of direction is required," Merit continued. "It doesn't mean you are giving up... But perhaps going east was only the motivation that you required at the time. Maybe you received what you needed from taking that original action, and now, it may be time to reassess your next steps."

Thyra raised a thoughtful eyebrow.

"It is true I would never have found you otherwise," she reflected in a quiet, almost solemn voice. "Perhaps that was always the true purpose in the end, even though I could not have known that at the time…"

Merit nodded, and Thyra flashed her a brilliant grin. She looked incredibly relieved all of a sudden, and like a massive burden had been lifted off her shoulders.

"I feel so much better. Thanks, Merit, for your wise words. I am excited about going home with you."

And so, once the decision was made to go, everything went really quickly. All in all, the trip back to Scotland only took them five weeks. Most of that time was spent at sea, in spite of Thyra's resolve to never set foot on board a ship again. But from Egypt, it really was the quickest and cheapest way to go. They sailed across the Mediterranean, through the Straits of Gibraltar, and straight up the deepest Atlantic Ocean to land right onto the shores of western Scotland. And now, Thyra allowed herself to smile in pure pleasure once again, as Merit snuggled deeper into her arms for added body heat.

"Tonight, we'll sleep in a comfortable bed, inside a warm house, and with a solid roof over our head," she promised. "And I will make you the very best…"

Thyra had been about to describe what she would cook for her lover that night. She was planning on making a selection of her all-time childhood favourites, a real feast of flavours, washed down with some of Hrorek's best quality mead; when a piercing scream suddenly echoed through the air, startling them both quite badly. It turned out that Thyra had lost none of her warrior instincts. She was instantly on her feet and reaching for her sword.

"Stay here," she instructed. "I'll be right back."

And before Merit could even reply, she jumped over the fire and disappeared through the forest. Merit watched her vanish with her mouth wide open in surprise. But she was only stunned by this high-class disappearing act for a second. She threw the covers off her legs, and instantly jumped to her feet to follow. She was not the type to stay behind and wait obediently whilst her lover was off tackling unknown dangers on her own. *She should know better by now…* she reflected, shaking her head in disbelief. She reached for her own knife, slid it through her belt, and bolted after Thyra.

CHAPTER THIRTY-TWO

The kid looked only about ten, if that, and Thyra spotted him long before he was even aware of her presence. He had slipped and fallen down into a steep ravine, and he was struggling to climb out of it. Going at it in the manner that he was, all frantic and uncoordinated, he was much more likely to fall the rest of the way than to get himself out of trouble any time soon. She suspected he was the source of the terrified scream they had heard. It would be quite scary indeed to find yourself suddenly airborne and falling through the air the way he must have done. Thyra hooked her feet onto a nearby tree root for support. She laid herself onto her stomach, leaned as far as she could into the deep gulley, and threw out her hand.

"Here, grab on to me," she ordered.

He looked up, startled out of his skin it seemed at the sound of her voice so near. He really had not seen or heard her coming. Thyra was surprised at the look of pure fear she saw instantly flash through his eyes when he spotted her. She leaned forward a little more and shot him a reassuring smile.

"Hey, it's okay. Take my hand, I'll get you out."

She saw his gaze light up over her necklace.

"Volsung?" he exclaimed.

Thyra frowned at the unexpected question. *Damn it, kid,* she thought in irritation. *Haven't got time to establish credentials here...* He was standing on top of two unstable boulders which were typically covered in moss and wet leaves. Below him, there was nothing but three hundred feet of wide open air. If he slipped now, he would fall to his death.

"Yes, Volsung," she hissed. "Now come on, grab my hand!"

He did it then, launching himself up toward her and only just managing to reach. Thyra got a firm hold of his wrist, grabbed onto the rest of his small body, and pulled him up easily. The second he was on top, and safe, he scrambled to his feet and tried to run away from her. But she had kind of expected he would. She held onto the leg of his trousers and gave it a sharp yank, bringing him down in the process. The kid had more fight in him than she had anticipated though, and she barely avoided getting kicked in the mouth when he struggled.

"Wait," she muttered. "Wait, I just want to talk to you."

"They're after me," he panted. "They're close! Let me go!"

Thyra tightened her grip on him. He had obviously hurt his shoulder in the fall, because he instantly winced in pain when she did that, and tears came to his eyes.

"Ow! Let go!"

"Look, kid, I really don't want to hurt you, okay?" she insisted. "And I can help with your shoulder too. Now, stop fighting me for a bloody second, will you? It'll hurt less."

The more he struggled, the more curious she became about him, and about who he was so anxious to escape. They were close to Volsung territory now, and this should have been a safe enough area. She gave him a closer look. He had short blond hair and piercing blue eyes that reminded her a little bit of Tait. His clothes were dirty and torn, as if he had been running through the forest for a while. And he looked so scared...

"Who is after you?" she asked.

Now, he started to cry for good.

"Asger," he said in a murmur. "Bjarke."

Thyra froze in place and her entire body went rigid. She swallowed thickly, and a wave of dizziness suddenly washed over her. As the blood drained from her face, she tried hard to regain control. No, she must have heard him wrong... She had to have heard him wrong.

"What did you say?" she murmured.

But the kid had noticed her moment of hesitation, and he darted to the side out of her reach. In a flash, he was off again. Although he did not go very far this time either, because when he looked up, he found another woman standing in front of him, blocking his way. Merit looked over the kid's head toward her partner.

"Thyra? Everything okay?" she asked.

Instinctively, she reached out a hand to stop the boy from scampering off into the woods. He did not struggle against her as hard as he had done against Thyra, simply because she did not look like such a fighter. He stared at her uncertainly.

"Hi," Merit smiled, before returning her gaze to Thyra.

She noticed that her lover was extremely pale, as she knelt in front of the child once again and rested both hands over his shoulders to command his complete attention. She was careful not to hurt him, and he seemed to relax a little bit more. Merit's presence certainly helped.

"What's your name?" Thyra asked him.

"Erik."

"All right. Who did you say is after you?"

"Bjarke!" the child repeated, throwing a fearful look over his shoulder at the same time. "I ran into him and a few of his men earlier. They saw me. I'm sure they're after me."

"Big, blue eyes, red beard? That Bjarke?" Thyra insisted.

"Yes. Bjarke of Asger," he confirmed.

Thyra stared into his eyes as she let out a slow exhale. The kid was not lying, and the fear in his expression was genuine. This piece of bad news felt like a punch to the stomach to Thyra. She got to her feet and met Merit's gaze. She gave a single shake of the head. Merit instantly stepped forward to rest a reassuring hand over her arm.

"It's all right," she murmured. "Are you okay?"

"Yeah." Thyra shrugged. "Yeah, fine. I just... I just..."

She shook her head again and brushed cold sweat off her forehead with the back of her hand. *Bjarke is alive...* She took a few deep breaths to calm her pounding heart, and tried to figure out how it could be... And how she of all people could not know this! But life had been so chaotic back then, she reflected, right after Kari's death. And Hrorek had been convinced that Bjarke was gone for good, too. It was easier to go with that idea than to believe that he was still out there. Thyra had wanted him dead so badly then. Once again, she had chosen to see only what she wanted to see. And for the four months that she was there with the Volsung, helping to rebuild their village, there had been no word of Bjarke either. So, it was easy. She had not travelled over the mountain to the Asger village. She had not been to check on any of the people there, or even to see her father. Only just now did Thyra feel the true horror of this. It hit her hard. *How could I not go back to see my own father...?* All of a sudden, she realised the insanity of it all. She had been in a crazy state of mind at that time. In a daze, not thinking straight, and struggling to come to terms with everything that had happened... And then, she had just left it all behind, hopped on a boat, and disappeared. Thyra gave a sharp, frustrated exhale at the thought of it. Yes. She had been quite mad...

"Hey," Merit insisted, still worried.

Thyra gave her a little stronger smile.

"I'm all right," she assured. "Don't worry."

To start beating herself up for what she had done or failed to do would get her nowhere. She had acted in the best way she could with what she had. She could not judge or condemn the woman that she had been then, just hope that she could do much better now. She was convinced that she would. So, it was fine. *Keep your head up and keep going.* Thyra brushed Merit's fingers with her own. She looked at her again, anchored herself in those deep black eyes.

"Thanks," she murmured.

"Thyra, are you sure that you're all right?"

"Yes. But we have to get back to camp now, kill the fire, and get a move on. If Bjarke is around here, we cannot afford to get caught out in the open."

Merit nodded, instantly ready to go. It was one of the things Thyra loved about her. Merit was so kind and gentle. And yet, underneath that soft exterior she was as strong, brave, and fearless as a hundred warriors put together. And she thought like one, too.

"Already took care of the fire, just in case," she declared.

Thyra shot her a warm, approving look.

"Good job, partner," she said.

Merit appreciated her saying that. She loved being Thyra's friend, and her lover. She relished being her partner in all things even more. And she realised what a nasty shock the sudden discovery that her brother was still alive must have been. She could see it in her eyes, how shaken she really was. Thyra had told her about Bjarke in great detail, and Merit was not looking forward to an encounter with the man. Indeed, it was time to go, and quickly too. Thyra turned to their young companion.

"You Volsung, kid?" she asked.

"Yes. I am Chief Hrorek's son."

Once more, Thyra did a swift double take. That Hrorek was now commander-in-chief of his people was no surprise. But she raised an ironic eyebrow at the second part of the statement.

"Hrorek doesn't have a son."

The boy instantly flushed bright red.

"Adopted son," he murmured.

Not for the first time that morning, Thyra wondered how many more surprises awaited her along the way. She had not even been gone a full year, yet so much seemed to have changed.

"Have you heard of *The Shining One*?" she asked him.

"Yes." He shrugged. "Sure, I have."

Thyra nodded, smiling faintly at the indignation she could hear in his voice. She was not doing very well with this kid so far, she reflected. Well, apart from having pulled him out of a life-threatening situation, of course. But perhaps she needed to give him a little something more that would ensure he really understood who she was, and that he could trust her absolutely completely. She pointed to the torc around her neck.

"Well, *The Shining One*," she told him, "she gave me this."

This obviously gave him pause, as it would to any Volsung who had heard the story of the legendary Kari Sturlusson. Erik stared at the shiny gold necklace with massive interest. His eyes went from it back to Thyra's face a few times, eagerly assessing her. She smiled. She could almost see the cogs spinning wildly inside his head, as he started to put two and two together and make sense of the story.

"Your name's Thyra?" he wondered.

"That's right. Formerly of Asger."

His eyes suddenly grew wide, but not from fear.

"Thyra!" he exclaimed. "You're her! You came back!"

Merit chuckled at the way that his expression suddenly turned from suspicious and painfully awkward to openly fascinated and delighted.

"That's right," she confirmed. "This is *Her*. I am Merit."

Erik appeared fully recovered from his earlier mishap now, and full of curiosity about the two women. They quickly walked with him back to their small camp, collected their things, and were on their way again in under two minutes.

"Stick with us," Thyra invited. "You'll be safer."

"I know!" he exclaimed. "I heard what a great warrior you are!"

Thyra exchanged a quick, loaded look with Merit. And then, something happened at that particular moment. It felt as if two important yet separate pieces of herself suddenly collided, embraced, and integrated. Thyra felt totally whole for the first time in her life. It was both a mental and physical event, and the surge of energy in her body made her feel extremely warm. It was like an inner power source had been turned on. The young, emotional, impulsive warrior that she used to be, and the much wiser, grounded, compassionate woman she had become finally merged into one. Merit was attuned to shifts of this kind, and she noticed it happen when it did. It was a subtle thing, a particular variation in the energy that surrounded her lover. Merit detected renewed strength and confidence flowing through her, two things that Thyra always had in abundance, but now, it was as if everything negative that she had also carried before was gone. The things that had stood in her way, emotions like hurt, guilt, and even remaining anger suddenly were no more. Thyra stood straighter, taller. Her face was more relaxed. It was as if her light finally shone true and bright for the first time, just as it was always meant to be, with absolutely nothing to dim its power.

"You know what?"

"What?"

"I'm feeling kind of good," Thyra murmured.

Merit squeezed her hand. She gave her a loving look.

"Yes," she agreed. "I can see that. Good for you, Thyr."

And she grinned at the nonchalant way that Thyra swiped the boy's hand off the side of her belt when he attempted to touch her sword.

"Not a toy, kid," she informed him.

"I've never seen one like that before."

"Uh-uh," Thyra said.

She was walking fast, intent on reaching the Volsung settlement as quickly as possible, and not paying much attention to him. The boy trotted alongside her, his eyes barely leaving her face for even a second. He had heard so many stories about the mysterious Thyra from his dad and some of the warriors; he knew she had been *The Shining One*'s best friend, and Hrorek's as well... He had heard how hard and relentless she was on the battlefield. For Erik, now seeing Thyra in the flesh was a little bit as if the legendary god Odin had suddenly descended from the skies and introduced himself to him.

"My dad told me you're a brilliant fighter," he blurted out enthusiastically. "And that you can handle a weapon almost as well as he does."

It could have been just a simple coincidence when Thyra suddenly stumbled over a hidden root in the ground at that particular instant, and almost went flying, but Merit did not think so somehow. She suppressed a chuckle at her unconscious reaction. Thyra shot her an amused grin in return. She raised an eyebrow. *Almost as well, hey...*

"That's right, Erik," she drawled. "Almost, but not quite."

CHAPTER THIRTY-THREE

After finding out that Bjarke was still alive, the second sign that not everything was going so well was when they made it closer to the Volsung camp, and instantly encountered heavily armed, highly-alert warriors guarding the area. But Thyra recognised most of the men amongst them, and she immediately called out a greeting. They came running. Merit was pleased to notice how happy and excited they all appeared to see Thyra. The adopted Volsung woman was greeted warmly by everyone they encountered, and a feeling of joyful celebration could soon be felt in the air. Their small group was let through, and invited to proceed to the village for food, drink, and some rest. Erik was beaming as he led them on, marching proudly in front of them. Clearly, he was taking full credit for bringing Thyra home. Merit was amused to see the kid act so possessive of her partner, recognising a strong case of hero worship in the making. And she laughed when a woman who turned out to be his mother came running as soon as they entered the settlement, to give her boy a swift slap on the backside.

"Erik, where on earth have you been!" she exclaimed. "I told you to stay in camp, didn't I? How many times do I have to say it? I've been looking all over for you!"

It was fair to say that she was not impressed with his little runaway stunt. And as Thyra and Merit stood watching the scene, waiting for the woman to turn her attention to them, a strong male voice suddenly echoed behind their back.

"What are you doing here, Viking?"

Merit tensed, instantly worried at the belligerent tone she could pick up in the man's voice. Thyra went still. She pursed her lips and slowly turned around to face the tall, threatening-looking warrior. He seemed to have appeared out of nowhere, and now he stood watching them both with an angry look on his face. Powerful arms crossed over his broad, solid chest. He had a serious, focused, intense look in his clear blue eyes. And he was much bigger than Thyra; all muscle, hard and unyielding, clearly not a man to be messed with or taken lightly. Thyra returned his gaze, her own face impassive and not betraying any emotion. Her body language sent him a message that was loud, clear, and simple to understand though. If he was after a fight, she would be more than happy to give him one. She was not scared of him. He seemed to recognise that, and the hint of challenge shining in her eyes. He nodded sharply toward her.

"What do you want?" he muttered.

Thyra gave a small shrug that made Merit hesitate and look back at the man again. Was there something else going on here between these two?

"Well. Some food and a cup of mead wouldn't go amiss," Thyra muttered. "Think you can manage that, warrior?"

He did not react immediately, and by now, Merit was really intrigued. This was such a strange thing for her lover to say... Thyra continued to stare easily back at the man. And after a couple more seconds, it eventually became too much for Hrorek, who could no longer maintain a straight face no matter how much he tried. His mouth twitched. Thyra grinned in victory.

"Gotcha," she said.

Hrorek's eyes sparkled in pure joy at the cheeky comment, and he burst out laughing out loud. He instantly stepped forward, slapped a pair of rough hands over her shoulders, and pulled her into his arms for a powerful hug.

"Thyra, it's good to see you, my friend!" he exclaimed.

"You too, Hrorek," Thyra replied, smiling widely.

Merit finally relaxed for good this time, and she breathed a sigh of relief. So, this was the man her lover had told her so much about then. Thyra's best friend, her ally, and the protector who had kept her going through all the worst of times. Merit liked him instantly. And as the two friends continued to embrace, she stood watching them both with a brilliant smile across her face. Indeed, this was a beautiful sight to behold, and a wonderful moment to be able to witness.

"I really missed you," Thyra murmured, too low for anyone else to hear. "I missed you a hell of a lot, you know?"

Hrorek tightened his grip on her shoulder.

"Me too," he whispered. "You have no idea."

He finally let her go and pulled back to take a good long look at her. A slow grin appeared over his lips as he did so. She had changed. Physically, she looked even stronger than before, a lot more relaxed, and extremely confident with it too. There was definitely something else as well, something which used to be there when Kari was alive, but instantly disappeared the night she transitioned. Hrorek stood watching Thyra for a moment longer, thoughtfully, trying to figure it out. And then, he noticed Merit standing there. He was instantly taken aback by her looks, her raw beauty, and the strong aura of love and protectiveness that emanated from her as she gazed at Thyra. Suddenly, it all made sense to him.

"Introduce me to your mate, warrior," he smiled.

Thyra's eyes softened as she turned back to Merit. She held out her hand to her and pulled her close against her own body. This was an awesome moment for her. These two were the people she loved the most in the entire world, and at long last, they were all finally standing in the same place together.

"Hrorek, this is my partner," she explained. "Her name is Merit."

Merit held out her hand to him, but Hrorek shook his head, gave a soft chuckle, and pulled her into the same sort of hug he had just given to Thyra.

"Merit, welcome to my Volsung family," he told her.

There was so much genuine, heartfelt emotion in his voice when he said this that Merit suddenly felt a lump form in her throat. She pulled back, but she held onto his hands for a moment longer. She flashed him a fierce, brilliant smile.

"Thank you, Hrorek," she replied. "Thyra told me a lot of great things about you. She loves you dearly, and it is wonderful to finally meet you."

He returned her smile, looking happy.

"Thanks, Merit, for looking after my friend."

Thyra wrapped a strong arm around her lover's shoulders.

"What about you, Hrorek?" she asked.

Hrorek introduced them to his wife, Freydis. She was a beautiful woman with long flowing black hair, clear green eyes, and a confident, straightforward attitude about her which Thyra appreciated from the start. She also liked to see the light in her eyes when Freydis looked at Hrorek. It was obvious that she was deeply in love with him, and so was he.

"Freydis' husband was killed in the village attack that day," Hrorek murmured to Thyra as they all walked back toward his house. "We got together shortly after you left. Life is good with her, and with Erik."

"That's wonderful, Hrorek," Thyra approved. "He seems like a great kid, and I am glad you found Freydis too. Her eyes shine when she looks at you."

Hrorek's face broke into a huge smile.

"Yes. She's the one for me."

"And hey, you're Chief now, too?"

He nodded with a small chuckle.

"I never considered myself commander material, you know that," he admitted. "I was quite happy doing what I was doing before. But it sort of happened quite naturally over time, and I think I am doing all right with it now."

He stopped and turned to face her.

"Thyra, listen. I need to tell you something…"

"That's all right, I already know," she interrupted. "Erik was running from Bjarke when Merit and I came upon him. I couldn't believe it at first when he said that… But I guess that's true, uh?"

"Yeah. I'm afraid so."

"What happened then? What's been going on here, Hrorek? How bad has it been?"

Thyra was full of burning, urgent questions, and for the next two and a half hours, they all sat together in the small house that Hrorek and Freydis shared together. Freydis built a warm fire. Hrorek distributed food around the table, and all the best mead he had to share. They caught up on each other's lives over the past few months, and the current situation at home.

"It all started happening early summer," Hrorek explained. "We heard reports of clans rising up against each other in the south. Then it all went quiet again. But one day, the news came through that the Asger clan had re-formed, again under your brother's command."

Thyra shook her head in dismay.

"Where was he all that time?" she asked. "Do you know?"

"Hiding somewhere, lying low and licking his wounds, I suppose. The Asger suffered heavy casualties, just like we did. Thyra, your father is dead, too. I'm sorry…"

Thyra stared into the fire in silence for a few minutes, as Merit gently rubbed her hand over her thigh under the table in a soothing gesture. She was feeling strangely empty. Not tired, not sad; but deeply annoyed, frustrated, and thoroughly fed-up with the whole situation. It was coming up to a year now since everything had exploded into violence and war, and in so many ways, nothing had changed at all. They were back to square one once again.

"Asger's been moving around a lot the last few weeks. With his men, he has been trying to organise the warring clans into a bigger fighting force. Back to his old tricks, I suppose. So far, that's all it's been," Hrorek said, glancing at Thyra.

"So far?" she repeated darkly.

"Yeah. They've been bickering amongst themselves about territory shares, strategy, and overall command mostly. Bjarke's not been making any real progress in the direction he wants."

"Maybe not, but all the same, he's getting bolder, isn't he?" Thyra pointed out. "He's been making incursions into Volsung land, right? Your own son was running from him when Merit and I found him."

Hrorek gave a heavy sigh at the reminder.

"That's fairly new behaviour, actually, but you're right," he admitted. "Bjarke is indeed getting bolder…"

"And that is never a good sign," Thyra interrupted.

"I agree with you. And you know, he is clever with it too. He does not normally show his face around here. Otherwise, it would be much easier for one of us to take him out and put an end to this whole charade."

Merit shivered at the fierceness of his words. She leaned against Thyra for added warmth and reassurance. She was grateful when her partner held her a little closer.

"All the same," Hrorek continued, "our men have been busy fighting small bands of isolated warriors over the summer. Things are heating up between rival Viking clans in the area. It's not just Bjarke, you know?"

Thyra just shrugged impatiently. Fighting between Viking clans was nothing new. She had grown up in that world of constant threat and violence. She knew. But it did not mean that she had to be happy about it now, and act like it was something normal to expect.

"We know what Bjarke is doing," Hrorek added. "He'll manage to get the groups he wants united eventually, either by choice or violence. And once he's done that, he'll come after us once again. Seems there is no way out of this vicious circle, Thyra."

He stood up to throw more wood onto the fire. He paused to lay a gentle kiss over his wife's forehead. Thyra saw the tender way that she clasped his hand in return, and the burning look in her eyes when she smiled at him. Again, she was glad for her friend that he had found someone to love him in this way, just as she had Merit.

"Anyway," Hrorek concluded. "This is where we are."

He sat himself back down rather heavily, locked eyes with Thyra, and gave a frustrated shake of the head. He reached for the bottle of mead and refreshed all their drinks.

"We are going to have to fight," he declared. "There is no other choice to be made. Not anymore, and certainly not where Bjarke is concerned."

Thyra remained silent for a short while after this. It looked as if Hrorek did not expect a specific answer from her anyway.

She turned to her partner instead and looked into her eyes. She observed the beautiful tiny sparks of lights that reflected in her dark pupils from the fire.

"How are you doing?" she murmured.

"Oh... I'm fine," Merit replied with a smile.

She said that so easily and casually, but Thyra spotted the worried look in her eyes that she was trying really hard to hide. She noticed how tightly Merit was holding onto her hand. She felt the tension in her body.

"Hey," she whispered. "It's going to be okay, I promise."

Merit gave her a quick nod, and even flashed her another bravely confident grin. In response, Thyra felt a rush of love and affection toward her, and a huge amount of admiration as well. It was Merit's turn to be far from home now, far away from her own world and all that she knew and made sense to her. She had dropped absolutely everything to travel with her partner to a strange and foreign land. Thyra did not take her commitment lightly, even though she knew that Merit loved her. But this was not the point. Everything must look threatening to her here, she realised, especially all this talk of war and violence. Thyra hated to plunge her into such a cold, dark world. At the same time, she realised that Merit would never abandon her. She would stay with her and stand by her side always, no matter what the dangers involved. Thyra was acutely aware of the fact that it was her job to keep her partner safe and protected. She had failed before. Now, there was no way she was going to allow that to happen, or for Merit to get hurt. She brushed a gentle kiss of reassurance over her lips. She smiled at her again. She was glad when Merit finally started to relax.

"Don't worry," Thyra murmured. "There is another way."

CHAPTER THIRTY-FOUR

They argued about it late into the night. Hrorek was convinced that Thyra's idea would never work, and that she was wasting her time.

"Kari tried it, and it's hopeless," he pointed out.

"No, it isn't," Thyra insisted calmly. "And Kari did not just try it, she made it work. That's why she was known all over the land as *The Shining One*. Her strength came not from fighting, but from refusing to engage in violence. People respected her for that. I know most of them envied her as well."

Hrorek shook his head. He did not look happy.

"You were her second-in-command," Thyra reminded him gently. "You were her friend, and you knew her for far longer than I did. You were on board with her approach before.... Why are you so reluctant to adopt it once more?"

She watched him as he stood by the side of the fire, staring pensively into the flames with the occasional ghost of a smile crossing his features. After a while, she went to rest a hand over his shoulder.

"Talk to me," she murmured.

He glanced at her and gave a small sigh.

"I'm reluctant," he finally admitted, "because of only one thing."

"What?" she asked impatiently.

He grinned at the eager look on her face.

"Me," he shrugged. "I don't think I'm strong enough to do this."

Thyra frowned in disbelief, and he laughed again at her expression. Before then, Hrorek had liked her immensely. And now, he did so even more because she also reminded him increasingly of Kari. Strong, intense, laser-focused. Certainly not willing to suffer fools gladly, and yet with an unshakable faith in the good that was to be found in all people. Not wanting to consider the possibility of failure for even one second, and totally confident in her abilities, and in his own as well.

"But I know how excruciatingly hard it is to achieve what Kari did, Thyra," he explained. "I saw how difficult it can be to forge and maintain those peaceful alliances. And after her death... Well. Everything just fell apart."

Thyra gave a light shrug.

"I'm not afraid of hard work," she declared. "And I want to uphold her legacy. So, will you help me?"

He flashed her a brief smile and returned his eyes to the fire. His heart was beating a little faster all of a sudden. Listening to Thyra speak in this way reminded him of many conversations he had shared with Kari. She had asked him once if he would help her achieve her vision of a peaceful Viking world. Alone, it would have felt to him like a mad dream, but with her, it all became an exciting goal. Now, once again, he could feel the familiar longing in his heart to do more; to be different; to create a better world for his children. He chuckled.

"Ah, Thyra," he murmured. "She would be proud of you."

Thyra instinctively touched her fingers to her torc.

"I hope so, although I am not doing this just for her, you know," she reflected. "This feels right to me as well. I told Kari that I would be the strongest broken link. I will not perpetuate hatred and violence. This ends here."

Hrorek raised a careful eyebrow.

"And that means with your brother too?"

"I don't feel any hatred toward Bjarke," Thyra replied. "Not anymore. When I found out that he was still alive, I was shocked and disappointed, that's true. But I guess that's mainly because I realised what it meant. That we were not safe. I will work on changing that. Kari told me once that I have to be the change I want to see in the world. So, it's up to me to create my own peace. As for Bjarke, I really do not feel any particular emotion toward him anymore. I feel nothing, in fact. It's all just gone."

Hrorek could see that she was speaking the truth. She stood in front of him, blue eyes sparkling in the light of the fire, and with a look of absolute determination on her face.

"Will you help me?" she repeated.

Hrorek nodded slowly. He took a deep breath.

"Yes," he promised. "I will stand by your side, Thyra."

∞

Over the weeks that followed, they travelled incessantly, criss-crossing the land to go speak to dozens and dozens of separate clans. Up and over the mountains, close down by the sea, or along the shores of magnificent lakes. The Volsung contingent travelled light and as a small group. It was just Thyra, Merit, Hrorek, and three of his best warriors. The days were short and bitterly cold, and the going was tough at this time of year. But they had good horses, and they were highly motivated.

"It's the perfect time to do this," Thyra promised. "I can feel it."

Everywhere they stopped, she pleaded her case for peace. The first time that Hrorek heard her speak, he was astounded and delighted to discover how good she was. It was like she had been born for this very purpose. Thyra was compelling. She was persuasive without sounding pushy, and convincing without appearing unreliable. She was able to quickly find common ground with the people that she wanted to recruit to her cause, and make fast, yet deep, meaningful connections with them. She was clever, witty; audacious, and even brash when she needed to be. She was not afraid to ask the hard questions and trigger emotional reactions in the people she talked to. She made them angry sometimes. She was relentless. But she spoke from a rock-solid ground of tremendous love and compassion. She talked about everything and everyone she had lost to violence and war. She shared her most personal experiences, and people related to her in a powerful way. It was not long before rumours started running across the land that *The Shining One* was back...

"I am proud of you, Thyra," Merit murmured to her one evening, after one of those highly emotional, hard-hitting talks.

They had found a small cave to spend the night. They were on their way back to the main Volsung settlement after several long hard days of travel and intense meetings. This last trip had been a particularly resounding success, since they had convinced two extremely influential local clan chiefs to accompany them to speak to Asger. Of course, it was always going to come to that. They all knew they would have to involve Bjarke eventually. Thyra snuggled close to her partner under the warm fur cover. Across from the fire lay Hrorek and his men, fast asleep already.

"I am proud of you too, Merit," she replied softly. "I could never do this without you."

Merit looked into her eyes.

"Yes," she whispered. "You would."

Thyra smiled. She gave a light shrug.

"I love you. Thanks for being with me on this."

"Well, yours is not an easy calling," Merit admitted, "but I am as committed to your success as you are. You know, I could never be with someone who just sits around and waits for things to happen. With every talk you deliver, you shine a little bit brighter in my eyes. I keep falling in love with you, Thyra, harder and better with every passing day..."

She sank her fingers into Thyra's thick and tousled locks and delivered a scorching kiss to her which made Thyra's head spin and tingle deliciously. She closed her eyes and grinned in pure abandon.

"You're beautiful, inside and out," Merit whispered. "I love you."

And then, she proceeded to show Thyra exactly how much she really meant it. She made love to her as if for the very first time. She did not rush. She made every single kiss extra-special, slow and intimate; she lingered over each caress, delighting in the strong body that always came so beautifully alive for her. She made love to Thyra as if she was the most precious thing alive in the universe. And for Merit, she really was. They were careful not to wake the men, of course. The next morning, Thyra overslept. She was the last one to get ready. Hrorek commented on it, unaware of the real reason for it.

"You're not getting sick, are you?"

He looked puzzled when the two women simply exchanged an amused look and burst out laughing. A few seconds later, he looked at them again. Thyra caught his eyes, flashed him a dirty grin and a lewd gesture. Hrorek shook his head, and he laughed.

"Whatever, Thyr," he muttered. "Whatever."

Later on that day, they made it home in time for the first snow of the year. Everything seemed to slow and settle down with it. And the next morning dawned really bright and sunny. Thyra finally got to introduce her partner to her land at its most magnificent. They both wrapped up warm and took one of the horses. Thyra rode in front, and Merit sat behind her with her arms locked tightly around her waist. They did not go very far, just on a short loop around the village to the lake and back. But Thyra made sure to hit all of her favourite spots along the way, everywhere that had the best and most expansive views. It was more than enough for Merit to realise that Thyra had not exaggerated about the beauty of the place when she had first described it to her, back when they were in the desert. It really did sparkle in the sunshine, and everywhere that she looked, snow and ice glinted and twinkled in the pure mountain air.

"This is absolutely breath-taking," she declared.

Thyra smiled in pleasure and satisfaction at her comment. She loved the mountains, and she really wanted her partner to be able to appreciate their true splendour as well.

"You like it?" she asked.

"I love it!" Merit exclaimed.

"Good." Thyra nodded. "Are you cold? Want to go back?"

"No, not yet," Merit protested. "We've only just started!"

Thyra shifted her position on the horse, just so that she could twist back a little, lock eyes with Merit, and steal a kiss from her. She loved to see the excited and happy look on her lover's beautiful, delicately sculpted features, and she suddenly realised that she had not felt this good in a very long time. In fact, it was also a while since she had felt the need to retreat within herself and hold her private meditation sessions where she always connected with Kari.

"What is it, Thyr?" Merit murmured.

She had noticed the sudden deep rush of colour to Thyra's cheeks, the thoughtful look on her face, and the quick flash of delighted surprise that shone through her eyes not long after.

"Do you remember that time when you told me that when we are together, you feel complete?" Thyra asked her.

"Yes, absolutely. And I still do."

Thyra smiled, and she gave a little nod.

"Well, at the time when you said that, I was not quite there myself yet, you know?"

"I know that," Merit replied gently. "And now?"

Thyra gave her a fierce, burning look in response.

"Right here, right now is everything I could ever want or even ask for," she said.

Her voice trembled from the overwhelming intensity of the powerful emotion that suddenly washed all over her. There were no adequate words to describe how insanely brilliant it felt to her to be with Merit, but she tried anyway, because she really wanted Merit to know.

"I would not change a single thing about my life with you, my love, not even if I could do it," she declared. "When I am with you, Merit, everything is just perfect. I feel whole and complete. Thank you for loving me the way you do. Thank you for being so brave and amazing. I am going to make this peace process work, you know?"

"I know," Merit murmured intently in reply. "I don't doubt it for a second, Thyr."

Thyra flashed her a bright, confident smile.

"I will do it for you," she added. "For us, and the rest of our people. I'll keep you safe, Merit. And I will not allow anything or anyone to stand in the way of the rest of our lives together. I promise."

CHAPTER THIRTY-FIVE

True to her word, and throughout the rest of the long winter months, Thyra continued her tireless efforts at diplomacy. She invited local chiefs to come over for food and drink; she carried on meeting with them regularly, and building relationships with their friends, families, and current allies. Little by little, she started to make really good progress. She even sent word out there that she wanted to hold friendly talks with Bjarke and the rest of his group. She let it be known to anyone who might be listening that it was not too late to make peace. The past could never be changed, but it was over now. It was still possible for everyone to enjoy a good future together. Alas, no response ever came from the Asger side. And it also became clear from her numerous conversations with the clan leaders that Bjarke was not a popular man with most groups anyway. Thyra had always suspected this was the case, and it was a relief to be able to confirm it. She was not surprised to hear her older brother often described as a bully, a liar, and definitely not the sort of man who could be trusted. Unfortunately, it also seemed that Bjarke had useful contacts and helpful friends in low places. This put him in a great position to easily recruit any mercenaries he needed, and all sorts of freelance warriors whose only allegiance was to the money he assured them he could provide.

"I don't know where he is getting it from," Thyra replied when Hrorek asked her about Bjarke's money. "I guess he's got his hands in some dirty business. All I know is that the more united we can all become over here, the more difficult it will be for him, or for anyone else for that matter, to launch a successful attack on any one of us one day."

"That's right," Hrorek approved. "Let's keep at it, then."

They did just that. And throughout the wider Viking world, Thyra's name soon started to become extremely well-known, and even famous in some far-out, difficult to reach places. Now, it was she who was referred to as the mighty *Shining One*. The notion that she was creating a powerful, strong alliance for peace and cooperation across the land began to gather momentum. Her work began to draw a lot of attention, at home and abroad. And then, it became quite relentless. Hrorek was delighted with the results, and so was pretty much everyone else involved.

"It is a myth that people enjoy war," Merit reflected to her partner one day. "What they truly want is what you are building for them right now, Thyr. Safety, peace, hope, and happiness. Keep going, my darling. I am with you all the way."

Toward the end of the winter, the future was looking really good for the Volsung people once again. Merit had acclimated extremely well to her new life in the mountains. She loved it. Thyra was delighted to be back home. They were happy. Things were definitely improving and looking up. That is until one freezing cold evening when it started to get dark a little early, and Erik failed to show up for dinner. Freydis was immediately full of anxiety about her only son's whereabouts.

"Hrorek, something must have happened to him," she exclaimed in instant panic. "You know how much he loves his food. You know what the boy's like, right? He has never failed to come back at the end of the day before…"

"We'll just get out there right now and look for him then," Hrorek decided. He gave his wife a strong, reassuring hug at the same time. "Don't worry, we'll find him," he promised.

He took both Thyra and Merit with him to go check the area nearest to the mountain side, a popular spot with Volsung boys for playing and climbing. He sent a few other men looking in the opposite direction, toward the deeper forest where Erik liked to spent some time too.

"I'll have to have a strong word with the boy when we find him," he grumbled to Thyra. "After Freydis lost her husband... Well. Let's just say that this is really hard for her whenever the kid goes wandering off like this."

At first, Hrorek himself was not really worried though. The child had a wild, adventurous spirit, and he knew that. Erik had probably just gone a little too far out and lost track of time. He would be tired and hungry when he got back, nothing worse. But after several hours of searching for him with absolutely no result, Hrorek too started to grow a little anxious and suspicious.

"This is strange," he muttered.

As if to make matters even worse, it started to snow quite heavily again. It was one of those freak weather storms that sometimes happen in the mountains at the change in between seasons. They all regrouped at the break of dawn, not far from the lake. By then, the entire Volsung village was out looking for the boy. Freydis had joined the search party too. She looked pale, exhausted, and like she had spent most of the night crying. As a misty grey light washed over the land that morning, Hrorek caught up with the different search groups.

"Anything? Any sign of him anywhere?" he asked.

The answers unfortunately all came back negative. After a quick pause for some food and a warming drink, they all spread out again to continue the search.

"Something's wrong, uh?" Thyra murmured to Hrorek.

He nodded, his face tight with unspoken concern.

"Yeah," he muttered. "For sure."

A little while later, Merit found herself walking with Thyra, Freydis, Hrorek and several of his men, inspecting every inch of ground that was right by the side of the lake. She was the one who spotted the only clue that had been left behind.

"Over here," she exclaimed. "Look at this!"

On the trunk of a nearby tree, a single kid's shoe had been nailed to the bark with a long, thin arrow. It was a message all right, a dark and disturbing one.

"Erik's shoe," Hrorek roared. "What the hell…"

Thyra stared at the arrow, her heart suddenly beating much faster inside her chest, as she recognised the familiar carving that was edged into the shaft. She remembered how her brother had always loved to personalise his weapons. His *death toys* as he called them. She swallowed hard.

"It belongs to Bjarke," she murmured.

This could only mean one thing, and Freydis instantly burst into tears at the realisation.

"My son has been taken," she moaned. "Asger has him! Oh, Hrorek, no! Not Erik, not my baby, please!"

Hrorek was livid with fury. Thyra stared at the arrow for several long seconds. The men were silent. Everyone jumped when a single rider suddenly appeared in front of them. Hrorek rushed forward, his face a solid mask of burning rage, but Thyra stopped him in his tracks.

"Wait," she advised.

She was right to ask him to do that, as this was a messenger from Asger. Bjarke, he told them roughly, wanted a meeting. At noon on the same day, at a location not far from this one. And yes, he did have the child.

"Tell him we'll be there," Thyra responded sharply.

"You alone," the man barked at her.

"Never!" Hrorek exploded.

The messenger shrugged, as he turned his horse around.

"Your choice," he spat. "Come alone, or the kid dies."

He galloped off without waiting for an answer. Thyra stood watching him go with a sinking feeling in her stomach. She was feeling a little sick now. Things had all been going so well... But she should have known what would happen. She should have remembered Bjarke's devious ways. Once again, in the blink of an eye, he had managed to gain the upper hand.

∞

Merit watched in dreadful silence as her partner got ready to leave the relative safety of the Volsung settlement. There had been precious little time to prepare for the encounter with Bjarke, even though Hrorek had dispatched a couple of his most trusted warriors, mounted on fast horses, with an urgent message to their closest new allies. *'We need your help'* was the request. But the likelihood of any sufficient help arriving in time to make a positive difference was slim, if not non-existent. Merit had not even pleaded with her partner not to go. She knew that Thyra would never back down on this, not when a child's life was at stake. Merit herself felt hollow inside, totally helpless, and petrified at the thought of losing Thyra. When her lover walked over to her, to say goodbye essentially, she struggled not to cry.

"Merit?" Thyra said.

She was wearing fighting garments. She had exchanged her desert sword for a Viking one. She wore heavy arm bracers once more, and a layer of protective leather over her chest. She looked focused, serious, and quite dangerous too. But her smile when she looked at Merit and rested her hands over her shoulders was all Thyra. It was incredibly warm, loving, and as always, only concerned about Merit's well-being.

"Are you okay?" Thyra murmured.

Merit gave a small shrug. She really did not want to answer that.

"So, what's the plan?" she asked instead.

Thyra instantly gave a sharp nod.

"Hrorek is coming with me," she said.

"Is he?" Merit exclaimed. "Great! But I thought…"

Thyra glanced toward her warrior friend, who was busy getting ready on the other side of the room. Hrorek was putting on his battle gear, getting his focus straight before the next fight, whilst his distraught wife stood by his side, helping him as best she could.

"I know I'm supposed to do this alone," Thyra said, "but Hrorek disagrees with me on that. He won't let me do it. He understands what it could mean for Erik… but he says that it's a risk we need to take."

Her expression darkened. She lowered her voice to be sure that no one but Merit would hear her next words, especially not Freydis.

"You know, Bjarke never plays fair," she reflected. "He is a liar and a prodigious cheat. For all we know, Erik may already be dead…"

"I understand that, Thyr," Merit interrupted anxiously. "So, why do you need to go?"

Thyra shrugged only briefly.

"Because if there's even a single chance that he's still alive out there," she murmured, "I am never going to give up on him."

Merit was not surprised at the reminder. She had expected nothing less from her brave, loyal partner, and she loved her even more for it. Still, Thyra's decision scared her to death.

"There must be another way..." she insisted, eyes full of reluctant tears. "You know what Bjarke really wants is to see you dead, right? And you're just going to walk out there, and face him all alone..."

"I won't be alone, Merit," Thyra repeated. "Hrorek will be right next to me, and our warriors will be hiding around the field. At the first sign of trouble, they'll go for it. Our best allies are on their way. This is as safe as can be."

Merit looked away, as a single tear rolled down the side of her cheek. She shook her head.

"Merit," Thyra whispered. "Please, don't..."

"Stop trying to make me feel better," Merit exclaimed, as she suddenly looked up again. "This isn't safe at all, and you know it. Our allies are miles away! The meeting is taking place in an open field, and our warriors will not be able to stay close to you. You are taking a massive risk! It's too big, it's..."

She finally could not contain her tears any longer. She started to panic.

"I don't want to lose you, Thyr," she cried. "I have a bad feeling about this. You said you would not let anything stand in the way of the rest of our lives together, remember? I don't want you to go. Please, stay..."

Impulsively, Thyra pulled her into a tight embrace. She did not know what else to do, or even say. The truth was that things might well go horribly wrong out there. But what else was she supposed to do? Turn her back, and walk away? If they wanted a chance at life together, she really had to do this. She did not want to die, no way, not anymore; and she would fight like hell to get out in one piece.

NATALIE DEBRABANDERE

"You have to trust me," she whispered. "I can do this."

Merit clang to her as if she were falling. She had never felt so scared. And then, Hrorek called out.

"Thyra. Time to go."

Thyra looked deeply into her lover's eyes. She hated to see her so terrified and upset. She did the best she could to reassure her.

"Trust me," she repeated fiercely. "I will come back to you, and we will spend the rest of our lives together. I am not going to leave you behind. I promise, Merit. Okay?"

Merit forced herself to nod.

"Okay," she whispered in a broken voice.

She wanted to smile but could only manage a weak one. Everything felt completely wrong to her at that precise moment; totally out of control, and she desperately did not want to let Thyra leave. But her lover was already pulling away. Merit reached out for one last embrace. She took her face in both her hands, gave her a hard, rough kiss, and she stared into her eyes for a second longer. There were a few words that she absolutely needed to say. It was important to do this now, for Thyra's sake. And so, Merit did it.

"I love you, Thyr. I do trust you. I'll see you when you get back, my love."

Thyra flashed her a grateful smile. This was exactly the sort of encouragement that she needed from Merit at this particular instant, and she also realised how hard it must be for her lover to let her go.

"Thank you," she murmured.

"Thyra!" Hrorek barked. "Going, now!"

Thyra winked at Merit. She gave a light chuckle and rolled her eyes in mock irritation at the big bearded warrior's unlikely behaviour.

"He shouts when he's nervous. But don't worry about it, Merit. I love you."

And with one last smile and a brief caress, Thyra was gone.

NATALIE DEBRABANDERE

CHAPTER THIRTY-SIX

In the end, Thyra and Hrorek did not go out to face Bjarke alone. At the very last minute, Hrorek made the abrupt decision to assemble his entire contingent of warriors, some ninety men in total, at one end of the field where the meeting was to take place. And then, only himself and Thyra walked out toward the middle of it, as agreed, as soon as the Asger group showed up at the other end.

"Bjarke's not going to like this," Thyra murmured.

Hrorek shot her a sharp glance. She sounded anxious.

"What, you want to die?" he snapped.

She shook her head, her eyes riveted onto the approaching figure of her murderous brother.

"No," she replied.

"Good. For your information, I don't care whether he likes it or not. One wrong move on his part, and I will give the signal. Our men are ready. And so am I. If we need to fight to protect ourselves, we will. Is that clear?"

Thyra nodded. It was crystal clear.

"I'm ready as well," she confirmed.

As they approached, she was slightly relieved to see that Bjarke only had about fifty or so men with him. Obviously, she did not know how good these fighters were... And he may have a lot more with him hiding somewhere in the nearby woods.

"Told you to come alone!" Bjarke exclaimed in fury, as soon as he was within shouting distance.

He was the only one riding on a horse, and as he came even closer, Thyra was shocked at his appearance. He had put on a lot more weight, and his skin appeared almost purple from too many swollen blood vessels in his face. He was completely bald now too. *Is he ill?* she wondered. He certainly did not look well. Even the man's voice seemed to have changed. Somehow, it did not sound anywhere near as strong and commanding as before, and neither did he. But the hatred in his soul was still there though, burning harshly through his puffy, darting little eyes. Thyra thought of Tait, and she reminded herself that her older brother was an extremely dangerous man. Sick or not, no matter what, she had to be careful.

"Where is my son?" Hrorek growled.

Bjarke came to a stop in front of them both, but he remained sitting on his horse. He spared Hrorek a single hateful glance and gestured to one of his men. Thyra looked in that direction. Her heart swelled in her chest at the sight of Erik, covered in dirt from head to toe, eyes red from crying, and looking petrified. But he was alive. Alive.

"Let him go," Hrorek demanded.

Bjarke gave a self-satisfied grin, and he enjoyed making him wait. He did what he did best, pushing and provoking people into hatred and fighting, as he relished recounting the awful way he had treated Erik.

"Have to admit, the boy takes a good whipping," he said. "Only cried a little bit at the end of the second one. Not bad, considering he's a Volsung dog."

Thyra could feel Hrorek's seething anger in the way that he stood so rigidly, with his left arm just brushing against hers. She made a conscious effort to relax her breathing.

"I propose an exchange," Bjarke declared eventually. He looked toward his sister, eyes glinting with sinister passion. "She comes with us. I let your son go."

Thyra's breath briefly caught in her chest, and she gave an involuntary shiver. She had not thought of that, so focused was she on creating peace for her people, and a good life for herself and Merit. But of course, it made perfect sense. Bjarke was not here to talk or negotiate. He was still stuck in the past, going after unfinished business. Merit had phrased it perfectly even less than an hour before. *Bjarke just wants you dead.* Thyra gritted her teeth at the thought that he was only here for her. This was bad. They were going to have to fight.

"I am waiting," Bjarke said.

Next to her, Hrorek gave a low, dark chuckle. He rested his hand on the handle of his sword. Thyra knew what would happen next. She realised they were probably only mere seconds away from descending into absolute mayhem. She tensed.

"Tell you what, Asger," Hrorek said, "why don't you send my son over here now, and I'll let you live; how's that for a good bargain, uh?"

But Bjarke just burst out laughing at the remark.

"You hear that, men?" he bellowed. "The Volsung beast is giving me options now!"

Some of his warriors chuckled in the background, obviously what was expected of them. But most remained quiet and carried on observing the scene in dangerous silence.

"I would take the offer if I were you," Hrorek remarked.

Thyra shot a quick glance toward the warrior who held Erik in his grip. The tip of his knife was resting against the side of the kid's neck. She could see a spot of blood showing on his skin. As Bjarke carried on laughing and taunting Hrorek, Thyra made eye contact with the young boy, and sent him a reassuring smile.

Erik noticed. He kept his eyes on her, wide open and wild. He was scared, obviously, yet fully alert and paying close attention to her. *Good*, Thyra thought. When everything suddenly kicked off, he would have to move fast.

"Thyra," Bjarke suddenly called. "Come on, now. Let's go."

Thyra took a single step forward, to stand deliberately in front of Hrorek. He shot her a furious look. She heard him hiss in disapproval. Toward the back of the field, behind a thick row of protective Volsung warriors, Merit was keeping her eyes firmly fixed on her partner. She tensed as well when she saw her move toward Bjarke. She dug her nails into her palms hard enough to make them bleed. *What are you doing? Thyra, no!* But Thyra had no intention of offering herself up to slaughter.

"Bjarke, I am not going anywhere with you," she stated.

She noticed his face turn immediately sour. Thyra stopped paying attention to him then, which she knew would anger him even more, and she took another confident step forward. She reached for her sword with her right hand. Behind her, Hrorek grew even more rigid. But in the next second, Thyra just threw her weapon on the ground. She opened her arms wide, and she stared at the group of warriors armed to the teeth who were assembled in front of her. She flashed them all a bright smile. This was their make-or-break moment.

"You've heard of me, right?" she declared in a strong, clear, and powerful voice. "I am Thyra of Volsung. People call me *The Shining One*. This is Hrorek, commander-in-chief of our clan. Now, this is what's going to happen. The kid is coming with us. You are going to turn around and leave. Men, I stand for peace. I do not fight in anger. But I will unleash hell onto your souls if you ever try to hurt my people. My warriors are the best in the world, and only waiting for my command. The choice is yours: leave or die."

It was a compelling speech, even though Thyra suspected it would not have much effect. But she had wanted to make it clear to those men what would happen if they chose to fight. They would die. She could feel Hrorek next to her, ready to pounce. In the very next second, a demented Bjarke yelled out his battle cry. And then, all hell really did break loose across the field.

"Attack!" Hrorek screamed, and the Volsung came rushing forward.

Before anybody else could even move, Thyra's short knife was out of her hand and through the neck of the warrior who was standing close to her. She had cleverly positioned herself right in front of the man who held Erik. As the warrior dropped dead at their feet, she picked up her sword from the ground once again and reached for the boy's shoulder at the same time. She slashed her blade across the chest of a would-be assassin, cutting short his mad run toward them. As the first of the Volsung support fighters arrived on scene, Thyra managed to drag Erik to the side. There was a clear path off the field and to safety in front of her. She looked into his eyes.

"Go," she urged. "Run back and find Merit!"

In a flash, he was gone, running as fast as his legs would carry him. Thyra immediately turned around and threw herself into battle.

Soon, she was covered in the blood of the warriors she slayed. Bitter sounds echoed all around her as she carried on fighting. The clashing of swords, and the crushing of bones. Men grunting and screaming in pain. Oh, how she hated all this... But the thought of Merit kept her going. Thyra would not allow a single one of these killers to pierce through their line and gain access to her. She would murder them with her bare hands if she had to, gauge their eyes out, and tear at their throats with her naked fingers and nails if it ever came to that. Thyra was totally committed, and absolutely focused on her mission. Win, or die. It was simple. Then, in the middle of this nightmare, a shout suddenly went out.

"Tryggvason is here!"

Thyra whirled around and stared toward the mountain, her heart pounding. She gave a loud shout of triumph when she saw him. Right there on the hill that rose east of the field, Leif Tryggvason, their closest ally going all the way back to the time of Kari had arrived. And not only that, but it looked as if he had brought his entire army along with him. Thyra had no idea how they could have made it over so quickly, but this meant that they were now assured of a complete victory against the Asger group. She carried on fighting with renewed hope and energy. Bjarke's men were beginning to run away in panic. One of them collided with her as he attempted to make his frantic escape. She punched him in the face, easily knocked his sword out of his hand, and grabbed him by the shoulders. She spun him around and gave him a sharp push in the right direction.

"That way," she snapped. "And don't you dare come back."

As he stumbled off the field, running for his life, Thyra tried to catch a glimpse of Bjarke next. If she knew him at all, he had probably long ridden off to hide somewhere else by now, but this time, she wanted to make absolutely sure. All around her, the Volsung warriors were walking with their swords raised up high in the air, already celebrating victory.

"Hrorek?" she called.

Thyra slowed down, and she started to get her breath back. *Where the hell is he?* Only when she finally spotted her dear friend, safe and in one piece, did she allow herself to relax a fraction. Hrorek was standing on the other side of the field. He was watching the Asger warriors run away with a big smile on his face, laughing hard at the sight of them all looking so scared.

Thyra allowed herself a small smile as well. *All right. Everyone's okay. This is over. It's over…* She started walking toward him, only to realise pretty quickly that something felt odd about this scene, somehow. What was it? *Hrorek…*

All of a sudden, it dawned on her what it was, and Thyra understood what appeared so familiar about him standing over there. Her heart sank. This was her dream. This was the exact scene she had been shown during her experience inside the Egyptian temple. Except that Hrorek had been injured then, and bleeding to death in the snow. Instinctively, Thyra glanced toward the forest, close to where Hrorek was standing now. She spotted something glinting through the trees. It was Bjarke. Still on his horse, still a big threat, and reaching for his bow.

"Hrorek!" Thyra screamed, and she started to run.

CHAPTER THIRTY-SEVEN

Hrorek did not hear her call. Thyra sprinted across the field toward him. *No, no, no! Don't let this happen!* When Hrorek finally noticed her, he turned around, grinning wildly.

"Thyra. We did it!" he exclaimed.

"Get down!" Thyra screamed at him. "DOWN!"

He looked puzzled. He frowned. Before he could react, she finally got close enough to him, but it was too late then. Bjarke's aim was true for once, and his arrow flew fast and straight toward its intended target. If Thyra had not thrown herself at Hrorek and knocked him to the ground, her brother's arrow would have sliced through his exposed neck, killing him instantly. As it was, it hit her in the middle of her back, piercing through her layer of protective leather like a hot knife through butter. Thyra collapsed.

"Get him!" Hrorek shouted.

As a significant number of Volsung and allied warriors, led by Tryggvason himself, disappeared into the forest to deal with Bjarke, Hrorek dropped to his knees in front of Thyra. She was lying on her side, with her right hand clutching at the centre of her chest. Bright-red blood spurted at an alarming rate through her fingers.

"Thyra, no," he muttered through clenched teeth. "Damn it, no!"

He immediately took off his tunic, rolled it into a tight ball, and applied it against her wound. The arrow had gone straight through her. She was breathing hard. Hrorek had seen injuries like this one before. Of course, he had. The last time had been with Kari. He shook his head, as hurtful tears welled up in his eyes at the memory. Thyra glanced at him, and even managed to flash him a brief smile.

"I'm fine. It's nothing," she murmured. "Hrorek, where... Where is Merit?"

Merit had seen her lover fall, and Hrorek instantly get down by her side. She knew that it must be serious when neither of them got back up. She flew across the field, acute fear at the thought of how badly Thyra must be hurt making it really hard to breathe. She rushed to her side, instantly paling at the amount of blood that she spotted in the snow when she arrived.

"I'm here, Thyr," she exclaimed. "It's all right. Let me see."

Thyra gave another faint smile. She met her gaze.

"Hey... I think... I think I need your magic hands," she sighed.

She lay on her back, staring up fixedly toward the sky as Merit quickly undid her vest, lifted her bloody tunic, and had a better look at the wound. She flashed a sharp, terrified glance toward Hrorek. He nodded, his face a picture of grief. They both knew that this was bad. They had to stop the bleeding, otherwise Thyra did not stand a chance.

"Merit?" she murmured.

"Yes, darling," Merit replied.

She leaned over her partner and ran a soothing hand through her hair. She struggled to keep smiling. She really did not want Thyra to see how scared she was.

"It was like in my dream… I'm glad…"

Thyra winced in pain as Hrorek applied more pressure over her chest.

"Harder," Merit told him.

She returned her attention to her lover.

"Keep talking to me, baby," she urged her. "Glad of what?"

"Glad I could change it… It's like Asim said to us… I knew when… I knew…"

The words died on her lips, as she suddenly smiled again, and stared intently toward something that appeared to be right over Merit's shoulder. The look in her eyes was so sharp that it even made Merit turn around for a brief second. But there was nothing there. When she looked at Thyra again, she realised that her eyes had closed.

"No!" she exclaimed.

Merit gripped harder onto her shoulders. She tried to keep her conscious.

"Thyra, I need you here. Open your eyes. Stay with me!"

Merit looked to the side when Hrorek suddenly grunted in frustration, as another piece of his tunic became saturated with too much blood and totally useless. Thyra was still bleeding heavily. Merit started to feel faint. She leaned over her partner, held her face in both her hands, and attempted desperately to keep her awake.

"Come back to me," she pleaded. "Thyra. THYRA! WAKE UP!"

A significant crowd of Volsung fighters and villagers had assembled all around them. People stood watching in grim, respectful silence, as another *Shining One* apparently lay dying. Freydis was amongst them too, holding tightly onto her son. The boy stood with his arms wrapped around his mother's waist, and both were crying silently at the sight of the wounded Thyra.

Everybody looked on, hoping and praying for a single miracle. Hrorek too had not given up. He was still working his hardest to save his best friend. He slapped her hard across the cheek. He shouted in her face.

"VIKING!" he yelled. "OPEN YOUR EYES, NOW!"

But even though both he and Merit were screaming at her, their voices quickly started to fade away for Thyra. A warm feeling of relaxation washed all over her. There was no more pain. *No more pain…* And all of a sudden, Thyra felt herself grow lighter once again. She sat up and looked all around her. The people were gone. The snow had disappeared, too. She spotted wild swallows flying high in the bright blue sky above her head. It was hot, and Thyra took a single deep, invigorating breath. She smiled as she realised that she was back at the lake once more, on a glorious summer morning. And right there in front of her, with their arms open wide, stood her beloved Kari and Tait. Thyra started running toward them.

∞

"I love you, Thyr. Please, come back to me…"

Merit whispered those words to her unconscious partner often during the days that followed the battle. Thyra did not die in the field. The bleeding stopped eventually, and they were able to carry her safely back to the village. They laid her on a comfortable bed inside the small house Hrorek had given her, and then, Merit asked to be left alone with her. She cleaned her body, and applied a tight, protective bandage over her torso. She rubbed soothing oil into her tired muscles. She covered her with clean, sweet-smelling sheets. And then, she simply got to work doing what she was so good at.

"This will help, my love. Can you hear me? I'm here, Thyr."

Merit practiced the healing arts that she knew so well, with unwavering commitment and unflinching belief that her lover would soon wake up. She did not leave Thyra's side for even a second, and she barely even stopped to eat and sleep herself. At night, she would lie awake against her body with her hand resting lightly and reassuringly over Thyra's chest, feeling her heart beating against her palm.

"She's strong," Hrorek approved. "She'll be fine."

And yet, Thyra remained deeply unconscious. Something was wrong, and Merit could not figure out what it was. She kept working with her, doing her energy healing, but she was scared. Three days went by in a single flash. The Volsung received a lot of pledges of support and allegiance from other Viking clans during that time. Leaf Tryggvason, their best ally, had come back victorious from the forest on that fateful day as well. He carried the dead body of Thyra's brother strapped onto the back of his horse. A single slash of his own powerful blade had rid the world of Bjarke forever.

"Now, we will have peace in this land at last!" Tryggvason declared in a booming voice.

Hrorek stood watching Asger's body for a few thoughtful seconds. He felt deep satisfaction at the sight of him finally dead. Bjarke would never hurt anyone else now. Hrorek remembered the harsh battle that had cost Kari her life. He recalled Thyra's reaction when she had pulled her twin brother's head out of that bag. He could still hear the raw and heart-breaking scream that she had given when she had walked out alone into the forest that night, following Kari's passing. Hrorek was never going to mourn for Bjarke, that was for sure.

"Thank you for coming to help us, my friend," he told Tryggvason.

The warrior just gave a brief smile as he shook his hand.

"Glad I did. That's what this alliance is all about, uh?"

"That's right. And we'd do the same for you."

Tryggvason clapped a strong hand over Hrorek's shoulder.

"I hope your friend makes it," he murmured. "She deserves to enjoy the fruits of her labour now, and we will need her help going forward. Our work will never be over."

Hrorek forced himself to smile.

"I know it won't. She'll come back."

He went to spend some time with Thyra after that, just sitting by the side of her bed with Merit, watching her sleep. He hated to see her like this, looking so lifeless and still. He missed her so much. And Tryggvason was right, he reflected. She should be wide awake right now, enjoying being with him, with Merit, and all of their people.

"This isn't right, Thyra," he told her. "You have to wake up, my friend."

But for Thyra, it all only just felt like the blink of an eye, not the actual long days that she spent with her eyes tightly closed, completely unaware of the rest of the world. She ran toward Tait and Kari and fell into their waiting arms. Being able to see her brother's smile once more was like feeling her heart beating for the first time. And gazing into Kari's loving green eyes, as the woman held her safely in her arms, had the power to make it stop completely.

"You came back," Thyra whispered.

"No, you came back," Kari corrected gently.

As they started walking together, Thyra held tightly onto her hand. It all felt a little strange to her, but mainly good. Yes, it was good indeed, and getting better and better.

"I'm not sure what's happening," she murmured.

"Just relax," Kari told her. "You're okay now."

She flashed her a warm smile. Her eyes lingered over her face.

"You kept your promise to me, Thyra," she reflected. "You really have become the strongest broken link. Walking the path of *The Shining One*, spreading peace and understanding along the way... I am proud of you."

And as Kari let go of her hand and started walking slightly ahead of them toward the light, it was Tait's turn to embrace his sister. He wrapped his arms around her shoulders, squeezed her affectionately against him, and shot her a brilliant smile.

"I missed you so much, Tait," Thyra exclaimed.

"Missed you too, Thyr. I'm glad you're here, sis."

They carried on, but then, Thyra hesitated.

"Where is Kari going?" she asked.

Tait glanced at her. He gave a delighted chuckle.

"Home," he exclaimed. "We're all going home now."

Thyra felt a sudden stab of anxiety hit her deep in the pit of her stomach. She came to an abrupt stop, as Tait and Kari continued walking in front of her. She realised they were both getting ever closer to a brightly-lit, door-shaped opening in the middle of the lake that sparkled like a thousand diamonds.

"Wait!" she called after them.

Kari immediately stopped walking. She turned back.

"What's wrong, Thyr?" she smiled. "Don't worry. You'll be with us, and safe. There's nothing to be afraid of now."

"Is this where I couldn't go with you the last time?" Thyra asked her in a halting voice. "When you told me I couldn't stay, and that I had to go back?"

"Yes. Last time, you were not ready."

"And now, it's my time?"

Kari nodded gently.

"Yes," she replied.

Thyra stared intently toward the opening, breathing harder in understanding now, as Kari stood holding her hand on one side and Tait on the other. They were both waiting patiently for her to make the first step. And Thyra wanted to go with them so badly that it even made her chest hurt. The light was calling out to her too, singing a sweet embracing song that felt just like total warmth, safety, joy, and eternal bliss all rolled into one. It was almost impossible to resist. Part of her did not even want to try, and yet… Thyra took a single deep breath. She glanced at Tait first, then toward Kari.

I love you both so much…

"Kari?" she murmured.

"Yes, Thyr. My love."

Thyra locked eyes with her. She was pretty sure from the encouraging, earnest expression on her face that Kari knew exactly what she was going to say to her next, and that it would be all right when she did. Thyra gave her fingers a gentle squeeze, and when Kari nodded in approval, smiling, she let go then; and of Tait's hand as well. She took a step back from the light.

"I love you," she whispered. "And I can't wait to be with you both forever. But first, there is another promise I want to keep."

NATALIE DEBRABANDERE

*

EPILOGUE

*

"Kiss me," Thyra whispered.

Merit rolled over onto the thick blanket they had spread out onto the ground. They were in Thyra's favourite outdoors spot, which offered perfect views of the lake and the white mountains in the background. It was still a little bit cold to be spending time outside like this, but Thyra had lit a warming fire, and they were tightly snuggled up together under several heavy blankets of fur. Quite simply, Merit was feeling wonderful. She looked into her lover's clear blue eyes and brushed a single lock of hair from her cheek. She raised an impatient eyebrow toward her, faking irritation at the demand.

"I was just reaching out for that drink you asked me for. At least let me get it for you before you start asking for something else..."

"No, I want you to kiss me first," Thyra insisted, grinning. "Please, Merit?"

Merit giggled, and she immediately gave in to the gentle, tempting request. She laid a single teasing kiss over her partner's lips and lingered a little longer before she pulled back.

"Better now?" she asked.

Thyra's smiled widened.

"Yeah," she sighed. "Great."

She was still feeling weak from her injury but getting better with every passing day. Merit would never forget waking up with a start that morning, five days after the battle, to find that her lover was awake at last and gazing at her tenderly, as Merit slept with her head resting over her shoulder.

"Merit... I love you."

These had been Thyra's very first words upon waking up, and her next ones were to ask for food. Lots of it. Since then, Merit had slowly nursed her back to full health with a steady regime of carefully selected meals, and a selection of what Thyra chose to call *'disgusting potions'*, but which Merit stubbornly maintained were in fact efficiently designed *'healing herbal remedies'*. As Merit handed her a cup of something liquid now, Thyra stared at it suspiciously. Merit burst out laughing at her expression.

"It's mead, Thyr."

"Yeah?"

"Yeah."

Thyra took a sip of the delicious brew.

"Thank you," she whispered, smiling.

"You're welcome. But it's only because I love you," Merit replied.

Thyra gave her a thoughtful look, and she was silent for a moment. She closed her eyes, and she smiled again as Merit ran her fingers through her hair and leaned over her for another kiss. Thyra exhaled slowly. She gazed at the tall mountains in the background, and the glittering waters of the lake.

"Hey," she murmured.

Merit raised her head to meet her gaze.

"Hey you," she whispered back.

"I saw Kari again, you know? When I was, uh..."

"When you were in the spirit world?" Merit encouraged.

"Yeah." Thyra smiled. "Yeah, I think that's what it was."

Merit sat up a little straighter, eyes shining in amazement and curiosity as her lover started to relate for the first time the full story of what had happened to her on the other side.

"I noticed you are not wearing your torc today," she said.

Thyra momentarily touched her fingers to her naked neck.

"It's a chief's torc. Hrorek should wear it."

"Thyra," Merit protested gently, "it was a present from your Kari... It is much more than a simple chief's necklace, and you know it. What happened out there? Are you okay?"

Thyra nodded openly in response.

"Yes," she said. "I feel great. I don't need the torc anymore. Kari is always with me, you know? Actually, I even feel like she has become a part of me. The torc helped when I was not strong enough... But now, I really am. I know what I'm doing, and I know what I want."

Merit gave a faint smile.

"And what is that?" she asked.

"You," Thyra replied simply.

"You already have me, Thyr."

"Well, that's true," Thyra conceded. "But when I was with Kari this time, Tait was there as well. They both came for me. They said that if I wanted to, I could follow where they were going, and stay."

Merit sat listening in stunned silence as Thyra described to her what it had felt like. Her heart beat harder when her lover explained how difficult it had been for her to resist the pull of the light, and how much she had wanted to go. Thyra gave a little shrug then, and flashed Merit a brilliant smile.

"What made me choose to come back was my promise to you, Merit," she murmured.

Thyra sat up, and she took her lover's hand in hers. She reached into her pocket for the small silver ring that she had asked one of her talented warrior friends to fashion for her. Not only was the man a gifted fighter, but he was also a talented craftsman in his spare time. And he could keep a secret, too.

"I promised to keep you safe, and to spend the rest of my life with you," Thyra said, as she slid the ring over her partner's finger. "I came back to be with you. This ring is a symbol of my love for you, Merit."

It fit perfectly. Merit stared at it in wonder.

"Thyr, it's beautiful," she murmured.

She glanced at Thyra, who was smiling softly, watching her, and she was suddenly overcome by a strong wave of emotion. She threw her arms around her neck and pulled her into a tight embrace. She kissed the side of her face and ran her fingers through her hair.

"I love you so much," she murmured.

"I had our initials carved into it," Thyra explained. "And I got one for me too. Now, people will know exactly what we mean to each other."

Merit's eyes filled with tears as Thyra slipped her own ring on and spread her fingers to show it to her. She thought back to that night on board the ship when she had first met Thyra. She remembered her long and lonely nights of captivity after she was taken as a slave. It was all worth it for this moment.

"You came back to be with me," she whispered. "You chose me over eternity with the people you love the most..."

"Not quite," Thyra interrupted, smiling gently. "Eternity would never be complete without you, Merit. So, it's just going to wait for us a little bit longer."

They kissed again, and shared a long, passionate embrace. Merit lay against Thyra's body with her hand resting safely and protectively over her heart. They spent the rest of the afternoon like this, gazing out over the beautiful mountains, and holding on to each other. They enjoyed a long and happy life together and died peacefully within mere seconds of each other. First, Merit went; and then, Thyra followed her. It is said that joyful laughter could be heard all over the sky that night, as they reunited with each other for the rest of eternity, and with their friends amongst the stars...

THE END

***

NATALIE DEBRABANDERE

ALSO

BY NATALIE

DEBRABANDERE...

UNBROKEN

"I couldn't stop reading. Heart-warming love story, full of intrigue, suspense, and a touch of terror. Loved it."

STRONG

"Raw and heart stopping action in Afghanistan. As a Marine, the main character deals with the stress of battles and loss. Great story, highly recommended."

ASHAKAAN

"What a fantastic book! I love a good Sci-Fi adventure with a strong female lead who can kick butt, outsmart the bad guys but not totally, and fall in love."

FELUCCA DREAMS

"Excellent writing! Awesome love story! The sensuality between the characters is palpable. Natalie Debrabandere keeps hitting hit out of the park!"

LOOKING FOR ALWAYS

"One of the purest love stories I have read. Original and captivating story line, amazing characters. This book keeps you hooked until the very last word. Great job!"

...

…

And:

BEYOND THE QUEST

"Fast-paced, addictive, full of twists and turns! A riveting, exciting tale of love and adventure!"

OF SCARS AND DUTY

"OMG, Major Williams rocks!
A kick-ass Sci-Fi military Lesfic!"

Keep up to date with Natalie's work on Facebook @ndebrabandereauthor & nataliedebrabandere.com

Thank you for reading!

Made in the USA
San Bernardino, CA
10 January 2019